TAKE IT ON FAITH

A Friends-to-Lovers, Second Chance Romance

JESSIE MARIE

To anyone who's chased a dream, made a wish, had faith: this one's for you.

One

Of course I would see him for the first time in two years while I was struggling.

Mother insisted on seeing the dress in her three-way mirror. Never mind that I didn't have a car. *Catalina has a car, doesn't she?* I could see Mother's pursed lips in my mind. *Go with her. I need to see this dress outside of the store before you walk down the aisle in it.*

So of course, that left me and Cat struggling to get a firm hold on my wedding dress, to shove it into the back of the car. Cat's car would be in the shop that day, so we had to rent one. Unfortunately for me, the problem with a ball-gown wedding dress was precisely what I envisioned: too much dress, not enough space.

"Just push it in." Cat let out a little grunt as she attempted to move it through the doorway of the car. One lone drop of sweat trickled down her face and I feared that any minute, she would explode. "Why did we rent such a tiny-ass car to pick up this monster of a dress?"

"Hindsight is a bitch." I let out a curse as I jammed my

finger between the dress and the car door. "We have no choice but to keep trying."

"Alicia?"

I turned my eyes toward the voice like a man follows a siren's song. My watch beeped at me frantically. *Take a breath. Take a breath!* I tipped my head back to meet his eyes.

Andrew.

A clean Caesar had taken the place of the high-top fade I was so used to. His lips—which almost always held a frown of some sort—seemed more tender-looking than before. More lush. More kissable.

The graphic-T / loose jeans combination of our high school days had faded into fitted jeans and a plain white tee. The shirt molded to the curves of his arms, bunched up a little on the hill of his bicep. It conjured up pictures of long hours spent at the gym or doing pushups. I could see Andrew in my mind's eye, at the squat rack or at the bar doing chest presses, sweat pooling at his collarbone or soaking his shirt. I practically salivated at the thought.

I longed to run my fingertips over his broad shoulders; my heart sped up at the thought of my fingers getting tangled in his shirt. Looking at him that day, I wondered if he was going to burst through the shirt if he turned the wrong way. While the thought of a semi-naked Andrew was always enough to make me blush, my heart ached for the stick-thin Skinny Minnie that earned him the nickname in high school. I met him when he inhabited that body, had lustful teenage thoughts about him even when he was a beanpole. It felt wrong, somehow, that we had grown into adults.

Despite all the delicious ways that time had done him well, he was still Andrew Parker. His light brown eyes still held the gentle mischief, the leisurely and calm confidence I remembered from so long ago. His eyes roamed over my wedding dress, and then over my face, possessing it and staking his claim. His gaze stopped at my lips then flashed back to my eyes. I knew that even with my dark skin, he could sense the blush, everpresent in our early days, creep over my face. He smiled.

"Hey." I tried to continue with our arduous task, but Cat took this moment to do her best statue impression. *Traitor.* I glared at her and tugged on the dress for emphasis. "How've you been?"

"Good," he said, looking back toward the dress. I felt the familiar tingle as his voice—smooth, low, and warm—wrapped itself around me like a blanket straight from the dryer. His eyes flashed back to mine again. "You're getting married."

"Two more months!" Even to my own ears, I could hear the false note of cheer. Andrew tilted his head a little, a small frown playing between his brows. My traitorous heart melted at the sight even as my watch beeped again. My hand itched to smooth his brow, the way he did for me all those years ago.

He tapped his palm over his fist before deciding to shove both hands deep into his pockets. He looked away from me, squinted into the distance. A muscle ticked in his jaw.

I flashed back to the memories of Andrew's face not even twitching when I felt like I was coming unraveled. Of the two of us, I was always the one on the move—tapping my fingers, pacing. His slow, easy heartbeat had been my anchor, and his calmness was always comforting. I paused at what I saw now.

"I saw you the other day, coming out of a coffee shop. It didn't look like a good time to talk, though. Seemed like you were arguing with someone on the phone."

"Probably was." Something in my voice made him

narrow his eyes. I flashed back to all of those times when I was constantly fighting with some guy or another, Andrew looking on with interest and slight disapproval. Not much had changed in that department—just that I was fighting different people now. Different battles.

"It made me realize that I couldn't call you." When I raised my eyebrows, he coughed and looked away. "I don't have your number saved in my phone anymore. After, you know, everything."

So he did it. The full purge. My heart lurched. I could feel the tears threatening to come up, so I blinked and looked down at the dress as I spoke. "I can text you. Is your number the same?"

Our eyes met over the gown with an almost audible *click.* He took a deep breath, and I could almost hear the echoes of our conversation, so many years ago, playing in his head as well as my own.

"Yeah, it's the same." Almost as if it had a mind of its own, Andrew's voice lowered, the deep resonance betraying his surprise and pleasure.

I dipped my head briefly, a curt nod. "Talk to you then."

"If we were ever to stop being friends, I'd do a full purge," I announced. Out of the corner of my eye, I could see Andrew stop chewing and hit pause on the Goosebumps *episode we were watching.*

"A full purge?" he asked.

"Everything that even remotely reminded me of you would go."

"Everything?"

"What are you, an echo?"

He chewed slowly, staring at the screen as he thought. I could almost smell the smoke burning from the effort.

"I'm surprised, is all," he said finally. "That's not really your thing."

"My thing?"

"Who's the echo now?"

"Minnie." I turned to him, a warning in my eyes. I scratched my knee then toyed with the skin around my fingernails. "Cut the enigmatic bullshit and say it straight. What do you mean it's not my thing?"

"First of all, you're a memory hoarder. That would never work." As I opened my mouth to protest, he continued, "Secondly, we've spent countless years together now. We met in our senior year of high school. We're almost out of college. That's thousands of hours of memories. You could forget all that?" He looked up from his cereal. His spoon remained suspended over the bowl as he searched my eyes. I felt a shiver and a slow burn inhabit my body. I hated it when he looked at me like that.

"I would have to forget." I could feel the waver in my voice as I swallowed. "I wouldn't have a choice." My face flushed with the confession, and then looking at him became too much. His eyes showed an understanding of something more, something that, at that time, I had yet to grasp.

He reached out to grab hold of my chin, tilted it toward him. I could see a question there, but I didn't know what he was asking. What he was really asking. Finally, he sighed as his fingers moved from my chin and returned to the spoon. He considered the Lucky Charms as he spoke.

"No amount of purging could help me get over the loss of us," he said. "I wouldn't even bother trying."

"So what was it like? Seeing Andrew after all these years."

I shrugged and gave the barista my card and looked around the tiny coffee shop. "First of all, it's only been two years." I gave Cat a sidelong look. "Secondly, it was regular." *So regular that my heart almost jumped out of my body.* "I didn't want to be rude, but I don't want to see him ever again. Especially after everything that happened last time."

"Yeah? Is that why you were ogling him? Because you don't want to see him ever again?" Catalina smirked.

I sighed.

"So are you ready to tell me something real, or are you gonna lie to my face some more?" She stirred honey into her green tea.

I picked at the skin around my nails then frowned in surprise. *I haven't done that in years.* "He's always been attractive; that hasn't changed," I admitted. "I like the beard on him. And he's filled out in a not-so-bad way…"

"So you *are* gonna lie to my face."

"That's not a lie!"

"Alicia, you might as well have tried to lick him from head to toe, the way you were looking at him."

"*Catalina!*"

"You pretend to be a prude, Alicia Jones, but you are *not*. And you may try to lie to yourself and to me about your rampant, insatiable lust for Andrew, but I'm not lying to no-damn-body. Including you." She flicked invisible lint off her arm. "You've been attracted to that man since high school. You couldn't get enough of him then, and you can't stay away now. Not to say I blame you. Andrew says he doesn't work out, but for someone who never hits the gym, he sure does have a nice, round, tight ass—"

"Jesus, Cat, aren't you happily married?" My face burned even brighter. "And *I'm* the one supposedly lusting after Andrew?"

"Just because I'm married doesn't mean I'm blind. Andrew is a snack. And just because you're *getting* married, it doesn't mean you have to be blind, either. Besides, you're marrying Michael *because* he's a hot piece of ass. Don't be so uptight. And don't try to tell me any different," Catalina said over my protests. "Because you're definitely not marrying him for his mind."

"That's not fair." I swirled my coffee distractedly. *Andrew had a mind that any nerd could get lost in.* "Michael makes me feel like no other man has. He's warmhearted, and responsible, and compassionate, and—"

"—doesn't have an intellectual thought in his head." Catalina rolled her eyes. "He's one turkey short of a feast, Alicia, believe that. I don't know how he's getting through business school, let alone overseeing a whole-ass retail store. And he's a fucking *bro*. He's the complete opposite of you. What do you talk about with him, anyway? Other than the weather and himself."

"He's stable, has a good job, good family background, loves kids, will be a great father, is taller than me," I said, using my fingers to list his attributes. "He has potential but most importantly, he's great in the here and now. He's everything I could want in a future husband. Unlike Andrew."

"So you're marrying him because he's not Andrew." Catalina pursed her lips. "Look, Alicia, I get it. Andrew broke your heart—"

"—here we go—"

"—and no one can compare—"

"—Cat—"

"—but this is worse than settling. This is emotional suicide. Marrying Michael will be like watching paint dry for the next fifty years of your life. How can you be okay with this?"

"Because." I turned to her. "Michael is the one. Period." *He has to be.*

So after all that you went through with this number all those years, you still kept it?

I laughed. *Yeah, I couldn't get rid of it. Memories, you know.*

Naturally. When did you ever pass up an opportunity to hoard your memories? I could almost hear Andrew's murmur of a laugh through the text. I could hear it echoing in my head, the richness of it filling my soul. My whole body went hot, heat pooling between my legs, and my watch beeped. *Take a breath.*

Don't fix what ain't broke, right? But the real miracle is that your number is the same. I'm surprised.

Fair. But ask me how many phones I've had since...

I frowned at my phone, looking for the spinning wheel of death at the top of the screen. My phone was as serene as an early morning lake. *The dramatic pause for effect,* I thought, sucking my teeth. *Typical Andrew.*

Anyway, he continued, **we should get coffee tomorrow. Catch up.**

I twisted my engagement ring around my finger as my mind scattered in several different directions. My skin felt like it was on fire as I remembered how things ended. On the other hand, I couldn't ignore the dull ache in my heart.

What will it be like? Will we go back to the way things were? Does he still smile the same?

Does he remember?

IDK, I said finally. I chewed my lip, fiddled with my ring again. ***Let me check with my fiancé first.***

There was a long pause, to the point where I wondered if Andrew would respond.

You have to check with your fiancé first? For coffee?

My nostrils flared as my nails tapped on my desk. The scorn in his text almost singed my hands. *Deep breaths,* I told myself. *Stop letting him get to you.*

Yes. Michael and I are a team.

Okay, Jones. Whatever you say.

I'll let you know by tonight.

Great, he said, as if it was already decided. **It's a date.**

Despite myself, I smiled.

"Did you pick up your dress?"

I rolled my eyes at the phone. My mother could be so short these days.

I snorted to myself. *Just these days?*

"What was that?"

"Yes, Mother, I picked up the dress."

"And everything is in order?"

"Yes."

"Good." I heard her shuffle around some papers on the other end. I sighed. Even when planning her only living child's wedding, she was still working. Still dictating. I breathed deeply, feeling the air expand within me. *Keep it cool,* I reminded myself. *Keep the peace.*

My relationship with my parents was tenuous at best. We kept it civil lately because of the wedding, and because they loved Michael. They thought he had great potential in business, if not football, which ultimately led my father—a sports attorney with connections to agents—to take Michael on as a client.

He's fantastic. Unlike that other boy you used to date. I could hear my mother's cool voice in my head, see the slight wrinkle of her nose as she thought of Andrew. Who, by the way, I never dated. But those were just semantics to my mother.

"Is there anything else?" I sighed. I looked at my watch, then at the time on my microwave. I shifted so that my feet dug into my couch. "I'm at my apartment, but Michael should be here any minute."

"No, nothing else." She shifted the papers again. "And how is Michael doing? You two are only two months out from the big day. Any wedding jitters?"

"Nope, he's as solid as ever," I said, unable to keep a slight edge from my voice. Michael, as solid as ever. His heartbeat was even steady when we kissed.

"Well, as we say, happy husband, happy wife."

"Doesn't the saying go, 'happy wife, happy life'? Shouldn't he be trying to keep *me* happy?"

"Alicia, don't start getting all bent out of shape. You know taking Michael as a client means a lot to your father. Michael's family has connections that we couldn't have even dreamed of. This could be the thing that makes or breaks your father's firm. We need Michael to be on board."

Michael, Michael, Michael. I made a face at the phone to avoid snapping at Mother. If I heard any more about this partnership that Michael and my father were working on, I'd go insane. "It's fine, Mother. I understand."

Fine, fine, fine, everything's fine. Isn't it, Ace?

It was as if Andrew was in the room with me. My heart jumped to life at the thought of him. I frowned and turned away from those thoughts. *Remember,* I thought. *Things have changed. You have a future marriage to think about now.*

"...need anything else," my mother finished. I quickly searched my brain for the last sentence that she said. God forbid she caught me not listening.

"I will," I promised. "Goodnight, Mother."

"Goodnight," she said just as Michael was walking in. Sighing in relief, I hung up the phone and smiled at Michael. "Hey, you."

"Hey, yourself." As I watched him saunter across the room, I marveled at the god that was my future husband. His muscles rippled with each step he took. While Andrew favored a basketball player physique, Michael was all football. Wide, broad shoulders. Biceps the width of my leg. Watching him stroll across the room, brazen confidence apparent with each step, he practically set my body on fire. We hadn't had sex yet, at Michael's insistence. Ever the traditional one, he wanted to wait for marriage because he felt like *it was the right thing to do*, as if he was protecting my virtue somehow. Still, it didn't stop me from picturing my legs wrapped around his torso, could almost feel him drive into me as I uttered irreverent prayers to our bedroom ceiling.

I studied his full lips, looked into his hazel eyes. A grin flashed across his face, dimples making their delectable appearance.

He bent down to briefly touch his lips to mine then dropped his bag to the floor. A slight flash of irritation zipped through me before I tamped it down. There was a hook specifically for Michael's bag, but he refused to even acknowledge it. Though I could appreciate that Michael felt at home wherever he was, this was still *my apartment*. My apartment, my rules.

I didn't mention it to him, though.

"How was the talk with your mom?" he asked as I fought my irritation.

"The usual. Straightforward." I grimaced. "She says hi, by the way."

"Hi back." He grinned at his own joke.

"How was the gym?"

"Good." He flexed and kissed his bicep. "Making gains. This will be my year, babe. I feel it."

"Yeah?" I turned to him as he dropped to the couch and propped my feet on his lap. "Did something happen?"

He started to rub my arches and I hummed my satisfaction. "Yeah. The starting running back pulled a hamstring. The trainers don't know how long it's gonna take him to recover."

I raised my eyebrows. "Yikes. That sucks for him—probably hurts, doesn't it?" Michael frowned as if that didn't even occur to him. "But it's good for you," I added hastily.

He shrugged. "Yeah. It's a step in the right direction."

We sat in silence, lost in our own minds for a moment, before I cleared my throat. "So, I wanted to ask you something."

"Yeah?" He reached for the remote and turned the TV on. A laugh track played softly in the background. "What's up?"

"I ran into Andrew today." I fiddled with my ring for the third time today. "He wanted to grab coffee and catch up."

Michael flicked through the channels absentmindedly. "Is this the same Andrew that your mom hates?"

I rolled my eyes. "Yes."

"Didn't she say that you two used to date?"

"But we didn't." I almost couldn't stop myself from flicking my thumbnail against the pad of my forefinger. The rapid *fft fft fft* sound couldn't be heard over the TV show's loud explosions.

"It's fine with me, then." Michael shrugged. "It's not like you had feelings for the guy."

A small seed of guilt swirled in my stomach. "Right."

The next day, Andrew and I met at a coffee shop in our hometown. As I waited for Andrew—who was running late as expected—I looked around the large room. Baristas scurried about with half-empty containers of this liquid or that, the manic, almost hysterical atmosphere reflected in their eyes. The barista manning the pick-up line pasted a falsely bright smile to her face as a woman gestured sharply in front of her. Looking out the window, I saw a sign boasting **FOUR NEW LOCATIONS!** *Must be a chain,* I thought. *Definitely not Andrew's style. I wondered why he picked it?*

"This was the only coffee shop in our town that I could find that we hadn't been to." I turned around to see Andrew standing behind me, hand on the back of his neck, eyes sheepish, mouth turned down in a sour grimace. "But I know about your love affair with coffee, and I didn't want to risk our first meeting since…everything"—he coughed—"without coffee, so I chose here. For a fresh start and all that." As if realizing that he strung too many sentences together at once, he stopped abruptly and shoved his hands in his pockets. I watched him for a moment before looking around again. Finally, I turned to him with what was hopefully a reassuring smile.

"You did good, Minnie," I said. "Let's get some coffee."

We took a few steps to integrate ourselves into the line waiting to order. As I browsed through the menu, Andrew cleared his throat. I met the mischievous gleam in his eye with a frown of my own.

"So," he said. "Your fiancé let you out the house then." An uncharacteristic smirk twisted Andrew's lips. *Although,* I thought, *who's to say it's not like Andrew to do that? We don't know each other anymore.*

But did we ever?

"He didn't 'let me out.'" I sniffed. "I am free to go where I choose. I *chose* to ask him."

"As opposed to sneaking around?"

"As opposed to not honoring his wishes, despite being in a committed relationship."

Andrew made a noise of approval. "Fair point."

I murmured my agreement, smoothing my skirt. Andrew frowned slightly, gesturing with his chin at my legs. "When did this happen?"

"When did what happen?"

"When did you start wearing skirts?" He gazed at my legs as I blushed. "Short skirts, at that. I thought you hated your legs."

I shrugged, tapping my hand against my thigh. "Things change. And they're not so bad. Michael loves when I wear skirts." I flushed deeper as Andrew's eyes met mine with a raised eyebrow. I returned his look with defiance coursing through my veins. *Say it. Say that you're disappointed that I changed for anyone; I dare you.*

"Things do change, I guess," he murmured. His refusal to say it made me avert my eyes. But I should've known. He never rose to a fight or picked one. Except that one time.

As I looked out the window to avoid his eyes, I said, "So. What's new on your end? I'm at a disadvantage. You already saw me struggling with my wedding dress."

I turned to him just in time to see him smile into his tea. "Yeah, that was pretty great. Would be great to see you in it. I bet you look like a princess."

I rolled my eyes. "Yeah, a big, poufy princess." I grumbled as Andrew's smile grew into a full laugh. "They will roll me down the aisle in a haze of taffeta."

"I'm surprised that you agreed to it." He took a long

pull of his tea. "The Alicia I knew couldn't be made to wear any dress, let alone a princess dress."

So there it is. The judgment. I shrugged, taking a sip of my own drink. "Sometimes, you have to make some concessions."

"Like marrying a Neanderthal and wearing a dress you hate to an event you wouldn't be caught at otherwise?" Andrew pulled his lips inward and pulled his eyebrows together. "What happened to you in the last two years, Ace?"

Somehow, the heat of Andrew's scorn was harder to stomach after a couple of years of not having to. I closed my eyes, counting to ten, before I gave up on that idea. "Life happens, Andrew, and we all grow up. Or some of us do. Life is about making hard choices, compromising for the people we love. So I participate in a wedding reception because my future husband wants to throw a party. So what? I'm not giving up world peace. Besides, that Neanderthal, as you call him, treats me well. We have a great life together."

"Do you actually love him enough to marry him, or are you just scared?"

"Is this why you invited me to coffee? To demonstrate your utter disapproval for the life that I've chosen for myself? Emphasis on chosen, by the way."

"No, I didn't." He sighed and ran both of his hands over his hair. My heart pulled at the memories the gesture invoked. *When you do that, you look like a wet cat,* I used to joke.

"To answer your question, nothing's new on my end. Still writing. Still not making any money." He laughed without humor. "Still working at a job that I hate."

I hid a smirk. Andrew's inability to keep a job was legendary. "Where are you now?"

"A home-décor mom-and-pop store. I love the owners, but I will die a fiery retail death if I don't quit soon."

"But what will you do for money? Do you have any savings?"

Andrew shrugged.

I shook my head. "Still living on a prayer, I see."

"Now who's the judgmental one?"

I held up my hands as I dipped my head in concession. "Fair point. Let's move on to less incendiary topics."

"Before I agree to that—how've you been? No bullshit."

How are you holding up, Ace? No bullshit. He used to ask me this so often that it became part of the lexicon of our friendship. At first, I hated it; he never asked to actually give a solution. Or rather, he thought that asking and listening to the answer was a solution in and of itself. For me, I needed an actual solution, actual things to work toward.

But now, after everything, hearing it again—*How are you holding up? No bullshit*—my body melted with the recognition.

I shrugged. "Managing. You know how that goes."

Andrew tilted his head, hearing the evasion in my voice. "Alicia."

I inwardly shivered at the way he said my name. Andrew was never a forceful person until he said a person's name. Until he said *my* name. He spoke it like a man who was used to being obeyed. He spoke it like a king, like I was his. We used to fight about it all the time.

Don't say my name like that, I used to say.

Like what? he would ask.

Like I'm meant to obey you.

Then don't answer like you want to obey.

Then and now, I didn't know which feeling was

stronger: my longing to hear him speak my name again or my fury that he thought he could command anything out of me.

"This is me, Ace. You know you can tell me anything."

"Do I?" I met his eyes. "How did that work out for me last time?"

He nodded slowly, taking the hit with pinched lips. "You're right. We have a long history of…" He spread his hands wide, indicating the unspeakable. "We can't start over, nor can we start where we are. So how do we fix this?"

I shrugged, fiddling with my coffee. "I don't know if we can."

ndrew had been a menace from the start.

We met under unfavorable conditions. I was waiting outside of our high school, on a frigid Monday night. I stamped my feet impatiently, trying to make my individual toes feel like part of my foot again. I feared that if I opened my mouth, all of the moisture there would turn to ice, but even the exhalations from my nose burst forth in a cloud of icy smoke. I shoved my hands deep into my fleece-lined pockets, but nothing helped. I couldn't take my mind off of the wintery fingers of death wrapping themselves around my body.

"Waiting for someone?"

I jerked my head toward the voice, a little to my left. I hadn't seen him standing there before, but there he was: a tall, shadowy, lanky form leaning against the brick half-wall next to the school. I immediately frowned, despite the fact that doing so in this cold made my forehead hurt. Anyone that tall, that could sneak up on me, was too quiet to be trusted.

"Something," I said finally. I squinted into the darkness. "The sports bus."

"Ah, so not a senior then." I could hear the mischief in his voice, speaking of years of little brother syndrome and pranks gone wrong—or right.

I opened my mouth to tell him about himself but thought better of it. Instead, I said, "Yes, I'm a senior. Are you?"

"Yes. Which is why someone's coming to pick me up." His voice was, decidedly, too smug for my liking. Let's take that down a notch, shall we?

"Seniors should have their own cars though, no?" I could hear the smugness in my own voice. "So wouldn't that make you less of one, as well?"

He paused to think about this and I gave myself a mental high-five.

"I suppose it does," he finally replied. Satisfied, I turned away from him. Take that, asshat.

"What's your name?"

My irritation instantly flared back up. I pushed on my fingers, trying to work the numbness out of them as I looked for the bus. The one time Danny is late, I have to deal with this guy, I thought to myself. I hoped that maybe if I was silent enough, he would get the hint, but no. This lanky stranger seemed to have an endless amount of patience—and ways to irritate me.

"Alicia Jones," I said. "Most people call me Ace."

I frowned at the lie. Only my friends and teammates call me Ace. Why did I tell him that?

"Ace, huh. Is that your street name?"

"Where is your ride?" I asked. "Or do you have nothing to do but sneak up on unsuspecting people and pepper them with questions?"

He murmured a laugh and my breath caught in my throat. My watch, which kept track of my heart rate, beeped *to let me know that it was too elevated.* Take a breath, *I could almost hear it chirp. I inhaled deeply and regretted it. I was almost sure that my nostrils were frozen over.*

"Not in the mood to talk," he mused. "Okay." I breathed an inaudible sigh of relief as I felt him turn away from me in the darkness. I did a little hop in place to continue my bid for increased body heat—although, I noted, I wasn't feeling that cold right then. Something about the timbre of his voice, the warmth and familiarity in his tone, made me want to kick him. Or listen to his tongue taste the flavor of my nickname. But who knew which was true?

"What sport do you play?" he asked. I let out a sustained groan. This kid never shut up, it seemed.

"Gymnastics," I replied, bracing myself for the inevitable. Because people just couldn't resist asking me—

"...a little tall for that?"

I bit down on my lip, hard, to keep the words in. My mom was always on me about my cursing. How will you ever get married, using that language? We're better than that, Alicia. You can't go around being a stereotype of your race and gender. Don't be the angry black girl.

"Nope," I said instead.

"I see."

The quiet rumbling of a diesel engine almost made me leap for joy. The chill in the air, coupled by this too-inquisitive stranger, made the bus a true godsend.

"Have a good night, Ace," he said, putting emphasis on my nickname. I shivered at the sound, though I convinced myself it was just the cold. This kid, whose name I didn't even know, reminded me of warm blankets on a cold day, or friendships that lasted a lifetime, and it was utterly disconcerting. And his voice. That voice could make even the most stoic girl blush.

*I pushed the traitorous thoughts from my mind and
snorted. If I was lucky, I'd never see him again. If I was
unlucky, too, I thought before I could stop myself.*

"So how did your date go?"

I looked at Catalina over the spread of cupcakes and
tried to remember that she was my best friend. "It wasn't a
date."

Catalina and I were at Bea's, a boutique bakery down
the street from my apartment. Michael insisted that they
had the best desserts in town, so we changed the vendor
last minute. When he first suggested it, my immediate
thought was *no.* From the outside, the storefront seemed
tiny, incapable of handling an order for the hundreds of
guests my parents invited to the wedding.

But stepping inside the cozy shop was like walking into
a delicious piece of paradise. The mouthwatering vanilla
scent wrapped around my body like a hug. The size of the
shop helped to make it feel comforting and familiar, and
the warmth of the clerks made me feel like part of a
family. It was the very opposite of the cold, almost sterile
look and feel of the bakery my mother had chosen. So, I
went with Bea's.

Catalina licked some frosting from the tip of her finger.
"Sure. How long did it take you to actually look at his face
and not his arms, or his crotch, or his tight ass?"

It was then that I concluded that counting to ten was
the most unhelpful advice to give someone who was full of
rage, and my mother knew nothing about actual, genuine
feelings. "I did none of those things." I chose a bite-sized,
caramel-colored cupcake and inspected the sprinkles. I

wrinkled my nose a little. *Who puts rainbow sprinkles on wedding cupcakes?* "I could only stay for about fifteen minutes."

"Why? Did you have something else to do?"

"No." I sighed. "Andrew is just as judgmental as he used to be. I could only stand to be around him for fifteen minutes."

Catalina waited with raised eyebrows.

"I mean, why does everyone have such a negative opinion about my fiancé?" I burst out. "Michael is the kindest man I've ever met. And he loves me. What is so wrong with that?"

"Maybe because you can't bring yourself to say that you love him." Catalina shrugged as I glared. "Just saying."

Though I continued to glare at her, a small wrinkle formed in the smooth fabric of my future. I could feel it growing, spreading.

"I do love him." My voice grew stronger with every word. "He's the only man I've been with who accepts me for the person I am today, instead of trying to get me to be the person I was before or a person I never was. He plans for *this life*, not for a distant past and *what-ifs*. I need that in my life, Cat. You, of all people, should understand that."

Catalina sighed, too, and rested her hand on my arm. "I get it, Alicia," she said gently. "I do. But is safety and security worth risking the greatest love of your life?"

"But see that's the thing," I said. I turned so that her hand naturally fell off of my arm. "Andrew was never and will never be the greatest love of my life. He never felt that way about me in the past, and I don't feel that way about him now."

That wrinkle grew just a little more.

Three

I slumped over my desk with my head in my hands, watching the calendar swim before my eyes. *Marriage license, 2 p.m!* It shouted at me. One more month and legally, I was a married woman. Two more months until the wedding. My heart sank a little, and I frowned. *What's that about?* I wondered.

"Alicia!"

I snapped to attention as my boss—excuse me, my *supervisor*—came to my desk. She insisted I call her my supervisor because "it speaks more to our collaborative leadership style here at Browne and Sons." Collaborative, my ass. What was collaborative about booking all the associates' appointments and flights and taking calls? I knew they only hired me because they worshipped the ground my mother—Quinta Jones—walked on. I think my boss actually said, one time, "...anything for Quinta." There's nothing collaborative about nepotism.

I plastered on my work smile. "Yes?"

"Do you have the finalized travel plans for my conference this week?" She tapped her foot impatiently.

Inwardly, I rolled my eyes. I didn't know anyone under the age of forty who tapped their foot when they were waiting for something. Except my boss, one of the law firm's partners. Sorry, my *supervisor*.

Outwardly, I kept my smile in place. "Yes, I have them right here." I found the internet tab with the flight and hotel itinerary. "You're all set to leave this Wednesday at 10 a.m."

"Good. Were there any additional details?"

"Everything should be in your inbox."

"Good." With that, she walked away.

I sighed and turned back to my screen, tapping my nails against the desk. Looking around to make sure no one could see my screen, I clicked on the tab with my personal email inbox. At the top was an email with the subject line, *About your inquiry*. Taking a deep breath, I clicked on the message.

Monday August 6th

To: AceJones@gmail.com
   From: MannoxPhotography@mannox.org
   Subject: About your inquiry

Dear Alicia Jones,

We thank you for submitting your photos to our contest. Unfortunately, we do not feel that your style embodies the look and feel of our company. We invite you to call us at your convenience if you have any questions.

We wish you the best of luck on your photography journey.

Warmly,
    Mannox Photography

I let my breath out with a *whoosh*. I moved the email to my "Rejected" folder and clicked through a few more emails. I had known it was a long shot, so I wasn't surprised by the rejection. And it wasn't like I was planning to quit my job, anyway. *Mother would have a heart attack.*

But so what if she disapproves?

The thought surprised me a lot more than the rejection letter. I looked at myself in my tiny desk mirror and a defiant face looked back at me for a second before transforming into my Work Appropriate Face. *So what?* was not a question that you asked in the face of my mother's generosity. It wasn't just my boss—supervisor—that would do "anything" for Quinta. That seemed to be the general consensus around these parts even if my mother no longer worked at this firm.

But even as I tried to iron out that question, and keep my life wrinkle free, the question became sprinkled throughout my day. *So what if the coffee machine breaks down and I don't fix it?* I thought as an associate cussed out the offensive machine. *So what if the flight is at 9:45 a.m. instead of ten?* I thought as my boss/supervisor came to complain. *So what if I want to leave this godforsaken job? What does it matter, anyway?*

"What does it matter, anyway?" I snapped my head toward Andrew. He continued to look at the sky, completely unaffected by my eyes on him. I could tell that he noticed because he smiled slightly in that way that he does when he knows he has my attention.

"So your parents don't agree that you should be a gymnast." He pointed to a cloud that looked like a penis and I snickered. "Is it hurting your chances of going to college?"

"Not really." I tapped an unnamed rhythm on my thighs. "If anything, it strengthened my applications. I got into five different schools, two of them Ivy Leagues."

"Okay, then, so what if you're a gymnast?" Andrew turned to me then, his cherry-wood-colored eyes meeting mine. "What does it matter to them?"

"You know how they are," I muttered. I picked at the skin around my pointer fingernail and watched the blood rush to the spot. "It's easier to give in than to fight it. I'm still living with them. I depend on them for money, for resources."

Andrew gently put his hand over mine, and I stopped worrying the skin. "You mean, it's easier to give up than to fight it."

My lungs burned with the fire of a thousand suns. "I'm not giving up completely. Besides, what am I supposed to do? I don't even have a real job. I'm only eighteen. They support me."

He turned back to the clouds with a decidedly holier-than-thou air. "Then get a real job."

"So you're just giving up then?"

We were practicing yoga in my living room when I

broke the news about my rejection to Cat. I figured that it wouldn't be a big deal. Very few people even knew I loved taking photos, so it wasn't like I had a following of any notoriety. But Cat had been my best friend since she stole my crayons in kindergarten. If anyone was going to call me out on not following my dreams—other than Andrew—it would be her.

I sighed long and low at my own willful ignorance. I should have known that Catalina would never let my dream go quietly into the night.

"It wasn't meant to be." I pushed my hips into downward dog and breathed deep through my nostrils. "It was stupid, anyway. I submitted my photos on a whim. I figured that the prize money would pay for any last-minute wedding things. Asking them about their job openings was just a side note."

Catalina grunted as she flopped into child's pose. "Okay, but you've loved doing photography since you were a kid. Being rejected has gotta hurt, even if just a little."

I shrugged as best as I could in the pose. The TV yogi walked her feet up toward her hands and I followed. "It wasn't my best work," I admitted. "I submitted the flowers and pond stuff."

"The safe stuff, then." Catalina stood up and brushed off her leggings. She watched as TV Yogi lifted her foot into tree pose. "Typical fear of success. Why are we doing yoga again? I hate this shit."

"It's good for flexibility"—Catalina waggled her eyebrows as I rolled my eyes—"and heart circulation, and peace of mind, which I need right now. Besides, this is my damn apartment. What do you mean by 'fear of success?'"

"Fear of success is when people get in their own way on their path to achieving their goals, for fear that they will be too good." Catalina looked at the tree-pose variation and shook her head. "You do this every time you get close to getting what you truly want and need."

"What does that mean?"

"Take last year, for example." Catalina sat on the ottoman and crossed her legs. "You had the opportunity to take photos at Ana's wedding. I know that Ana was your brother's wife, but you two are pretty close, so it would have been a great opportunity. Did you take the gig?"

I studied my fingernails.

"Exactly. And what do you love to do most, even more than watching gymnastics?"

"Event photography."

"Point made. Fear of success."

I scratched my knee and picked at a scab on my elbow. "That wasn't me getting in the way of my own success," I said. "It was me trying to avoid the wrath of Quinta Jones. Can you imagine if I even *attended* Ana's wedding after everything that's happened, let alone take photos for it?"

Catalina narrowed her eyes. "Since when does your mom run your life?"

I lowered my eyes to the ground. "Since always." I looked at Catalina. "We are in a good place right now. If I rock the boat, it will cause a major blowout, and the wedding will be ruined. And you know how hard Michael has worked to make sure everything is okay."

"How hard *Michael* has worked?" I'm sure the whole eastern seaboard felt the scorn of Catalina's eye roll. "News to me. Last I heard, he couldn't be bothered to look at silverware for the wedding, let alone do actual work for it. And anyway, why is it more important to make your mother—and Michael—happy than it is to pursue a career that's actually sustainable? You can't work at your mom's old law firm forever."

I shrugged. "It's just a couple more months, and then I

only have to talk to my mom on holidays and birthdays," I said. "Sure, I work at her old law firm, but it's not like she visits them. Besides, we only talk about wedding stuff, so once the wedding is done, we'll have nothing else to talk about. If I only have to make her happy for this one day and never really talk to her again, it's worth the sacrifice."

"Is it though?" Catalina said. "Is it really?"

Catalina's argument wasn't new. I had been fighting this fight with everyone I knew—except my parents, and Michael—for years. Once Cat left, I rolled up the yoga mat, trying to push a similar argument, from years ago, from my head.

Dante, my late brother, was always pushing. He pushed me to apply to the best colleges, even ones that were on the opposite coast. He pushed me to fight against that part of me that just wanted to stay hidden. And most importantly, he pushed me to listen to what those closest to me were saying even if I thought it was complete nonsense.

Consider the possibilities, he would say. *You never know.*

I closed my eyes and leaned my back against the ottoman. My watch beeped as it monitored my heart rate's steady climb. I could feel the tears gathering in my eyes as I pressed my knees to my chest, willing the anxiety, that elephant on my chest, to go away. *You're not dying,* I reminded myself. *Keep yourself in the present.*

I did all the things my former therapist told me to do. I thought of five things that I could see, four things I could hear, and so on. But nothing could stop the suffocating feeling that overcame my entire being, that feeling that this was, truly, the end.

After a few minutes, I felt my heart rate come back under my control, but Dante's words stayed with me: *consider the possibilities.*

Yeah, I've already done that, I thought, rising from the floor.

And look where it got me.

As if I didn't have enough to contend with, I couldn't get Andrew out of my head.

I saw a pair of friends walking down the street and felt the pang of loss. I would hear someone reveling in their food choice and would remember Andrew's reverence for the art of eating. He even showed up on my "People You May Know" on social media one day.

So, of course, I stalked him the next day.

Against my will, of course.

It was surprisingly easy; I didn't even have to friend-request him. His profile was up for the world to see. Under his "About" section, he listed *Writer* as his profession. I smiled to myself.

I quickly scrolled through his profile pictures. It seemed like he changed them every six months or so. In one of them, he was with a group of well-dressed men. In another, he was taking a bite out of a four-patty burger. I smiled. *Glad some things never change.*

As I scrolled down his page, I noticed the same woman writing on it. Sadie Johnson. *Who is this woman?* I frowned at her photo. She had big, brown eyes, smooth, dark skin, hair down to her waist (*probably weave,* I thought scathingly, though I couldn't be sure), and a heart-melting smile. In one photo, she was barefoot with oven mitts, wearing an apron stretched across a sizable chest. I looked down at my own chest and glowered.

She was with Andrew in many of his wall photos, smiling brightly at the camera or up at him. In some of the photos, he was smiling back at her. She was a little bite-sized version of a woman, all legs despite her height. I could see them doing cutesy things like baking together and having housewarming parties. *She can't be taller than like, 5'3"*, I thought to myself. *She probably fits right in the crook of his arm. I hate her.*

Suddenly, my computer chirped. I jumped a little and stared at the bottom of the screen. A message.

Couldn't resist, huh?

I frowned and then rolled my eyes as I recognized the photo and the tone.

But he couldn't possibly know that I was on his page, could he?

I took a deep breath before responding. ***Couldn't resist what?***

Adding me.

I looked to the top of his profile and saw the checkmark next to *Friends*. I groaned aloud. No wonder I could see all of his photos. We were already friends!

Catalina, I thought grimly. She did seem pretty intent on doing something on my computer last night. I must have left my page open.

Catalina did it. I rolled my eyes again though he couldn't see it. ***She had my computer the other night. Must have done it then.***

Lucky me.

My heart picked up speed. *Lucky him? What does that mean?*

I've been thinking about the last time we talked. I was an asshole, and I'm sorry. Truce?

I sighed. *He feels lucky that he got a chance to apologize. It's nothing more.* ***Truce. It's funny, I was just thinking about you.***

Good thoughts, I hope.

I rolled my eyes again. *He just can't help himself.* ***I was thinking about how you never looked at anyone the way you look at food. Is that still a thing?***

Yes. I've even joined a group of like-minded individuals. It's called People Against People Who Are Against Loving Your Food. We meet at lunch.

Charming.

I thought so.

ANYWAY...... What's new with you?

Not much. He paused, and I grumbled to myself. *You'd think that he would have taken a typing class by now, for God's sake.* **Going through some stuff.**

Going through some stuff?

Still echoing, I see.

Still shifty, I see.

I could almost hear his laugh through the computer. **I missed this.**

Not sure I can agree. I smiled, regardless. *So are you going to tell me what you're going through or nah?*

Just another breakup. They never get any easier. We broke up yesterday.

Sadie Johnson?

Another pause. **So you HAVE been stalking me.**

My face burned as I realized I had been caught. *Just curious.*

Uh huh. But yes, Sadie. I thought she was the one.

Does it count as being "The One" if she's one of many? Is that what you mean by the one? Would certainly clear things up.

Retract the claws for a bit, will you? My heart is tender.

As is your head.

Too soon.

I laughed aloud. Andrew's tender-headedness was the stuff of legends. His whole family had clowned him on a regular basis for it. Everything seemed to hurt his sensitive scalp. He could barely get a haircut without grumbling about how the barber was clearly trying to torture him.

No bullshit though, you okay? I chewed my lip as I considered what to say next. **Why'd she break up with you?**

She didn't. I broke up with her. Hence the whole "not the one" thing.

My breath quickened, and my lungs squeezed. It had to be a coincidence that he broke up with her right after he saw me again. I counted to ten before I responded.

So you broke up with her because she wasn't The One?

Yep. I can't waste any more time being with people who don't fulfill me.

Is fulfillment a double entendre?

Wow, Ace. How is that a double entendre?

It just is.

Whatever, Jones. You know what I mean, though. I found myself in a relationship of convenience. I was in it because it was nice. Easy, you know. Sadie was great but it was a lifestyle of complacency. I couldn't do it anymore.

I felt a pang of guilt as I thought about my relationship with Michael. It was definitely more about duty and opportunity than about love. *But what's wrong with that?* I thought angrily. *It's not so bad. And I do love him.*

Fine, fine, fine. Everything's fine. Isn't it, Ace?

I see. Sounds rough.

Oh, Ace. You're such an empathetic wordsmith.

Now who has to retract the claws?

This time, I knew that he was smiling. I could feel my own smile stretching across my face. I sighed.

So when are we gonna hang out again?

I paused. *Is this a good idea?*

Not sure I wanna hang out with you, Parker. It was too much fun the last time.

C'mon, Ace. I'll be on my best behavior.

I tapped my fingernails against the desk as I thought about this. Finally, I said, ***Guess I'm a glutton for punishment. What's your schedule look like for tomorrow?***

My schedule is decidedly freer, given the circumstances. When do you get off work?

5 PM.

Great. Meet at the old spot? Our park?

Our park. My heart sighed. *He still thought of it as our park, too.* Memories of us pointing out penis-shaped clouds—me, reluctantly, Andrew, enthusiastically—along with us sitting on the cement bench while it was still drying, flooded my memory. Our park. So much had changed since we christened it so.

Sure, I said finally. ***Works for me. See you then.***

Until then.

"So what do you think they did with it?"

I laughed and shrugged. "Who knows? It took them long enough to replace it."

"Indeed."

We both looked down at the new wooden bench that had replaced our old cement one. Andrew stroked the wood with one finger, teeth worrying his bottom lip. For a moment, I thought I saw a flicker of sadness in his eyes, but then he looked at me and smiled. I closed my eyes against the sudden onslaught of tingles, the breath knocked from my body with just one awkward-kid smile.

"How are your shoulders doing?" he asked.

I opened my eyes and frowned at him. "My shoulders?"

"Yeah. Are they comfortable up there by your ears?"

I rolled my eyes but consciously lowered my shoulders to their regular position. "Very funny."

"I like to think I'm hilarious, actually. A barrel of laughs, even."

"Yeah, maybe you should become a comedic writer. Or join Clown College."

"Alright, alright, Jones. You wanna sit or what?"

We both plopped down on this decidedly lesser bench and sighed. I unpacked our ice cream from my plastic bag and handed Andrew his cherry ice cream. He shook his head and pushed it away from him. "No, thanks."

I raised my eyebrows and turned toward him fully. "Andrew Parker, turning down food? Are you sick?"

"Nope, just watching my figure."

I gave him a once-over, feeling the laughter bubble up from the depths. When we were in high school, no matter how much he ate, Andrew never seemed to gain weight. Granted, he packed on the pounds now, seemingly all in muscle. I laughed to cover up the fact that I, too, was watching Andrew's figure. Or trying not to.

As I wiped tears from my eyes and hiccupped, he said, "Okay, you don't have to laugh that hard. Give me the Cherry Garcia so I can eat my feelings."

I handed it over and opened my Phish Food. "I haven't laughed that hard in years."

"Well, you never did laugh as hard at anything as you laughed at me."

We smiled at each other.

"So, you're getting married."

"I am."

"What's that like? What's he like?"

I sighed as I thought of Michael. Andrew frowned but didn't say anything.

"Being engaged is this in-between world," I said finally. "People can no longer ask you, 'when are you getting married?' but they move on to other questions. Harder questions. Like 'are you thinking about having kids?' or even 'how many kids are you going to have?'" I picked at the skin around the base of my nails, avoiding Andrew's gaze. "I feel more unsettled now than I did before."

"And your fiancé? What's he like?"

I shrugged. "He's great," I said. "Motivated, generous." I blushed. "Attractive."

Andrew smiled his awkward-kid smile again. "You love him."

I smiled, too. "Of course. And he loves me." I frowned then. "Catalina doesn't seem to think so."

"Is she still looking for the greatest love of your life for you?"

I laughed. "Yup. Even though I'm getting married in two months."

Andrew joined in with a laugh of his own. "Of course."

I scooped a spoonful of my ice cream. I rolled the ice cream around my tongue as I reminisced. "I'll never forget the time she tried to hook me up with Terry."

"Thomas."

"Whatever. It was a disaster. He actually had the nerve to say, 'the gymnastics team is good, for a bunch of girls.' For a bunch of girls! What a whole lot of what-the-fuck."

"You mean, you *weren't* good for a bunch of girls?"

When I turned to Andrew, ready to pummel him, I recognized the little-brother smirk on his face and rolled my eyes. "What? Was he wrong?"

"We were good for *anybody*, full stop." I caught Andrew's eyes. "Guys included."

We sat in a warm silence for a while, eating our ice cream. Andrew smoothed the top of his with his spoon before asking, "So are you still taking photos?"

I nodded as I licked all of the ice cream off of my spoon. Andrew watched. "Nothing has gotten picked up yet, though." I shrugged and fiddled with my spoon. "Same old rejection letter. 'Not a culture fit.'"

Andrew scoffed. "What does that mean, anyway? *Culture fit.* It's not like you're trying to promote photos of cannibalism. It's American event photography."

"I know, right?" I turned to him then, heat rising in my blood. "I'm taking photos of fucking rock bands, for Christ's sake."

He took a bite of his ice cream with vigor. "Do you have a picture of yourself anywhere on your submissions?"

I thought back for a moment on all of the emails I sent. "Yeah, it's in my email signature. Why?"

He nodded then, understanding twisting his mouth into a grimace. "Then culture fit refers to this." He gently rubbed his knuckles against my arm. My whole arm tingled with the contact. I quietly marveled at how compatible our skin tones were before shaking away the thought. "You don't often see black people on the rock scene. Think about it: how many black, female-lead rock bands do you see out there?"

"Not many. You have The Leroys, but that's pretty much it." I picked up my spoon again and considered it. "You're right, of course. I should've known better. I'll have to take my photo off of my signature."

Andrew turned to me then, defiance bright in his eyes. "Don't do that."

"Why not? I won't get hired if I don't."

"You will find a company that will hire you *because* you are who you are. You won't have to trick them into it. I feel it."

"Okay Ms. Cleo," I joked. He sighed impatiently, and I turned to see disappointment flatten his mouth. "What?"

"You still do that thing where you make a joke out of serious things." He faced forward on the bench and took another bite of ice cream. "And it's still as annoying as it was back then."

I coached my face into a neutral expression though I grit my teeth against my sudden anger. "What the fuck is *that* supposed to mean?"

"You can handle serious topics when it's not about you or what you can do, so why can't you be serious when you're in the spotlight?" Andrew took another slow bite, closing his eyes and humming low. This time, I watched him. His enjoyment of food surpassed almost everything else, including his love of frowning.

I grimaced and turned to face front. I played with the edges of my carton with my spoon. "Maybe if my photography isn't accepted by these companies, it means something." I tapped my spoon against the carton. "Or maybe I need to do something differently. Or maybe I should stop submitting my work." Andrew frowned but I held my hand up to stop his protests. "Sometimes, it's not about what the *right* thing to do is, but what people will accept." I sighed. "We can't all be a zealot for truth like you, Andrew."

He turned toward me with a frown. "So you'd rather do nothing, then?"

I shrugged. "I'm not doing *nothing*," I said. "I'm still taking photos. I'm still submitting my work. But I have a good job. Michael makes enough to support us both anyway. What, exactly, is my purpose of submitting these photos?"

Andrew thought about this for a moment, shoveling spoonful after spoonful of ice cream into his waiting mouth. Finally, he said, "Maybe we should talk about something else. In the interest of keeping the peace."

I nodded. "Agreed."

We sat in silence for a moment before Andrew spoke again. "So, tell me more about your fiancé. What's his name again?"

"Michael."

"Michael, then. Tell me more about Michael."

I shrugged. "I don't know what else to say. He's a little younger than us, only by a couple of years. Still in college, his last year." Andrew smirked, and I rolled my eyes. "Yes, I still date younger men."

"There was only one exception."

We looked away from each other. Neither of us wanted to speak his name aloud, but Nicholas was the one mistake in my dating history that neither of us could forget. After all, it led to the demise of our friendship.

I cleared my throat. "Anyway, Michael's a football player through and through. He's in line to be the starting running back on his college team. He also manages a branch of his family's clothing store, Clothing Line downtown. He's going to school to get his degree in Management and Finance."

Andrew whistled low. "Sounds like your parents' dream guy."

I rolled my eyes. "Yeah, and he's white to boot. They love him more than me."

Andrew tilted his head. "Yeah?"

I sighed into my ice cream. "Well, not really," I

conceded. "Or at least, that's what I try to tell myself." I turned to him then, remembering. "Speaking of parents, how are yours?"

Andrew smiled to himself. "They're good. They'll be happy that you and I decided to kiss and make up, as it were."

My brows snapped together. "Why's that?"

Andrew squinted, looking off into the distance, then looked down at his hands. "It was a tough two years. My parents were convinced that it all started when you and I stopped being friends."

I grimaced. "Well, I did keep you honest. And trapped in the real world."

He turned to me with that look of defiance. "No, not trapped," he said. "Anchored. Grounded." His eyes softened then. "I missed that, Ace. I missed you. Truly."

"Yeah?" I smiled a little. "I wasn't a wet blanket on your rainbow dreams?"

"Never."

"Never? Lies."

"Okay, maybe once or twice." I raised an eyebrow. "A few times."

I laughed and patted his thigh. "I'll take it. Nobody wants to be a perpetual Debbie Downer."

He smiled. "Truth." He looked at his watch and grimaced. "I probably shouldn't keep you much longer. It's getting late."

I looked at my phone and sighed. Three missed calls from Mother, a voicemail, and a text from Michael. *Home yet?* it said. *Your mom's been blowing up my phone.*

"Yeah, I gotta go." I rolled my eyes and showed him my phone. "Mother awaits."

We stood up and stretched. He wrapped me in a bear hug and I tried, as always, not to enjoy it. "Let's do this again," he said. "Invite Michael and we can all go to dinner at my parents' house next weekend."

I laughed into his shoulder. "You, me, and a football player? There's not enough food in their house."

I felt the smile in his voice. "They'll make it work." His voice turned slightly sour. "Because they *definitely* love you more than me."

"Hey, babe." Michael smiled as he smacked a wet kiss on my cheek. He dropped his bag where he stood and headed to my kitchen. "Want me to make something to eat?"

I moved the bag to the hook as I grit my teeth. I loved having my own space. Before Michael, I always knew where things were; I could navigate my apartment in pitch blackness without turning on a light.

But then, Michael happened. Almost immediately after he proposed, he started to encroach on my space. Soon, I started finding errant socks with no match, or bags piled up in the hallway. Worse, the invasion of my space hadn't gotten any easier with time. I could only imagine how much worse it would get when I moved in with him.

I plastered a smile to my face as I turned to him. "Sure. What are you in the mood for?"

"Spaghetti." He rummaged through my cabinets. "You?"

I shrugged. "I'll eat whatever you're making." I sat at the kitchen bar. "How was your day?"

"Good." He held up the spaghetti in triumph. "Associates didn't have any major problems with customers, which was a nice change. We did have an old-lady smuggling ring come through, though."

"An *old-lady smuggling ring*? What the fu— heck is that?"

I caught myself on the swear before Michael could frown at me.

He poured meat sauce into the saucepan and turned it on low. "They've hit up all the major locations in the mall and smuggled goods under their shirts or in their bras. Another manager calls them the Blue Haired Group." He snickered. "Because old ladies sometimes have blue hair. You get it?"

I rolled my eyes. "Yes, I got it. So have they been stopped yet?"

"Yeah, we caught them today."

I nodded. "Good."

"How was your hangout with your friend? Andy?"

"Andrew," I corrected as I grimaced. Andrew hated the nickname Andy. His younger twin brothers used to call him that, and it was the fastest route to a headlock. "It was fine. He invited us to have dinner with his family next weekend. He wants to meet you. You wanna go?"

"Sure, babe," Michael said easily. "Just remember that your parents planned that thing for next Saturday."

I let out a groan. "I completely forgot about that. God! Do we have to go?"

Michael smiled and kissed my forehead. He held out the sauce spoon for me to taste. "Yes, babe, we have to go. It's being held in our honor, so it's kinda the point that we go." I licked the spoon clean and sighed in pleasure. Andrew may know how to eat, but Michael knew how to cook. "Invite Andy. Kill two birds with one stone. I can meet him then."

"Andrew," I corrected again, frowning. "And I guess I could do that." I tried to picture Andrew mingling with my parents' high society friends. Something deep in my stomach twisted. I wasn't entirely convinced that my mother didn't still hate him.

"Do it, then." Michael shrugged. "It couldn't hurt."

The stove timer beeped, and Michael turned it off. He broke the pasta in half, little pieces flying everywhere. I ground my teeth together, watching some of the pieces fall underneath the fridge.

"Sounds like a plan," I said.

Won't that be weird? Doesn't your mom still hate me?

I laughed. *It's as if he's in my head,* I thought.

I guess we'll find out on Saturday. And I got the okay from Michael, so there's that. In fact, he suggested that we invite you.

How big of him.

I rolled my eyes at the screen. Andrew's sour, doubtful look popped into my mind as I typed. *I thought it was really sweet of him, actually.*

It'll be a pissing contest. And I'll be on his turf.

I frowned; I hadn't thought of it that way. *Michael doesn't think like that.*

I guess we'll find out on Saturday.

Andrew was silent for a while before another message appeared. **I'm sorry. I haven't even met the guy and I'm already making assumptions about him. Forgive me?**

Forgiven. I huffed. *I guess.*

Cool. What are you up to?

I looked at the piles of SD cards and camera equipment and shook my head. *Organizing. You?*

Staring at a blinking curser and a blank page. Trying to write.

Writer's block, huh. What's the holdup?

Silence for a moment. Then: **the love scene.**

I squinted. ***Don't you usually write fantasy novels?***

Yes, but the main character has a love interest. Which, you know, happens in fantasy novels, too.

Tone down the snobbiness. I rolled my eyes. ***So how are you gonna write the love scene?***

I don't know. It's why I'm stuck. If I knew how to write the scene, I wouldn't be stuck.

Feeling a little sensitive?

Nope, but thanks for making my day, nerd.

I smirked. Andrew had always worn his heart on his sleeve. *Some things never change.* **Didn't mean to make you cry, Minnie.**

Ugh, are we bringing that nickname back again?

Yes, because you whine like a Minnie.

Listen, Jones, one day I will find an equally demeaning nickname for you, and you will not like it.

Haven't found one yet, huh. What's the holdup?

I could almost feel the smile in his words as he typed. **I see some things never change.**

Likewise. I smiled, too.

He paused as if mulling something over in his mind. Finally, he said, **Okay, okay, I'll go to this soiree, if only to see the man who's vowed to put up with you for *supposedly* all eternity.**

My heart beat a suddenly frantic rhythm in my body. ***You'll go? Really?***

Truly. But once your mom spots me, I'm out.

Butterfly wings rustled against one another in my abdomen, and I felt like I was lit from the inside out. I smiled. ***Can't wait.***

"So…Ace. Good to see you again."

It was what I thought was another ordinary Thursday. I was, again, waiting for the sports bus in the cold, wintery Massachusetts air. I was so intrigued by the voice — or my mind was so numbed by the cold, who knew? — that I only sort of recognized that I turned around and almost hit him in the gut with my elbow. Unfortunately, I missed.

"It's you." I squinted up at him. We were almost eye to eye; he was a little taller. Impressive, I thought, despite myself. At 5'9", not many eighteen-year-old guys were taller than me.

Before I could stop myself, my eyes traveled to his face. His smile revealed rows of straight, white teeth, and only his bottom lip moved as he smiled, as if he had never moved through the awkward-kid-smile phase. But his eyes were intelligent, also appraising me. And he had a beauty mark, which was cute enough, I guess. His high-top fade was clean, the lineup, crisp. A guy who takes care of himself. I tried to press the smile from my face and failed.

I looked down at his sneakers, fully expecting a pair of Jordans to match the haircut but found Converses instead. His skin was a smooth caramel color, as if it had never seen a pimple in its life. Lucky, I thought.

I turned away from him just as he said, "Like what you see?"

I shrugged. "Not bad," I allowed, "if it weren't for the crew-cut body type."

"Crew-cut body type?" He asked, tilting his head to the side and squinting. "That sounds oddly insulting."

"You know," I explained, a wry grin making its way to my face. "It's like a mullet without the party in the back. All business. Straight to the point."

"What's that supposed to mean?" His eyes narrowed more until his irises were barely visible.

"You're a plank of wood," I said finally. "No junk in the trunk."

"I'm sorry, I didn't realize we were still using that anachronism," he said. I grinned wider. Definitely offended.

"You're a 2x4," I continued. I laughed then. "A regular plank of wood with extra sanding."

"I am not." His grumble, paired with his frown, made me snicker more. "And if you don't appreciate it, I can find several other girls who will."

"I bet," I crowed. I laughed in earnest as he picked up his bag and walked away. "What?" I asked. "Feeling a little salty?"

"No, but thanks for making my day, nerd," he grumbled.

"Listen here, Skinny Minnie," I said, pointing a finger at him. "You don't know it yet, but this is the start of a beautiful friendship."

The next day, as I was sitting at my desk, my email alert pinged. *Great. More rejection letters. Or an order from The Boss.* Sighing, I opened it and skimmed it quickly. Not believing my eyes, I read it again.

Wednesday August 8th

To: AceJones@gmail.com
   From: TheLeroys@gmail.com
   Subject: HELL YEAH!!

Hey Alicia,

*Thanks for reaching out to us! Your photos are EPIC!!
We actually just lost our photographer so we would love to
have you in the crew. You would start next week. Let's set up
a time to discuss your rates.*

Best,
Jean

Jean Lee
Drummer, The Leroys

*PS – If you have any writer friends or people who can do our
social media shit, send them our way! I'm tired of answering
all these fuckin emails LOL*

"I'm not surprised."

I looked at my phone then held it up to my ear. "What
do you mean, you're not surprised? I'm fucking shocked!"

"Ace, you've always had the ability, and the eye for it."
Andrew shifted the phone to his other ear. "I knew
someone would see it. And you kept your headshot on your
signature, right?"

"Yeah."

"Exactly." His voice warmed, and I felt the decadence
in it, like thick, warm fudge straight from the pot. "So
when will you start?"

"When will I start?"

"You really have to stop echoing me, Ace."

I scoffed. "I'm not gonna take the offer."

A pause. "Why not?"

"I can't just up and quit my job," I said. "They want me to start immediately."

"So?"

"*So*, my mother would kill me."

"And? Ace, you're a grown woman. You're almost twenty-five. No need to involve your mother."

"And what will Michael think? The Leroys tour all over the state. I would have to go with them."

"Are they going to tour outside of the state?"

"I'm not sure, but they only seem to tour in the Northeast."

"Okay then."

"You say that as if that resolves everything!"

"It does." Andrew's breath changed as if he had suddenly gotten up. I could picture it: he was probably pacing and frowning, like he does when he's come across a really exciting, challenging word problem.

"Think about it this way: you'll never be more than a few hours from home. Michael will always be able to get to you if his caveman needs arise." I grumbled at that, but Andrew continued. "Your mom can't even complain because it sounds like they're willing to pay whatever your rate is. You'd be a staff photographer for a *band*, Ace. That's great publicity for your whole family! Right up their elitist alley."

He did have a point.

"I'll have to think about it," I said finally. "It's still risky. I don't know anything about them as a company, and because they're a band, it's not like I'll be able to find who's worked for them."

"It may not be easy, but it's not impossible. Hemingway's a small town." I heard tinfoil crinkling and I smiled. *Of course, he's eating.* "You should be able to find at least one person who's worked for them. I'll help you."

"Yeah?" I grinned, feeling the blood rushing through my veins. "You'd do that?"

"Of course." I could feel his grin, too. "Besides, they still need a writer, right?"

I spent the rest of the day searching for any scrap of information that I could find on their former employees. Well, first, I responded to the email and told them I'd like to interview first. *Then,* I went fangirl crazy, and *then* I went looking for any scrap of information that I could find on their former employees.

"Did you find anything?" I asked Andrew as I was unlocking my front door. I threw my keys on the kitchen bar and put my bag on its hook. I sniffed. *Something smells good in here. Flowery, like roses.*

"Yes." Andrew rustled something that sounded like papers. "Turns out that their former staff writer is a writer friend of mine."

"And?"

"She loved working with them. *Loved it.*"

"Yeah?"

"Yeah. There's only one catch."

"What?"

Andrew paused, and I felt my heart sink. *They're all psychopaths,* I thought. *Great, there goes my dream.*

"They're a little...disorganized. Things change very quickly when they're on the road." Andrew's grimace showed through his voice. "I know that you're not a fan of that."

"Yeah."

"But other than that, she had nothing but good things to say about them. They all have a lot of fun, she said. The only reason she's no longer with them is because she had a kid. It'll be an adventure, for sure."

"For sure," I echoed. I sat down on the couch with a *plunk*. "Well, that's not unexpected, I guess."

"True."

"But still a lot, you know?" I fiddled with the hem of my shirt as I looked around my apartment. It was weirdly neat, as if Michael had finally picked up all his socks. *Guess he put the key to good use.* "It's a big adjustment."

"But could it be a necessary one?" Andrew opened his fridge, moved something heavy-sounding around. "This is your dream, Ace. This is what you're meant to do."

"How do you know that?"

"I just do," he said. Pride showed through his voice and I preened at the sound of it. "Alicia, this is what you're *born* to do. Don't you feel it?"

"I think you're turning into a hippie before my very ears," I joked.

"Listen, Jones, I've been a hippie from birth. Crunchy granola all the way. But no veganism. I love meat."

We both laughed.

"Well, I have the whole weekend to consider it," I said. "I'm interviewing with them on Monday."

"Good! So you have the whole weekend to fangirl, then."

I smiled. "How did you know that was on the agenda?"

"Because you've listened to the Leroys since at least high school. At *least*."

"How do you know *that*? Michael doesn't even know that."

"We went to school together, Alicia. I know you."

Oh yeah, I thought. *I forgot. This is Andrew.*

I frowned at that. *But I'm not that person anymore.*

He bit into something crunchy-sounding and chewed.

"You gotta try these chips," he said around a mouthful. "One of the customers came into the store the other day, and—"

"Can we talk about something other than food, Andrew? Fucking focus, man."

"Okay, okay, you have my full attention. But seriously, think about it. Working with your dream band. How awesome is that?"

"Truly awesome," I agreed. As I breathed in, my nose caught a whiff of the heavenly scent I smelled earlier. "Hold on, Andrew, I think Michael's here." I finally looked around me and saw the rose petals sprinkled on the floor. A brief flash of annoyance ran through me before I melted at the sight. And then panicked.

"Andrew," I said slowly. "What's the date?"

"It's the 8th, why?"

"Shit." I checked my watch and saw that I had an alert: *Happy Anniversary! 7 p.m.* "I gotta go. I gotta go."

"What happened?"

"I forgot my anniversary!" I groaned. "Michael's gonna kill me."

"Well, I don't wanna be a witness to a murder, so go." He laughed low. "I'll talk to you later."

"Okay, bye." I ended the call before Andrew could respond. I swiped my hands under my arms and sniffed. *I smell absolutely vile.* Sweat poured down my back. I looked at my watch again. Fifteen minutes until Michael walked through the door. *Shit, shit, shit.*

I ran to the bathroom and turned on the water. A hot stream of water poured forward. *Thank God.* I quickly turned it to shower mode and stripped off all of my clothes. Stepping in carefully, I wet my hair, watching the water run through the curls. I grabbed the conditioner and squirted it into my hair. I could hear my phone ringing as I ran my soapy washcloth over my body. *He's gonna kill me.*

"Alicia?" I heard. Footsteps came closer and closer. I quickly rinsed and shut off the water. I grabbed the towel just as Michael stepped into the bathroom. His face fell. "You're not ready yet?"

"I'm so sorry, I got out of work late, and then I was researching the Leroys—"

"What about the Leroys?"

"I didn't tell you?" I searched my memory and realized with a start that I hadn't. *I called Andrew first thing.* "The Leroys want to talk to me about being their photographer."

"Really?" Michael sat on the toilet seat and frowned. "Do they tour all over?"

"Just in the area," I said quickly. "I would never be far, just a few hours at most."

Michael made a noise of dissent. "How long would you be gone for each time?"

"I haven't even interviewed yet, so there's no way of knowing."

"So you don't even know if you have the job yet?"

"No, Michael, I don't." *How would I fucking know that?* I wanted to ask but held my tongue at the last moment. The last thing I needed right now was a *why do you use that language* talk. "That's what the interview is for."

"Okay, so nothing's set in stone." He breathed a sigh of relief. "That's good. It gives us time to talk about it."

"Yeah," I said though I could feel what kind of "talk" it would be. "I interview on Monday, so it gives us the whole weekend."

"Okay, good." He brightened. "Now, are you ready to have the best meal of your life?"

"Sure," I said. My sinking-heart feeling stayed, and I felt suddenly deflated. "Let me go get ready."

I picked at my steak absentmindedly as I thought about the photographer job. I could picture it: my heart slamming against my chest as my eye pressed to the viewfinder. My blood singing in my veins to the lyrics of my favorite Leroys song, *Take it on Faith*. I would feel the energy of thousands of hearts beating to the same wild drum solo. And then, there he is. Running his hands over my shoulders, down my body, his warmth enveloping me, his murmur whispering across the bare expanse of my shoulder.

We would fit perfectly together.

"...so I said to her, 'you'd better not put that picture frame under your dress!'" Michael slapped the table for emphasis and I jumped. I blushed furiously as I tried to suppress my thoughts.

"You alright, babe? You're not usually this jumpy." Michael frowned. "And you're picking the skin around your nails again. Did you read that article I sent?"

"Yeah." I put my hands under the table but kept picking. "Sorry."

"It's okay. I just don't want you getting some funky bacteria." He smiled and reached across the table to pat my shoulder. I tried not to grimace. "I worry about you, babe. You need to be taken care of."

I'm fine on my own. Always have been. The thought came with a bitter edge that tasted like burned toast and black coffee. "I can take care of myself, Michael."

"But you shouldn't have to."

"Why not? I'm grown."

"Yes." He frowned. "But we are one. Or soon to be, anyway."

"Yeah." I fiddled with my napkin under the table. "I know." The edges of my soap bubble of happiness squeezed until it popped. My shoulders sagged under the weight of reality.

I wasn't going to get the job. Even if I did, Michael would never let me tour with a band all across the state.

Well, I thought. *It was a great dream while it lasted.*

That night, as I was getting ready for bed, my phone pinged to let me know that I had a text. I picked up my phone and sighed heavily.

Did you talk to Michael about the gig?

I grimaced. *Yeah, but what's the point?*

A pause. **Did you just ask what the point is? Really?**

Oh no, I thought right before the phone rang. Sighing, I picked up the call and waited.

"WHAT'S THE POINT?" he thundered. "Ace, what happened? What did Michael say to you? 'Me Tarzan, you Jane, Jane stay home'?"

"Knock it off, Andrew." I sighed again, the will to fight exiting my body on my exhalation. "It was my decision, not his. It would put too much of a strain on our marriage, way too early."

"Or maybe it'll make it more durable. You don't know which way it could go."

"It's not worth the risk. No career is worth losing the man I love."

"So you're just gonna do the safe thing, then? Or the supposedly safe thing? What if this is your destiny, Ace?

You're just gonna give up the adventure of a lifetime for a sure-to-be-boring thing?"

"That *thing* you're referring to is my future marriage, Andrew. And anyway, my life is good as it is. Why mess up a good thing?" I shook my head. "Besides, this is how things are supposed to work out. Get married, settle down, have kids. Right?"

"Are you asking me or telling me? Because if you're asking me, I feel like you know what I'm gonna say."

"Maybe it was just a beautiful dream, and now it's time for me to wake up."

"Or maybe this safe choice is your nightmare, and you're supposed to wake up to your dreams."

Right, I thought. *Well, it's too late for that.*

Four

My mother would not leave me alone.

"Alicia, make sure to follow up with the caterers. We want to make sure they have the food ready no later than 7 p.m. And dessert should be on every table by 7:40 p.m."

"Alicia, we need to have the best silverware out on the tables. You know how Leticia gets about unwaxed cutlery."

"Alicia, call the florists and make sure they haven't put more than three sprigs of baby's breath in the centerpieces. And no red roses. It's too overdone."

"Alicia, make sure that you don't have your nails more than 3.5 centimeters long. People will talk," I mimicked later, recounting all of Mother's demands. Catalina snickered, and Michael frowned.

Michael, Jeremiah, Catalina, and I were all lying in various forms of laziness around Catalina and Jeremiah's couches, stuffed from dinner. It was a rare night that Michael had off, so we decided to hang out with Cat and Jer. As I related my day, finally out from under the watchful eye of my mother, Jeremiah rested his fingers in Catalina's wild curls. Michael and I sat on opposite ends of the couch, limbs hanging loosely.

The Last Supper, I couldn't help thinking before I suppressed the thought. It was Friday night, the day before my parents' big engagement party. I hadn't considered myself a Christian in at least a few years; something told me, though, that comparing my last night of freedom before social hell to Jesus' last night before he was crucified was probably sacrilegious.

"Make sure to have them painted," Jeremiah deadpanned. I gave him a fist bump of approval.

"I don't see the issue," Michael said. "Alicia's mom just wants things to be nice."

Jeremiah, Catalina, and I just stared at Michael until he shrugged. Picking up the last of the fries, he stuffed them in his mouth and asked, "Am I missing something?"

"Other than your manners?" Catalina raised an eyebrow. "Yes."

"Alicia's mother has been a coldhearted stickler for as long as we've all known her," Jeremiah explained. He weaved his fingers between Catalina's. "We've all known each other since kindergarten, so that tells you something."

"'Color *inside* the lines, Alicia. *Inside.* And don't be so messy about it.'" I rolled my eyes and Catalina pressed a laugh from her mouth.

"She doesn't seem so bad to me," Michael protested. "Maybe not as cuddly as most parents, but not terrible."

"Give it a year or two more," Catalina said. "You'll see."

"Don't poison Michael against Mother." I shoveled popcorn in my mouth. "She loves him. And clearly can't wait to have some high-yellow babies." Jeremiah, Cat, and I rolled our eyes in unison as we remembered my mom's many comments about my "midnight skin." I didn't know about colorism among black people until I realized that my mother's commentary on my skin color was not a compliment. It stung, at first, to come to the conclusion that I would be seen as lesser-than in even my family's eyes. Now, it was just an annoyance.

"She just wants what's best for you," Michael insisted. He puffed out his chest proudly. "And she knows that I'm what's best for you."

"Yes," I assured. "You are." As I moved closer to press my lips against Michael's, I could hear Catalina and Jeremiah fake-gagging in unison.

"Don't listen to them," I murmured. "They were insufferable in their first year of marriage. Don't get me started on their engagement year."

"We were just fine, thank you," Catalina sniffed.

I raised an eyebrow. "Define 'just fine,'" I said.

Catalina blushed as Jeremiah gave her a sly look. "I'm not mad about it," he murmured.

I gestured to them. "Point made."

"Speaking of the past, we bumped into Andrew on the way home." Catalina raised an eyebrow as I avoided eye contact. "He told me you have a new job opportunity?"

"Not really." I pressed my legs together and clenched my hands. "A band asked me to be their photographer, and tour with them."

"And?" Catalina pressed.

I shrugged. "I'm gonna pass on it."

"What! Why?"

"It's what's best for our family," Michael jumped in. "She'd be away for months at a time. And who knows what that life will be like."

Catalina cut her eyes at him. "So, this was a decision that you two made together?" Her eyes found mine.

I nodded, and Jeremiah frowned.

Catalina shook her head and sighed.

———————

"Mother, please stop worrying the dinner napkins. They look fine."

She ignored me and flipped the napkin over once more. "The governor will be here," she said. "And the Abernathys."

"What do they do again?"

"They're agents for several major bands. How do you not know this?"

"I work at a law firm that does tax law, Mother. How *would* I know this?"

"You like that one band. The wild one. What are they called?"

"The Leroys?" I suppressed an eye roll so hard that my eyes watered. "They're not exactly wild, Mother."

"The singer's hair is pink!"

"She has a few streaks of pink; the rest is natural-colored. And that's what makes them wild?"

"You watch your tone, Alicia Jones." My mother faced me directly and I felt my spine shrink. "You may be an adult, but I will not tolerate disrespect."

"Yes, ma'am," I mumbled.

"Good." She turned back to the table. "You might want to get dressed." She sniffed delicately. "Maybe take a shower first."

"On it." I took a deep breath and weaved my way through the tables. They were set precariously on the lawn because "Heaven knows we paid enough money to have all of this landscaping done," as Father put it. *Yes,* I could hear Andrew saying all of those years ago. *Heaven knows.*

"Wow, Ace, shower much?"

I spun just as I heard a murmured laugh behind me. Only one person could sneak up on me in the middle of the afternoon.

"You're here," I said. My heart beat fast with annoyance, delight, and desire in equal measure. I slapped his shoulder. "And unlike some people, physical labor does make me sweat. But maybe you don't know anything about that."

"I think I'm in great shape, thanks," Andrew replied. He kissed his sleeved bicep and turned out his fist to the side. "Though I'm sure I'm nothing in comparison to your muscle-head fiancé."

"Listen, I'mma need you to cut that shit out, Parker." I rested my clenched fists on my hips. "You haven't even met him. Maybe you two will end up in a bromance."

"Not likely." Andrew relaxed his pose. "Anyone who thinks it's a good idea for you to rot in this town is no friend of mine." His eyes roved my face. "You weren't meant to stay here, Ace. Don't forget that."

For a moment, I couldn't look away from his cherry-wood-colored eyes. As my breath accelerated, the rest of the world fell away. Andrew had been the former oasis for my heart, and it was hard to forget that. To forget him and the impact he had on me. His hand came up to rest lightly on my shoulder and he squeezed gently. I sucked in a breath, almost dying as memories and his scent flooded my nose. I never could forget how he always smelled like bonfire smoke.

"Of course, you found Alicia," Catalina said behind me. Andrew dropped his hand and I snapped to attention.

I shook my head as Catalina's tone registered in my brain. She sounded like she caught us doing something, which made me balk. *For fuck's sake, I'm marrying Michael!*

But I wonder what would've happened if I wasn't.

"Do you need something?" I asked sweetly, turning toward her. Her smile was equally saccharine.

"I could ask you the same thing." She raised an eyebrow. Andrew's eyes swiveled back and forth between us, his brow furrowed.

Catalina wrapped her tiny arm around my shoulders, whisking me away from Andrew. She sniffed delicately, matching my mother from minutes earlier.

"You smell disgusting," she said. "Let's get you ready for this party."

"Is all of this makeup necessary?" I grumbled as Catalina clearly ignored me and put on more eye shadow. "I have more makeup on than the entire cast of Moulin Rouge combined."

"It's not *necessary* because you have the smoothest skin I've ever seen on anyone except Andrew," she replied. "But the makeup is a bonus. It will make your boo forget his own name."

"Michael prefers me without makeup."

"Not that boo."

I cut my eyes at Catalina. She ignored it, per usual.

"Almost done," she chirped. She wrapped some of my curls around her fingers and gently let go. Like the obedient tendrils they are, they kept their suggested shape. Cat smiled, satisfied. "Okay, go look in the mirror."

I tentatively stepped in front of the mirror. When my eyes met in the mirror, I gasped softly.

Catalina had turned me into a bona fide princess.

My dress whispered against my knees. The bodice of the gold-colored dress hugged me gently, fanning out once it hit my waist. Layers and layers of gossamer silk made me feel like I was supported by clouds. I ran my fingertips down the fabric in wonder.

And then I looked at my face.

Big, doe eyes stared back at me in surprise. Gold eyeshadow sparkled around my eyes, and my skin glowed. My lips parted around teeth that stood straight and bright, in stark contrast with my skin. My hair had been in an old twist-out, stretched for days, which made it easier to put it in an updo. Small curls played around my temples and ears, while the rest was held back by a matching gold-colored, metal headband.

"Catalina." I found her eyes in the mirror and she smiled proudly. "Thank you."

"I did nothing but work with what you already have," she said. She looped her arm through mine. "Now let's find your man."

Five

I t turns out that Catalina had more pull with my mother than I realized. "I was able to invite some key people," Catalina said as we walked down the hall. I looked at her askance. She only smiled.

"Aunty Alicia?"

I turned to the voice I knew so well, a smile bright on my face. He smiled back, and my heart lurched. *So much like his dad.*

Justin Jones, my late brother's only child, seemed to be all gangly arms and legs. His growth, while predictable, was startling for his eight years. It was as if he had grown overnight even though I saw him two weeks prior. My vision grew fuzzy as tears gathered. I missed my brother every day, when I allowed myself to think about it, and here was his almost identical, though smaller twin. *If only he could see you*, I thought. *He would be so proud of the person you're becoming.*

"Justin." I bent down to wrap my arms around him. "So good to see you. So glad you came! Is your mom here?"

He nodded against my shoulder. "In the backyard."

I pulled away to look at him, and he beamed. "You're getting so big! You look just like your dad."

He shrugged, pride and embarrassment shining in equal measure. "Thanks." He brightened further. "Will there be cake here?"

"I sure hope so!" We grinned at each other. "What's a party with no cake?"

The three of us walked in unison down the hall, Catalina's arm still looped in mine, my other arm around Justin's shoulders. When we reached the backyard, I caught eyes with Ana, Justin's mom and my sister-in-law. She gave me a two-fingered salute and turned back to Michael. I snorted as Ana gestured wildly and Michael nodded while pulling on his beard. I could see his grimace from clear across the yard. *Typical Ana,* I thought. *Probably trying to get Michael to save the rain forest.*

Cater-servers weaved their way around the backyard with hors d'oeuvres and drinks. Most people within eye range were laughing or dancing, and the playful cadence of the band swelled. The undertone of the drum caught my heart and carried it along the bass line of the guitar. I clasped my hands to my chest so as to not get carried away.

I turned to Cat, and she squeezed my shoulder. "Thank you."

"Anytime," she said, and winked. Reaching around and tapping Justin on the shoulder, she said, "C'mon, let's go find that cake."

"Awesome!" He bounced on his toes as he walked away with Catalina. I smiled as I watched both of them go.

"And here, I was told that this party would be a wash."

I rolled my eyes before turning to Andrew. "Can't you

make an entrance like a normal person?" I asked. "Or at least, make some noise instead of sneaking up on me all the time."

"Can't promise that." His smile gentled as he took me in. "Wow, Ace, a shower really transformed you. Well done, my friend."

"Man, screw you." I laughed. Happiness bubbled over as I finally took him in. I touched his sleeve, and the fabric brushed against the pads of my fingers. The sleeves tapered subtly to his wrists, right below his watch. Though Andrew had the skinniest legs on Earth, I couldn't tell despite the well-fitting pant legs of the suit. His shoes, leather and subtle, were properly tied—a miracle by anyone's standards. Bringing my gaze up to his shirt, I noticed that it was an understated slate gray. The pocket square matched the hue of the shirt exactly.

I whistled low. "You're not too bad yourself, Parker. You actually own a suit? Or did you rent this one, too?" My laughter rang through the yard as I recalled what he wore for prom night.

When Andrew had come to pick me up that night, I surveyed his suit with a critical eye. Some of the threads had hung loose, and the sleeves were way too short. Underneath the jacket, he had on a bright purple shirt with a silky, darker purple tie. His pocket square had been yet another vibrant shade, but different hue, of purple.

On his feet, he had donned a shiny black pair of shoes. The shoelaces had come untied and were hanging loose, like the threads of his suit jacket. *At least the pants are the right length,* I thought. But Jesus, he had been a mess otherwise.

"You do realize that those are tux shoes, right?" I hid my mouth behind my fingers to quell the laughter. "You're a hot fucking mess, Parker. Where did you find this getup?"

"It was the only suit I could rent short-notice," he said sheepishly. I locked eyes with him. "I know, I know, you told me to get a suit weeks ago."

"Weeks. Plural. Emphasis on the plural." I sighed, pulling him into my house, and shut the door. "Let's see if my brother has a better suit. I think you two are the same size."

My vision sharpened as I brought myself back to the present. Andrew was speaking, so I attempted to focus on his words.

"I'll have you know, *Ace,* that I own many suits now." He cleared his throat and looked away. "I didn't have much of a choice."

I tilted my head, puzzlement furrowing my brow. "Why?"

"Sadie." He burrowed his hands in his pockets. "She… liked to go out."

"You mean, she was a bougie-ass woman." I smirked. "And you hated it."

"I did," he admitted. His eyes warmed as they met mine. "But sometimes, it's worth it. Like now."

I blushed as Andrew's gaze intensified just slightly. Before I could retort, I felt an arm around my shoulders and the sharp, alcoholic smell of cologne wafted over my nose. I closed my eyes as Michael said, "Hey babe. I just got away from Ana. What an intense chick."

"She's passionate." I slid his arm off of my shoulder. "There's nothing wrong with that."

Michael made a noise of dissent. "Sure, babe. Who's this?"

We both turned to Andrew. "Michael, this is Andrew," I said, gesturing to him. "Andrew, Michael."

They shook hands solemnly, eyes assessing each other.

"Pleasure to meet you, man." Andrew let go of Michael's hand. "Alicia told me a lot about you."

"Same." Michael's body tensed with a wariness I rarely saw. I looked on with raised eyebrows. "You two went to high school together?"

"Yeah, and college, basically." Andrew and I smiled at each other. Michael frowned. "We went to sister colleges," I explained. "They were practically down the street from each other."

"But we spent a lot of time on each other's campuses too." Andrew regarded me, smiling. "She was at my place when we found out about the Marathon Bomber—"

"And he was at my place when we were told to shelter in place –"

"And then there was that fun little adventure in your big chop moment—"

I smirked. "And your subsequent shit fit when I said the cut was just okay."

"I gave you a crown of glory." Andrew's sniff was equal parts miffed and indignant. "You looked like Buckwheat, and I saved you. You're welcome."

"Interesting." Michael gestured, and a cater-server appeared by his side. He took a flute of champagne for each of us and passed them around. "Well then, I'm glad I got to meet you in person, I guess. Here, let's toast." He raised his glass, and Andrew and I followed suit. "To old friends, new beginnings, and a love that'll last forever."

"Cheers," I said, and our glasses clinked together. We sipped in an uncomfortable silence.

Finally, I turned to Michael. "Let's dance."

He made a face like I was asking him to step over hot coals barefoot. "Babe, you know I hate dancing."

"It's our party; let's at least make the effort." I stuck my bottom lip out and batted my eyelashes, and he smiled a little.

"Compromise?" He took my flute and then Andrew's. "You and Andy catch up, dance a little. I'll schmooze with your parents' friends, so they don't bug you too much." He winked, and I laughed. He always knew how to get out of dancing, but I didn't mind this particular compromise, even if it meant dancing with Andrew. He was a terrible dancer, especially in comparison to Michael, but I hated talking to my parents' friends.

Andrew took my hand. "I guess I must take one for the team," he said. My heart sped up at the physical contact. He tugged on my hand for emphasis. "Let's do it."

I looked back at Michael. For a nanosecond, I saw an expression flit across his face. His eyes narrowed at Andrew's hand around mine. He pulled his lips between his teeth and his eyes looked almost feral, possessive. *He's jealous,* I realized. Before I could say anything, it was replaced by a friendly but smooth mask.

"Have fun," he said, waving. He disappeared into the crowd.

My uneasiness dissipated quickly. I turned to Andrew with a wicked smile. "Let me show you how it's done."

Andrew led me into a surprisingly smooth dip at the ending note of the song. Everyone clapped, and Andrew bowed.

"Thank you," the lead singer said. "We are the Bangers. But before we go for the night, we just wanted to say congratulations to Alicia and Michael, and we hope you have a long and happy marriage. To show our congratulations, we have a special guest joining me on the stage for our last song. Please welcome Yasmine from The Leroys!"

My eyes widened, and I looked to Andrew. He smiled and shrugged slightly. "I called in a favor."

I crushed his body to mine in a hug, pulled away, then hugged him again. "This is fucking epic, Parker," I whispered in his ear. "Thank you, thank you, thank you."

"You're welcome." He pulled back to look into my eyes. "May you have a long, happy, *healthy* marriage." He smiled sadly. "Consider this my wedding gift to you."

I tilted my head a little, my gaze roving over his face. Slowly, the party started to fade away. Something was going on with Andrew; I just couldn't put my finger on it. His mouth tightened slightly, like the skin around his eyes. He gripped my shoulders more firmly than he had in the past. And his eyes. Those cherry-wood-colored eyes. They were bright with the light of a thousand sunsets. My breathing quickened until I felt like I had been running a marathon. And I sure did hate marathons.

Almost as much as I hated this uncertainty.

Andrew dropped his hands from my shoulders and took my hand in his. "C'mon, Ace," he said quietly. "Let's show them how it's done."

I remembered when we danced at our high school prom.

We moved slowly to the tired beat of the band. I wrapped my arms around his shoulders, and his wrapped around my hips. Slowly, he moved me in a small circle. I sighed against his chest.

"I wish everything was this peaceful in my life." I held back the tears for fear of ruining my makeup. High schoolers can be cruel, and I didn't want to give them any more fodder. "Everything with Dante, and his illness…"

I felt Andrew's nod. "It sucks, for sure," he said. "Which is why this moment is so important."

I pulled back a little to look at his face. "This moment right here?" I asked. "Why?"

He looked at me, too, then, eyes shining with some unnamed emotion. "This is the moment your life changes forever," he said. "Can't you feel it? There's something in the air tonight that has sparked a flame in your heart. You'll look back on this moment five, six years from now and know that this was the moment that changed everything. I only hope that I'm there to see it."

And as I looked into his eyes, I did feel it. Something within me had clicked into place, the "aha!" moment I had been waiting for this whole time without knowing it. All of the sadness, all of the strife with my brother Dante and my parents, it all washed away, out with the tide. And my doubts, everpresent as I thought about the measure of my life, were bottled up like a secret that no one wants to keep. They, too, were whisked away with the tide.

Looking at Andrew, I knew that he was a part of this peace, this serenity in my life. He was my oasis in the desert, the eye of my storm. And I knew, when the time came, he would be there to witness all of it.

Six

"The woman of the hour!" Yasmine crowed. I plastered on what I hoped was my best smile and waved shyly. She enveloped me in a friendly bear hug and rocked me side to side. Pulling away, she surveyed me and whistled.

"Hot mama," she said. She grinned and dropped her hands from my shoulders. "I had no idea the badass photog Alicia Jones and this Alicia Jones were one and the same. But I'm so glad that you are!" She adopted a faux-serious face and put her fists on her hips. "Now I can beg —I mean, *convince*—you to tour with me and the band."

"Oh, I don't know—" I started.

"Nonsense," she cut in. "What's stopping you?"

Though Andrew was silent beside me, I could feel the urgency vibrating off of him. *Tell her,* I could hear him say. *Tell her that the only thing stopping you is yourself.*

I ran my palms over my dress. "Well, I want to get settled into married life before I start a completely new career."

"*Manita,* it looks like you've been taking photos your

whole life," Yasmine disagreed. "It's not new." Andrew made a noise of consent beside me, and I fought the urge to glare at him. "And what do you do other than taking photos?"

"I'm a lawyer's assistant." I shifted from one foot to another, trying not to pick the skin around my fingernails. *Terrible bacteria*, I reminded myself. *Gnarly, terrible bacteria.* "I work in my mom's old law office."

"Sounds like the very opposite of what you should be doing with your life," Yasmine said on a yawn. "Listen, the job is yours if you want it. None of this BS about interviewing first. I said what I said," she put in over my protests. "I know a fantastic photog when I see one, and your photos are phenomenal. We want nothing less for our band, so you're it. But let's make a deal." She leaned in closer and I followed suit. "Let's do a test run, see if it's a good fit. You'll tour with us for this month, and if you don't like it, no hard feelings. Hell, bring your fiancé. Make it an adventure." She straightened and clapped her hands together. "Do we have a deal?"

I considered her for a moment then looked at Andrew. He raised his eyebrows and shoulders. *Why not?*

I turned back to Yasmine with a grin. "Okay," I said. "Let me talk it over with Michael and get back to you. Can I let you know by Monday?"

"*Sí, claro,*" she said. Her smile reached the ends of her face as she slapped my shoulder with gusto. "I gotta head out but I can't wait to hear your yes on Monday." Her grin turned sly. "Catch you then. Nice to meet you, Andrew."

"The pleasure's mine," he said. And with a two-fingered salute, Yasmine disappeared into the crowd.

Andrew turned to me. "Isn't that dope? You're gonna do it, right?"

I sighed and grimaced. "I have to talk it over with Michael, first," I said. "He may not go for it."

"Go for what?" I heard behind me. Andrew and I turned to see Mother and Michael frowning behind us. Their facial expressions were so similar that it would be funny if it weren't so terrifying. My watch beeped, and I looked down at it. *Take a breath.*

"I actually have some really great news!" I said cheerfully. Michael's frown deepened as he looked from me to Andrew.

"What is it?" Mother asked. She crossed her arms over her chest and waited.

My smile faltered a little as I considered how to approach the topic. "Well, you know how I've been obsessed with the Leroys since high school?" Michael nodded but my mother just stared. "Well, their lead singer just offered me a photography job on the spot!"

Mother's eyes widened, and Michael frowned. "Really?" Michael asked. By the tilt of his eyebrows, I knew that this was not good news to him. I belatedly remembered that we were going to discuss the gig this weekend. Mentally, I facepalmed. When I caught his eye, he seemed to be asking, *Are you serious right now?*

"Yes," I answered to both his unspoken and spoken questions. "It's amazing. It's a once-in-a-lifetime opportunity. And they said you can go with them, too, Michael!"

"Wait a minute, how will Michael oversee the store?" Mother questioned. Her forefinger tapped a beat on her forearm. "He can't run it from the road."

Michael nodded. "She's right, babe." He frowned. "But this is a once-in-a-lifetime opportunity." Finally, he shrugged. "You might as well go," he said.

I looked at him askance. Not even a full twenty-four hours ago, he was against the idea, but he seemed to be at least somewhat okay with it now. *I wonder what Catalina said to him.* This had her name written all over it.

"Go without you?" I frowned. "But it would be right before our wedding."

"It's okay." He beamed. "Consider it my wedding present to you." I could feel Andrew's eye roll as strongly as if I had looked at him directly. I held back a grimace myself as I said, "Great! And it's not like I'll be alone."

"I know that, babe. You're going with the band."

"Yes, that. But Andrew's going as their staff writer."

A pause. "Andy's going with you?"

As I studied Michael, I could see that mentioning Andrew had the opposite effect on Michael. The subtle sense of possessiveness radiated from Michael, heating the air more than the late summer heat ever could. *And here, I thought it would be a good thing that Andrew was going.*

"I'm not going *with* Andrew, Michael," I said finally. "I'm going on tour with my favorite band, and Andrew will happen to be there."

"And you can just pick up and leave your job here, Andy?" Michael asked.

Andrew's lazy smile made me narrow my eyes. The practiced casualness of the expression reminded me more of a predator in wait than the Andrew I knew. "It's Andrew," he corrected. "And yes. My job gives me the flexibility to come and go as needed. They understand that sometimes, I have to do what I can to support the important people in my life."

A tense silence ensued in which the two men stared each other down. Though the fact that they so openly disliked each other made sweat trickle down my back, I also wanted to roll my eyes at the brazen display of testosterone. What was this, the 50s?

"Well, I guess it'll be good for Andy to go," Michael

said after a while. When my mother and I raised our eyebrows at him, he said, "He'll be there to watch out for her, be there for her when she needs to be taken care of." Andrew's eyes swiveled to mine, and I tried to hold back a grimace.

"I think Alicia would give me a wallop or two if I tried to be there for her when she didn't want me to, but I'm flattered," Andrew said. "How about this: I'll do it for the adventure." He smiled at me. "Protecting her is just a bonus."

Though I wanted to pummel him on the spot, I simply rolled my eyes. My mom frowned as if putting something together in her mind.

"Sounds like we have a deal," Michael said. He stuck out his hand for Andrew to shake. Andrew grabbed it firmly.

"Sounds like it," I said.

A few days later, I sat at my desk, almost bouncing from residual joy. The Leroys, a band I had followed since high school, wanted me to be their photographer so badly that they offered me a job on the spot. I couldn't believe it.

I was so wrapped up in my own thoughts that I barely noticed my supervisor waiting by my desk. "Alicia," she said, and I jumped. "Can you come in my office for a minute?"

My heart beat wildly in my chest. *I wonder what's going on.* Slowly, I stood up from my desk and stood in my boss's doorway. "Sure, what's going on?"

"Close the door, please."

With my heart gaining speed and sweat flowing freely

down my back, I obeyed. I hovered by a chair before taking the plunge and sitting down. "Yes?"

"I got a call from our IT department because they found strange activity coming from your computer station." My boss steepled her fingers together. "Do you know what they found?"

"No, ma'am." Out of her eyesight, I picked the skin around my fingernails.

"They found multiple job site tabs open in your internet browser, and something about photography submissions?" My boss frowned. "To bands?"

"Yes," I squeaked. I cleared my throat and said in a calmer voice, "Those were just random contests that I entered. Nothing serious."

"Well, it seems pretty serious to me," Boss said. "It seems like you're searching for another job. Have we not done right by you and Quinta? Is that why you're looking for other opportunities?"

"No, ma'am," I said quickly. "I appreciate this job. And the opportunities you all have given me."

Boss sighed. "But you don't love this job, and it's showing in your work." She handed me a sheaf of papers, the top one displaying her travel plans. "The hotel wasn't even booked, Alicia. If I hadn't caught that, I would be in New Mexico with no place to sleep. What do you have to say about this?"

"I'm sorry," I stammered. "It won't happen again."

"You're right, it won't." She sighed again. "I wanted to repay Quinta for all of her generosity, but I just don't see this working out. Effective immediately, you are terminated from your position. You are to pack up your things and head to HR to pick up your final check. A member of security will escort you from there. Do I make myself clear?"

I heard my boss as if we were both underwater. I couldn't believe it. *Fired?* I had never been fired from anything before. What was I supposed to do for money?

"Understood?" my boss prompted.

I gulped. "Understood. I'll start packing now."

I stood up slowly, holding onto the armrest for support. With small, quiet steps, I shuffled back to my desk to pack up my things.

"It's a good thing you're taking that photography gig, then."

I glared at Andrew with what I hoped was foreboding. As always, he ignored me.

We decided to meet at a lunch spot down the street from his job. I called Cat at soon as I was escorted out of my former job's building, but she didn't pick up. As my anxiety ramped up and I was almost in the throes of a panic attack, I called Andrew. He told me to meet him at the lunch spot.

"It wasn't supposed to be a permanent gig," I said. "I was supposed to go for a month and come back to *this* job. Who knows how much this band gig pays. Who knows if I'll be able to support myself."

"Weren't you planning on moving in with Muscle Man anyway?" Andrew asked. I rolled my eyes at the absurd—but accurate—nickname. "You should be set in terms of bills and whatnot. Plus, he's making corporate money, *and* he comes from a rich family. You'll be okay."

"Yes, but that's not the point. It wasn't in the plan."

"So?"

"So, I can't just uproot my whole life, Andrew. It doesn't work that way."

"Why not?" He sipped his soda. "Give me one good reason why it can't work that way."

"It's chaotic, for one." I ticked off the reasons on my fingers. "For two, it's irresponsible. Three, it's unreliable."

"Aren't those all ways to say that you want a life that's boring and static?"

"No, but safety is at the very foundation of who I am."

"Is it?" Andrew licked his fingers without a care in the world. "Or is it at the foundation of what you're told to be?"

I sighed. "The point is, I'm out of a steady job."

"So now you *have* to go tour with your favorite band. Sounds like a real problem."

"It is. What about you? Have you cleared it with your job?"

"Yeah." He shrugged. "They weren't too concerned. Still, it's a good thing Yasmine agreed to pay me to be their social media specialist."

I sighed again. "Lucky you. You have a job to come home to *on top of* working on the road."

"Listen, Ace." He turned to me. "You'll be fine. This is what you're meant to do, remember. Everything else will follow."

"Okay Deepak Chopra." I snapped the lid back onto my potato salad. "I'll see you in the morning, bright and early." I stood up and stretched. "Time to face Michael."

"What do you mean you lost your job?" I didn't think it was possible, but I was almost convinced that Michael's eyeballs would roll out of his head and onto the table. He shook his head back and forth, as if he couldn't believe what he was hearing. "How are we gonna pay for your apartment?"

"I'll talk to the band leader about it tomorrow morning and send you the numbers," I said. "But really, there's nothing we can do about it now."

"I know, but babe, you're usually much more careful than this." He looked at me, grimacing. "Why would you look up other jobs on a work computer?"

"I wasn't thinking about it, okay," I snapped. I sighed as Michael's grimace quickly morphed into a frown. "Look, I'm sorry. I'm disappointed in me, too. It was careless and stupid to look at other jobs on a work computer. But we have to deal with this now, so can we talk about what we're going to do?"

"Well, my job plus whatever my dad can lend us will cover our expenses." Michael's eyes moved back and forth as he did the calculations in his mind. "You'll probably get your first paycheck toward the end of the month, when your rent is due. That'll be your last rent payment anyway, considering that you were gonna move in with me. We will be fine." He sighed and ran his hand through his silky strands. "We just don't have any wiggle room for mistakes or added expenses in the interim."

I nodded slowly. "I understand. I'm so sorry, Michael. I don't know what got into me."

He smiled, patting my shoulder. I tried not to grimace. "It's okay, babe," he said. "Things happen. I've got it covered." He puffed out his chest a little. "I'll take care of it."

I pressed a kiss to his lips. "I have all the faith that you will," I said.

Seven

Mornings are already tough with the sun. Mornings without the sun are so much worse. We stood outside the bus, the next day, in the parking lot of my favorite park. The air was heavy with moisture, and the flowers housed dozens of droplets of dew. Fog, as if waking from a great slumber, lazily fit itself around every solid surface. I yawned through my second cup of coffee, trying to keep my eyes wide open to combat the lethargy refusing to leave my body. I looked around and saw that the band was no better. Jean Lee, the drummer, nodded off while standing and almost fell over. Kevin, the second guitarist, was actually asleep in the front seat of the bus. Philip, the lead guitarist, was the worst of them all. He grumbled for a full five minutes, to himself, with his eyes closed. I overheard something about, "fuckin' mornings, who signed us up for this shit?"

The only three that seemed even remotely conscious were Yasmine, Danny, the bassist who also drove the bus, and Andrew. The latter sidled up to me with a knowing smile.

"You know, morning people tend to die sooner," I grumbled.

He actually laughed, the jerk. "I live for today. You should, too, Ace. It's a beautiful day to be alive." He inhaled deeply. "Don't you feel it?"

"I feel extreme remorse for waking up so early, that's what I feel," I grumbled. I shifted my camera gear. "When did you get to be a morning person, anyway? You used to hate them."

Andrew shrugged. "I guess my perspective changed. I feel more productive at this time of day."

"No one should feel anything this early." I yawned for the fifth time in as many minutes. "Where's the first gig, again?"

"Harbor Café, I believe." I opened my eyes to see Andrew frowning at a piece of paper. His eyes widened and then flashed to mine. "It's several states over."

I stood up straight. "I think I heard you wrong. I could've sworn that you said that Harbor Café is several states over."

Andrew smiled his awkward-kid smile.

My breath quickened as adrenaline shot through my body. "It's *several states over?*"

"That's what the paper says."

I snatched the paper from his hand and scanned it quickly. I gasped. "*All* of these places are far from here. Not one of them is close to home." I pushed the paper into Andrew's chest. "I thought that we would be in New England the whole month!"

Andrew watched me closely. "Ace, are you okay?"

"No! No, I'm not okay. Michael's gonna *kill me.*"

Yasmine walked over to us, in the midst of a yawn. "What's with all the noise over here? Even the birds stopped chirping."

"I thought that we were gonna be in New England this whole month." I pushed my hair back with both hands as I paced in a tight circle. "Why didn't I look at the itinerary?"

"Alicia, *manita*," Yasmine said, watching me. "It's my bad. We thought we would be local, but then we realized we can reach *más personas*, more people, if we expand past the northeast. But you'll be back in time for your wedding, no prob. I promise."

"I wish I had known this sooner," I said. "Michael is gonna kill me for sure. And Mother. God, and Father. They'll take turns killing me. Bring me back to life, then kill me just to teach me a lesson."

"I understand that this is a change from the original plan," Andrew cut in. "But what's the big deal?"

"What's the big deal? *What's the big deal?*" I stopped briefly to glare at him. "You know my family. This is a big fucking deal. Also, this is *not* what I planned. This is *not* what I thought."

Yasmine and Andrew exchanged looks. "Is she gonna be like this the whole time?" Yasmine asked Andrew.

"I hope not," he replied.

"I can hear you two!" I exclaimed. My voice was as shrill as my nerves were frayed. As I paced, I could feel my breath getting quicker and quicker. Finally, Andrew stopped me with both hands on my shoulders.

"Alicia, listen to me," he said. My eyes snapped to his. "Were you planning to go home, for any reason, at any point in this next month?"

"No, but—"

"And is Michael taking care of things back home?"

"Yes, but—"

"And the wedding planning is being handled by your mom, correct?"

"Yes. But Andrew—"

"And your phone works, does it not?"

I sighed. I knew where he was going with this, but I answered anyway. "Yes, Andrew, it does."

He let go of my shoulders. "So, there's no problem, then." He smiled cheerfully. "Nothing has changed."

"But what if there's an emergency?"

"What if there was an emergency when you were shooting? Would you stop right then and there?"

I glanced at Yasmine then at him. "No."

Andrew spread his hands wide. "Then *nothing has changed.*" Andrew looked to Yasmine. "What time are we leaving?"

"Five forty-five—ten minutes," she said. She looked around at her bandmates. "Or whenever these sacks of lard can get moving."

"Good, that gives us enough time." Andrew looked at me. "Do you wanna pray?"

I stiffened and looked around. "Here?"

"Well, maybe not *right* here, but yeah."

I shook my head. "No, I'm good. But thanks."

Andrew watched me for a moment, head tilted to the side and a small frown playing between his brows. Finally, he shrugged. "Alright, well, I'll see you in a few. I'm gonna go pray." And with a two-fingered salute, he disappeared.

I turned to Yasmine, who was also watching Andrew. "Damn," she said. "If I was about a decade younger, I'd tap that in a heartbeat."

I grit my teeth against wanting to punch her. As the thought crossed my mind, I reared back. *Am I jealous?* After an assessment of my stance—balled fists, squared-off posture, thought process (*I will kill her,* I thought), and emotional state—it almost felt like I got a punch to my own gut. *I am jealous. Shit.*

I didn't know what to make of that.

. . .

As Yasmine predicted, we were on the road in ten minutes. Somehow, the band was able to rouse themselves enough to put their equipment on the bus and drag themselves up the bus stairs. Andrew bounced onto the bus while I practically fell on, dragging my appendages. Once we were all on, Danny closed the door and started the engine.

"Danny, you are a godsend," Jean Lee said from the kitchenette. She raised a fist in salute.

"Danny, Danny," someone slowly chanted. The voice grew in energy. "Dan*ny, Dan*NY."

It caught on. "DANNY, DANNY!"

Soon, the whole bus was chanting. "DANNY! DANNY!"

Danny rolled his eyes and pulled out of the parking lot. I'm sure the neighbors couldn't hear anything, but inside the bus, the band members created a ruckus.

"DANNY! DANNY!"

"YOU DA MAN, DAN!"

"FUCK YEAH!"

"DANNY'S THE SHIT, BRO!"

"HAVE MY BABIES, DANNY!"

"Alright, alright," he grumbled, pressing a smile from his lips. "Calm the fuck down back there!"

I looked around me then caught Andrew's eye. He smiled and shrugged as if to say, *Hey, what can you do?*

I sighed. This was going to be a long trip.

I used the first several hours of the trip to search for other jobs.

At first, Andrew looked on over my shoulder. Soon,

though, he squeezed his long-legged body next to mine in the tiny kitchenette booth.

"Of all of the places to sit, you chose *right* next to me. Really?"

"Yes, really. I know that I get you all hot and bothered"—I rolled my eyes—"but remember, you have a fiancé who loves you."

"Do you need something, Parker?"

"Just making sure you don't ruin your life." He looked at my laptop computer screen and frowned. "Looks like I just made it in time."

"What's that supposed to mean?"

"These jobs you're applying for." He pulled the laptop toward him. "Office assistant? Receptionist? Why? You don't even like office work."

"It fits the skillset that I have," I replied, moving the computer back toward me. "It's what I know how to do."

"Yes, it's *part* of what you know how to do," he said. "But it's not *all* of what you know how to do. For instance, you could take photos at a PL Hughes, if you wanted to."

"Family portraits in the mall?" I scrunched up my nose. "Babies and shi— stuff?"

"You can say 'shit,' you know," Jean Lee piped up. "We're all adults."

Someone snickered at her. "I'm an adult. I'm twenty-one!" she said, pouting.

"I know we're all adults"—I looked at Jean Lee and pressed a smile from my lips—"but my mother says that I need to work on my sailor mouth." I grimaced. "And Michael agrees."

Jean Lee let out a groan while Andrew looked at me, eyebrow raised. "He does?"

"Yeah." I blushed. "It's a long story."

"We have hours. Please, do tell."

"It's nothing big, Minnie," I said. I clicked on a new tab of my internet browser. "He just doesn't have great experiences with women who swear a lot."

"But he's marrying you. He doesn't think you're any different?"

Sensing an underlying statement, I turned to Andrew. "Spit it out, Parker. What is it?"

Andrew shrugged, shaking his head. Yasmine interpreted: "I think he's thinking what I'm thinking. What the fuck kinda guy are you marrying?"

"Agreed," Danny piped up from the front. "Does he know you're on the road with a rock band right now?"

"If he does, he must not know what *kind* of rock band. Did he listen to any of our songs?"

"I mean, what grown-ass adult expects his bride not to swear? What time period did he grow up in, the Victorian era?"

"Lighten up on Alicia, you guys," Kevin put in. "This is her first official day. Chill."

"The point is that you don't have to be or not be anything that isn't authentic to you. Not on this bus." Yasmine turned to me with a grin. "Feel free to let loose, Alicia. We're here to help if you need it."

Hoots went up all around, complete with lewd gestures and a low, murmured laugh from Andrew. I rolled my eyes.

"Noted," I said. "Now can I get back to what I was doing?"

"Andrew's right, though," Yasmine said. "If you *must* leave us at the end of the month"—someone pretended to sob in the background—"at least have the decency to do something epic. This life is too short to sit at a desk if that's not your style."

I sighed, clicking through all of my tabs. "But see, that's the thing," I said. "I don't know anything different."

"Then we'll teach you something different," Jean Lee said. The accompanying grin didn't make me feel better at all.

We finally stopped to take a break in a town just over the neighboring state's border. We all clamored off of the bus, some of us heading toward the bathroom. Andrew made a beeline for the diner and I followed.

When we got inside, I looked around. The walls were dingy, covered with photos of famous people who had visited the diner. *Home of the 5-pound slammer!* a sign said cheerfully. There were several photos of people behind a monster of a meat patty.

"Thinking about entering their contest?"

I rolled my eyes at Andrew. "Wouldn't dream of it, actually." I smirked. "You should give it a go, though."

"Is that a bet?" He tilted his head and smiled. "You gonna put up or shut up, Jones? I know how much you love to be proven wrong."

I narrowed my eyes. "You may have won all past bets, Parker," I said. "But one day, I will win."

"Face it, Ace. You're terrible at predicting outcomes."

"I am not!"

"Yes, you are. Matter of fact, I know how much you love absolutes, so here's one: you are *absolutely* terrible at predicting future outcomes. How's that?"

"That's an absolute that is not true." I sniffed. I crossed my arms over my chest. "I'll prove you wrong one day."

"But not today?" Andrew said, a sly smile creeping onto his lips. "Not ready to lose a bet yet?"

I scoffed. "I'm not setting myself up," I said. "It wouldn't be a fair shot."

Andrew shrugged. "Fine, wimp out if you want to," he

said. We followed the waitress to the booth in the back. "There's no shame in that."

I picked up the menu and scanned it quickly. "You will *not* goad me into betting that you can't eat that big-ass burger. Stop trying."

"What's a little friendly competition, though?"

"Andrew…"

"Ace…"

I sighed and put down my menu. "Can you just pick something to order, already? I'm starving."

The waitress came back with two waters and put them on the table. "Know what ya want?"

"Can I have a stack of pancakes, please?" I said. "And a side of bacon."

"Same," Andrew said. We handed our menus to the waitress and she walked off.

"Why do you do that?"

I dragged my eyes from the window and frowned at Andrew. "Do what?"

"Use that high-pitched voice when you talk to strangers?"

"You're really getting on my case today, Minnie. Can I live?"

"Seriously though, Ace. What gives?"

"I don't even know what you're talking about. What high-pitched voice?"

"Like this," Andrew said in an absurdly high voice. "You sound like a child." In his normal voice, he added, "Your regular speaking voice is much better. You actually sound like a grown woman."

"Please, do go on. I'm sitting rapt with attention."

"But for real. Your real voice has smokiness to it. It has a timbre to it that makes me think of campfires and warm blankets." He cleared his throat and looked away. "It suits you more than that high-pitched shit."

I blushed and looked down at my linked hands. "Thanks. I think."

I could feel Andrew's eyes on me, so I looked up. His eyes held a fire whose source I couldn't place. "It's a compliment, Ace. Take it confidently." He sighed and pushed his hair back. "I don't know what's happened to you in the last two years, but whatever it was, it wasn't good for your self-esteem. Though you weren't the most fearless—"

"What's that supposed to mean?"

"—your self-esteem is practically nonexistent now." He peered at me intently.

I pushed my shoulders back and stiffened my spine. "Nothing bad happened to me in the last two years. I wish you would stop saying that."

"I wish I would stop feeling it, so I guess we're even." We glared at each other for a moment before the waitress came back with our food.

I looked up in surprise as she placed the plates down in front of us. A mountain of pancakes sat high on the plates, a round dollop of butter parked on each stack. Steam rose off of the food in a delightful, lazy haze. Andrew grinned at me, disagreement seemingly forgotten.

"Let's eat," he said.

Eight

When we got back to the bus, Yasmine was missing. "Where'd she go?" I asked Danny. He jotted a number down in the margin of his sudoku puzzle. "Went to look for a gym. Wherever we go, she has to find a gym that'll give her a 30-day free trial, or a guest pass, so that she can work out. Crazy woman. But I suppose the endorphins are worth it."

"Yasmine works out?"

Danny looked up. "Yeah. How did you *think* she got those shoulders? Wasn't by chance."

"Oh," I said. I shrugged. "I didn't know."

"As well you wouldn't," Yasmine said as she walked onto the bus. "*No me preguntaste.*" I squinted at her, recognizing that she was speaking Spanish but having no idea what she meant. "You didn't ask me," she explained. "You can't know what you don't ask about. Is everyone here, Danny?"

He crossed off a few numbers. "Yep."

"Alright, let's find a place to park this baby. We'll stay

here for the day. I found a kick-ass gym down the way and I wanna try it out."

"Your wish is my command, boss." Danny tossed the sudoku puzzle onto the dashboard. "Everyone ready back there?"

"Ready," the rest chorused.

Danny closed the doors and started the bus. "Alright then," he said. "Let's head out."

We found a spot of open land in an RV park about twenty minutes later. In those twenty minutes, I heard not less than twenty complaints, all from Jean Lee, so I thanked our lucky stars that we found the park when we did. Danny looked ready to lose it.

Everyone but me, Yasmine, and Danny clamored off of the bus almost immediately. "Air," Jean Lee said. "Sweet, breathable air. Blessed wind, glorious sun on my face. I adore thee."

"You were on the bus for all of thirty minutes, Jean Lee," I heard Philip say tersely. "Relax."

"So, will the wondrous, most talented badass photog join me at the gym?" Yasmine put an arm around my shoulders and I grimaced. "You look like you hit the weights, too."

"I do cardio, mostly." I shrugged. "But I'm down."

"I'll go, too," Danny said. He struck a pose and I laughed. "Gotta impress the ladies. You know how that goes."

"Yes." I rolled my eyes. "Naturally."

Yasmine tapped a button on her phone with a flourish. "Lyft will be here in roughly two minutes."

We all walked into the gym a few minutes later and looked around. Danny headed off toward the back right corner, where the men were grunting and panting, sweat pouring down their faces. Women dominated most of the treadmills, bikes, and ellipticals. And, apparently, they were taking over in the cycling class in the room adjacent to the main room. The instructor yelled, "That's it, ladies! Push, push, push, you can do it!"

My eyes flashed to Yasmine's. "Where do you usually start?"

She grinned. "Gotta get your warmup in, right? Let's hit the bikes. I hate the treadmill."

I frowned slightly. "Why?"

She rolled her eyes and laughed. "I may have fallen asleep on one once." She grinned. "Or twice."

I frowned deeper. "But…how?" I sputtered. "And how did you manage to escape without falling and causing major brain damage?"

"It was more of a nodding-off than a true sleep," she said. "I woke up right before I fell off."

I whistled. "Close calls, then."

"*Sí*," she said. "*Claro.* Doesn't stop me from coming here, though."

"You're brave," I said. We climbed onto the bikes. "I wouldn't have come back."

"The gym is my happy place." She pressed a few buttons and began to peddle. "I couldn't stay away."

I nodded, considering. "I almost did stop coming to the gym," I said.

Yasmine looked at me askance. "Why?"

I shrugged self-consciously and began peddling. "Michael asked me to," I admitted. "Said that he didn't want me to get too muscular and manly-looking."

"Wait, he told you not to work out because he didn't want you to get too *muscular-looking*?"

I shrugged again. "Yeah."

"Didn't you say that he's a college football player?"

I tilted my head, confused. "Yeah?"

"Then he should know that women don't build muscle like men." Yasmine let out a breath. "We don't have the makings for it. The only time women get those huge muscles and the thick necks is when they're actively training to be bodybuilders. The layperson doesn't get that kind of physique."

"I guess." I peddled a little harder. "I don't think he meant anything harmful by it."

Yasmine didn't say anything to that.

We peddled in silence for a few more minutes before Yasmine stopped and stretched her hands above her head. "You ready to hit the weights?"

"Sure, let's do it."

We hopped off of the bikes and weaved our way through the machines. Stopping at a station with an Olympic bar, Yasmine said, "Hold down this station. I'll be right back." Whistling a lyric-less tune, she bounced over to the weight racks.

As I watched her ponder over a few head-sized weights, I heard, "Excuse me, are you using this bar?"

Turning toward the voice, I was startled to find an upper arm the circumference of my leg. My eyes slowly traveled the distance from bicep to eyes and was greeted with a pair of moss-colored irises. Twin dimples, like commas, danced in and out of the man's cheeks as he smiled. His peaches-and-cream complexion colored slightly as I continued my inspection. I followed the smooth slope of his nose down to a pair of full lips. My watch stayed blissfully, mercifully, thankfully silent.

"Um, yes." I cleared the squeak from my throat. "So sorry, um, my friend and I are starting our workout—she's over there, gathering some weights—sorry that it's taking so long—"

"Not a problem, princess." His grin grew wider as I blushed. "Hey, maybe after we leave here, we could grab a—"

"Nice, cold shower?" Yasmine said sweetly. She dropped the weights under the bar unceremoniously. "I'm sure my friend is flattered, but she's engaged."

Sensing danger in Yasmine's voice and teeth-baring smile, the man held up his hands in a conciliatory gesture. "Hey, I didn't mean any harm. You ladies have a nice day." He sauntered over to an Olympic bar about 20 feet away. One that, I realized, had been empty the whole time. Yasmine watched him load the bar with her lips pursed and her look sour. "Men," she muttered.

After watching him for a moment more, she turned to me. "Listen," she said. "I sense that I'm gonna have to say this eventually, so I might as well say it now. Because I like you, I'm not gonna even sugarcoat it, *bien?*"

Inwardly, I laughed. *She must like a lot of people,* I thought. In the one day that I had been with the band, she had given it straight to almost everyone. Instead, I said, "Got it. What's up?"

"Stop being so fuckin' apologetic for your existence, *manita.*" When I frowned in confusion, Yasmine sighed.

"Look, I heard you talking to that *pendejo* when I was gathering the weights. You were apologizing to him for taking the space, but look around you." She gestured to all of the empty bars. "There are at least three other bars that he could've used. He was flirting with you, *claro, pero* he was being purposely deceptive, asking if you were using the bar. He was asking about the space to get closer to you. All while ignoring that huge rock on your finger.

"Alicia, you have a strength and fire in you. And you're

a badass photog. And you're fuckin' tall as shit, *Dios Mio.*
Own all of that. Don't be a smaller, compressed version of
yourself. Stop apologizing for taking up space in this world.
Let that fire get some oxygen and grow into a force to be
reckoned with. Take up more space. Elbow a few people
out of the way, even. But above all else, only apologize for
things you actually did wrong. Otherwise, the words
become meaningless, *verdad que si?"*

Though I couldn't understand the Spanish trickling
into her speech, the meaning was clear. I nodded. Shame
shuddered through my body, leaving pins and needles in its
wake. Yasmine's look and my review of the situation with
Muscle Man made me wonder: when had I become this
version of myself?

Yasmine nodded. "That's better. Now, *manita,* go get
your weights. The real fun begins."

Something that Yasmine had (probably purposely)
neglected to mention was that she used to be a full-time
personal trainer before she gave it up to be a full-time
musician. The easy-to-manage, chill workout that I
thought I was going to have trickled away with each new
layer of sweat. Soon, I wondered if I had any water left in
my body. *No wonder Danny disappeared,* I thought. Even my
thoughts gasped for more air.

Toward the end of the workout, Yasmine handed me
one of her towels. I wiped the sweat out of my eyes grate-
fully. "How are you feeling?" she asked.

I looked at her with what I hoped was an incredulous
look, but in reality, was probably a slightly deranged look.

"Good." She took a swig of her water and then capped
the bottle. "You have to give your 100 percent to your
workouts. I could tell by the weights you chose—and that

BS that you told me earlier about your fiancé—that you've been coasting out of fear. That's why I made you put those pansy-ass weights back. Have you ever deadlifted before?"

"Yeah."

"How much do you lift?"

"Um." I pretended to think but really, I was delaying the inevitable. "Ten pounds on each side with the forty-pound bar?"

"Are you asking or telling?"

I sighed.

"So I repeat: how much do you lift?"

"Twenty pounds total, with a forty-pound bar."

"I want you to lift triple that, with the Olympic bar we used today."

My eyes bulged. "What?"

"*Me oiste, manita.*" Yasmine pointed to her ear. "I went easy on you today, but next time, we're going harder."

"This was *easy?* Are you trying to kill me?"

"No, you're our photog. We need you."

I glared at her before I could stop myself. She grinned.

"There she is! I want you to get angry. I want you to shed whatever it is that makes you feel like you need to bow to people who don't deserve your deference." Yasmine took another sip of water. "Think about it this way: if you're really just hoping to be a housewife, which is where you seem to be headed despite your photographic talent, you will still need to build strength. Weight-lifting will also help you manage the stress of dealing *con los muchachos* and a dunderhead soon-to-be husband. It will release endorphins in your body that can last a while after you finish lifting. You will be able to more easily push babies out. It will help you lift those children when they fall. Once they can walk, it'll allow you to play multiple rounds of tag without feeling as tired. When you have to do housework—which you will, because your husband probably won't contribute—you won't pull a back muscle picking up the laundry basket or scrubbing the toilets.

"But most important—and I want you to really hear me, *manita*—it'll increase your quality of life outside of benefitting your family. When you lift—and lift with the right amount of weight—you will gain a sense of peace, happiness, and strength. You will stop slouching and rise to your full height. You will take the reins on your life. And you will never look back on that trash life you were living before.

"And that's only if you decide to be a housewife." She grinned. "Just imagine if you decided to pursue photography full-time." She sighed happily as she re-racked the weights. "The possibilities would be endless."

Nine

On the Lyft ride back, I stayed silent as I processed everything that Yasmine said. *The possibilities would be endless. You would never look back on that trash life you were living before.*

Am I living a trash life? For a moment, I paused, turning the thought over and over in my head. Finally, I shook my head, dispelling the notion. My insides burned up with rage.

Who does she think she is, anyway? I thought. *She's known me for a minute. She can't possibly know what my life will be like.*

But does she see something I don't see?

I didn't have time to pursue that thought because we pulled up to the bus. The rest of the band and Andrew were sitting around a makeshift fire pit, the fire spreading its fingers to the sky. Andrew looked up and lifted a hand in greeting as we approached.

"Hey yourself." I sat down next to him and swiped his hotdog on a stick. "Thanks for the snack, nerd."

"My pleasure," he grumbled, watching me eat his perfectly cooked hotdog. "How was the gym?"

"Interesting." I swallowed and took another bite. "Did you know that Yasmine used to be a personal trainer?"

"No, but I could've guessed." He watched as Yasmine and Philip shadow-boxed. "The woman is a beast."

Frowning at the admiration in his tone, I said, "She's not *that* much of a beast."

Andrew's eyes caught mine, his interest making my breath catch. "Is that so?"

Before I could respond, Yasmine cleared her throat theatrically. We all looked up.

"Thank you to Andrew and Alicia for being here," she said. "And especially Alicia, our new badass photog. No offense, Andrew." She and Andrew smiled at each other. Applause, whoops, and cheers went up all around. I blushed.

"Now, onto more important business." Yasmine put on an official look. "Our first stop in our tour is tomorrow afternoon, in a café. I know that it's not ideal," she said above the grumbles, "but it's what we're working with. We are a band full of *colorful* people." She smirked at her own pun. "There aren't many rock bands of color out here, so we have to start off in some odd-ass places. But that's okay, because we're the Leroys, and we can make it work." More cheers were lifted into the night sky.

"Be ready to practice at 9 a.m," she said. "We leave at noon."

Later that night, as I was staring up at the bottom of the top bunk, a multitude of thoughts whirled through my head. *This is the dream. I'm the photographer of my favorite band. I get to really be here, brushing elbows with Yasmine fuckin' Torres. What a story to tell my future kids.*

But then I started to think about my future with Michael. *What if he tells me to come home? What if I'm not back before the wedding? What if this is all just some crazy adventure that won't lead to anything?*

What if I'm not good enough?

"Worrying again, I see."

I narrowed my eyes at Andrew as he squeezed into the already-tight space. "What the fuck are you doing?" I hissed.

"Saving you from your own mind."

"I'm fine." My watch beeped, and Andrew eyed it shrewdly. "Okay, so what if I was doing a little bit of worrying? That's normal."

"Sure, if it was only a little bit." Andrew shifted so that we were almost nose to nose. "And if it led to anything productive. Which it won't."

"How do you know that?" I sniffed, moving as far away from him as I could get. "And don't you have your own bed?"

"I'm gonna tell you what I think you were worrying about," he murmured. "Let me know if I'm close." He adopted a look that I assumed was supposed to be similar to mine. His eyes widened slightly, and his breath quickened. He bit his top lip. "I can't believe I'm on tour with the *Leroys*. This has to be a dream. This cannot possibly be happening. But what if it isn't? What if I'm dreaming? Or what if Michael calls me *right now* and tells me that I need to come home? And what would Mother think about this…*lifestyle?*"

"You don't know me," I grumbled though I blushed. Andrew gave me another shrewd look. "Okay, so what?

"I'm not trying to embarrass you, Ace," he said. "I'm trying to get you to see that these worries are not serving you. And you don't have to serve them." He finally, thankfully, slid off the bed. I stopped myself from whining aloud at the loss of body heat but didn't allow myself to think about what that meant. "Think about *that* next time you think about Michael's feelings in all of this."

The next day, Yasmine shook me awake. "Get up, *manita*," she said. "We're going to the gym."

I squinted at her through one eye. "What time is it?"

"Four a.m."

I put my pillow over my head and groaned. Yasmine took my pillow and let it flop to the floor. "Come on, *vaga*, let's get a move on. This is actually the best time to work out. Not many people go at this time."

"Do you wonder why?"

"Not at all. I don't even care that they don't. More space for me—you feel me?"

I threw my arms over my eyes. "No, I do not *feel you*. How could you do this to me?"

"Quit being so dramatic, *manita*, and earn that gorgeous body you have!"

I peeked from underneath my arms. "You think I have a gorgeous body?"

"Yes, and it can only get better from here. *Párate de ahí*." She gestured for me to get up.

I sighed and lowered my arms. "Fine," I muttered. "But only because you gave me compliments."

When we arrived at the gym, I looked around. Much like Yasmine predicted, there were only a handful of people in the facility. Most of the people worked there.

What surprised me the most, though, was the look of the gym-goers that *were* there. One man's arms shook as he lifted the dumbbells above his head. The extra skin around his triceps, hanging from age and trial, shook in celebration as its owner gripped the dumbbells above his head. Another woman, whose glasses kept sliding down her hooked nose, grunted with the effort of thrusting her hips through her deadlift. Though liver spots dotted her arms, the cords in them stood out just as much.

Still another woman bent as if sitting in a chair, the barbell resting neatly on the shelf of her shoulders. She bit her bottom lip as slowly, slowly, she stood back up.

Not one of the gym-goers was a day under sixty-five.

"I call it the early bird special." Yasmine looked around, a small smile playing on her face. "At almost any gym I visit, the elders are here early in the morning, working hard. They were some of my best, most dedicated clients." She patted my shoulder and headed toward the bikes. "Consider it your daily dose of inspiration."

That day, our workout made the last one seem downright laughable. Before, I had a break between sets; now, Yasmine packed other exercises in.

"Alternating sets," she said as I grunted my way through my squats. "You're still giving specific muscles some time to rest but working out other muscles in the meantime. Helps move your workout along."

"Or gets me closer to death," I muttered.

"That's another thirty seconds of planks, *manita*," she said cheerfully. She bared her teeth in a humorless grin. "You know the deal. Complaints will only get you more workout. Degrading comments about your body *or* comments in a defeatist tone will get you thirty seconds of planks, one minute for longer complaints." She smirked. "By the end of this month, you're gonna have a *very* strong core."

By the end of our workout, I was laying on the floor in

a pond of my own sweat. Yasmine threw a towel in my direction.

"That's enough for today. It's about"—she checked her watch—"Five-thirty a.m. Time for breakfast. Then, the band has to rehearse for a bit before we set up for the gig." She sniffed and wrinkled her nose. "And you'll clear out the gym if we stay here much longer, anyway. Let's get you to a shower, *apurate*."

Once we got back to the bus, I made the mistake of lifting my arm and smelling my own armpit. I made a beeline toward the shower, not stopping to say hello to the band or Andrew.

As I showered in the tiniest bus shower stall known to man, a small sigh of happiness passed through my body. The soap bubbles slid down my arms at a luxuriously slow pace, reflecting the full rainbow on their surface. The steam from the water rose to the top of the tiny bus shower, bumping its head on the ceiling and spreading its fingers across. The sounds outside of the bathroom, much like the colors within, came into sharp focus, setting my body alight with the cacophony of life.

As I was stepping out, I must have been lost in my thoughts. There's no other way that when Andrew stepped around the corner, I almost jumped out of my towel.

"Have a nice shower?"

With a scowl, I readjusted my towel. "You're such an asshat." My hand clutched it tighter. "What do you want?"

"I already told you what I want," he said. I waited, hoping that he'd shrivel from the heat of my glare. I had the sudden urge to cover myself more but tamped it down. *He can't see anything, and even if he could, he wouldn't want to.*

"What do you *really* want?" I pressed.

"Well, I figured that the band will be practicing for the next few hours. Why don't we go on an adventure?"

"Who said I want to go on an adventure with you?"

"Who said you didn't?"

I rolled my eyes.

"Anyway, think about it." He tapped his open palm over his fist and turned toward the front of the bus. "And hey, Ace?"

"What."

"Nice figure." He smirked as I growled and slammed the door to the sleeping area. Even through the pine, I could hear his murmur of a laugh.

"Where are we going?"

Andrew continued to look out the window, not saying a word.

"I mean," I continued, "if you drag me somewhere, the least you can do is let me know where we're going."

"Still don't like surprises, huh." Andrew hummed a lyric-less tune. It sounded a bit like "Row your boat." He contemplated the sky as he responded. "Don't worry, I'm not taking you somewhere to die."

"Not knowingly," I muttered. I sighed and tapped my fingers on my legs impatiently. "Can't I get a hint? Anything?"

"It's outside."

I gave him a sour look.

"Alicia," he said. Inwardly, I melted at the brazenness of the command. I tried to control the pang of lust that rippled through my body at the sound. "Just enjoy the ride, okay? We'll be there soon."

I sighed again, the beat of my fingers getting faster with each second. "Fine. I'll wait."

It didn't take much longer to get to our destination.

After about twenty minutes, the Lyft stopped at the edge of a what looked like a large cluster of trees. I looked at Andrew suspiciously, but his face remained neutral.

"Trees, Parker? Really?" I looked back at the forest. "I *just* got clean, and you want me to visit some fucking trees?"

He opened his door and unraveled his legs from the car. "Yes, Alicia, we're at a forest. Will you get out of the car already?"

Letting out a sustained grumble, I, too, unraveled myself from the car. Almost immediately, after I shut the door, the Lyft took off. I frowned. "Where are we?"

"McDowell National Forest." He started walking toward the trees. "I found it yesterday."

"When?"

"When you were at the gym." He turned around once he realized that I wasn't following him. "Alicia, what is it? Are you afraid of the trees?"

I squinted at him. "No, I'm not afraid of the trees, Andrew, Christ."

"Just Andrew is fine. And if you're not afraid of the trees, what is it?"

I paused, contemplating the towering droves of branches and leaves. It reminded me so much of the place Dante had wanted us to spread his ashes. *Just sprinkle me among the trees,* he had said all those years ago. *I don't want you to mourn my death but celebrate my life. And what better represents life but a forest?*

"It's nothing," I said finally. I put one foot in front of the other until I caught up to Andrew. "Let's do this."

About ten minutes later, we came to an open space. Trunks as wide as I was tall stretched up toward the sky, exploding into a dark green canopy. Rays of sunlight beamed down like the common depiction of God. Dust motes lazed in the light.

The burning feeling that had started in my gut spread through my esophagus and lent heat to my exhalations. My heart knocked against my rib cage in a frighteningly erratic pattern. My breath quickened with each step deeper into the forest, and my vision narrowed until I could only see a small pinprick of light directly in front of me.

When we got to the clearing, I stopped, my hands on my knees. Though I could only see a small bit of light, I sensed Andrew's rising alarm. "Ace?"

I closed my eyes and swayed, off-balance.

"Alicia?" I could hear Andrew's quiet footsteps come closer, tentatively. "Are you gonna throw up or something?"

"Stop talking, Andrew," I bit out. "Right now."

Andrew put his hands on my shoulders. Slowly, he increased the pressure until I was sitting on something hard. "On the contrary, Ace, I think talking is exactly what you need. Open your eyes and look at me."

I continued to keep my eyes closed, my breaths getting faster. *Don't let me pass out,* I thought. *Please don't let me embarrass myself.*

Andrew's hands engulfed mine. "Alicia, open your eyes."

After a few more breaths, finally, my eyes met his.

He took a deep breath in then let it out slowly. "Follow the sound of my breaths." He took another deep breath in and out. "Then you do it."

I watched his chest rise and fall. As I watched, I noticed a few curly hairs peeking out from the collar of his shirt. *When did he grow chest hair? Has he always had that?*

"Admiring my body, I see." When I looked at Andrew, he smiled. "Keep focusing on my breathing, Jones. Or focus on my chest hairs. Your choice."

I kept my eyes on his, following his breathing pattern. Slowly, gradually, my breathing matched his. Five minutes went by and my heart stopped pounding. My vision widened, and my peripheral came back into focus.

"Better?"

I took one last big breath and let it out in a *whoosh*. "Better." It was then that I realized that I was squeezing his hands. I let go with a flush. "Sorry."

"No harm done." He wiggled his fingers at me. As he stood up, his knees cracked. "You ready to eat?"

I frowned as he pulled a blanket from his backpack. "Eat?"

"Yes, Echo, eat." He pulled out a lunchbox. "Breakfast. It's 7:30 in the morning, remember?"

"How could I forget?" I muttered. I moved from the stump to the grass where Andrew was sitting. My stomach rumbled in agreement. "What've you got?"

Andrew pulled a tinfoil-wrapped package from his lunchbox. "We have fried chicken, biscuits, fruit, and pota- toes." As he spoke, he pulled the items out one by one from the lunchbox. He grinned sheepishly. "I eat dinner for breakfast."

"I see that," I said, eyeing the spread. "No judgment from me, though. I'm starving."

"As am I, so let's eat." Andrew rubbed his hands together and opened the fried chicken.

We ate in silence for a while before Andrew coughed. He swallowed and said, in a too casual voice, "So."

I narrowed my eyes. "So?"

"When did the panic attacks come back?"

I heaved a sigh and put down my biscuit. "Do we have to talk about this right now?" I asked. "I'm enjoying the ambiance of the forest you dragged me to."

"Yes, we do need to talk about it right now. Otherwise,

you'll try to get out of talking about it for the rest of the tour."

I leaned my head back and looked to the sky for guidance. Finally, I grumbled, "Fine. If I must." I sighed again. "They started coming back around the time I broke up with Nicholas."

"Before or after?"

"After."

"So after we stopped being friends?"

"Yeah."

"Oh." Andrew picked up his plate and lowered his gaze to his food. He took a bite. "How often do you get them?"

"Not often." I followed his lead and picked up my own plate. "Only when something reminds me of Dante." I looked up at the canopy of trees again. "He loved the forest. He wanted his ashes spread in the forest."

"I remember." Andrew grimaced. "I'm sorry, Ace. I know how tough it was last time—"

"Yeah," I interrupted. "But it's over now." I took a vicious bite of my chicken and chewed vigorously. Andrew watched me with an eyebrow raised. "It is," I insisted around a mouthful of food. "I haven't had a panic attack in weeks."

"But you just had one now." Andrew put down his plate, giving up pretenses. "So it's not over, is it?"

I sighed louder. "See, this is why I didn't want to talk about it," I said. "You're making it a bigger deal than it is."

"Because it's a big deal, Ace," Andrew shot back. "Have you seen a therapist about it?"

"Nope, because I don't need one. I'm fine."

"Oh you are? So you didn't just admit to having panic attacks? Ace, you're not fine. You're a mess."

"A mess? Since when does having a good job and a

good fiancé and a good fucking life count as being a mess? I've been just fine, thanks. This is the best I've ever been."

"You worked at a job that didn't respect you, you have a fiancé that treats you like a 1950s housewife and you're not even married yet, and you just had a panic attack in a forest because it reminds of you of your dead brother. How does any of that sound fine?"

"Who are you to judge my life, Andrew?" I slammed my chicken on my plate. "You *also* work at a job you hate. You have not had a steady, consistent romantic relationship in *ever*. You came on this tour because you have nothing to lose. You've always been known as flighty. You're doing worse than I am. At least I have Michael. You just want me to not be fine because *you* aren't, and you want to be needed. Well, I don't *need* you, Andrew. I'm living my life just fine."

"You're not, if you're having panic attacks every time you think of Dante. Seriously, Alicia, what the hell's going on with you?"

I sighed and ran my hands over my face. Finally, I looked up at him. "Listen, I'm sorry for overreacting," I said. "You're right, I did just have a panic attack, and you helped me through it, and I appreciate it. But everything else is good. I'm living the dream right now. We're on tour with my favorite band." I forced a bright smile to my face, and Andrew frowned. "Let's just forget it, okay?"

Andrew shook his head and picked up another biscuit. "Fine," he said.

We sat in silence for a few minutes more before Andrew said, "Janet had panic attacks, you know."

I looked up in surprise. Janet was one of Andrew's steadiest siblings, so the notion that she could lose her shit was baffling. "Really?"

Andrew nodded. "She has really bad social anxiety."

"Interesting. I didn't know." I swallowed my potatoes and steadily avoided Andrew's eyes. "I thought that you knew how to calm panic attacks because *you* had them."

"Nah, not my diagnosis." As I tried to meet his eyes, he squinted up into the canopy. "I'm more of a 'stay in my room for weeks on end, stop eating, yell and cuss at everyone who comes close' kinda guy."

"Depression," I said. He nodded without meeting my gaze. "When did you know for sure?"

"For a while now, but definitely since you and I stopped being friends. Had to go to therapy for a while there." He shrugged. "We all deal with loss in different ways, I suppose."

"Yeah. I suppose." I sighed, feeling the heaviness of our conversation. "Wow. I didn't know you went to therapy."

He smiled wryly. "You didn't ask. One could even wonder if you didn't ask on purpose."

"One could? Or you do?"

"Oh, I don't wonder about it." He grinned and finally looked at me. "Anyway, the past has passed. And what was it you said? 'It's over now.' I'm better now." He shrugged again.

"Therapy helped, then?" I asked.

"A little," he said. "And God. And sunlight."

"Ah, so you're a flower, then."

"The prettiest. And don't you forget it."

We smiled at each other.

We spent the rest of the time talking and laughing—and enjoying Andrew's favorite activity, eating—to the point where I almost forgot my earlier panic. By the time my "time to go" alarm went off, I knew the tension had melted from my shoulders.

I sighed, standing up and stretching my hands toward the sky. "As much fun as this is," I said, "reality awaits."

Andrew started packing the remnants of our breakfast into his bag. "It's a good thing that reality is just as sweet," he said.

Despite believing that as we left our forest oasis, when we got back to the bus, we found ourselves in the midst of chaos. I heard several different raised voices floating from inside. Andrew looked at me and frowned as he knocked twice on the door. It swung open to reveal Danny's stormy face.

"Get in quick," he grumbled. "Someone's bound to start throwing shit off the bus if I leave this door open too long."

My eyes widened, and I quickly followed after Andrew. We walked in just as Yasmine put her fingers to her lips and whistled.

"Hey, team, calm yourselves!" She shouted over the din. "One at a time, please! Phil, you first." I couldn't help but notice Jean Lee roll her eyes before Philip started speaking.

"This arrangement of 'Come for Me' doesn't work," he said in his characteristically flat voice. "The minor 3rd gives it a weird feel. And we never agreed to that for this song."

"But it gives it *life*," Jean Lee retorted. "We can't be bee-boppy every fuckin' song, bro. We're a rock band that's starting to sound more pop than anything. We have to stay true to our sound."

"Well, if we're staying true to our sound, and we usually sound 'bee-boppy,' whatever-the-fuck *that* means, then we *should* take out the minor 3rd." Philip smirked.

"Don't be a pretentious asshole, you mother—"

"Hey, hey, hey," Kevin said, holding up his hands. "Don't talk about Philip's mom like that."

"I would be talking about *Philip* that way, you idiot." Jean Lee rolled her eyes.

"No name-calling," Danny put in, tuning his bass.

"Look, you both make good points," Yasmine cut in, frowning at everyone in turn. "Jean Lee is right—we want to have variety in our sound, *si?* Keep the people entertained and all that. However, for this song—and for all our older stuff—we need to give the people what they want: consistency. So we're going with the major chord for 'Come for Me,' and we can take a look at the newer stuff for variation. *Estamos de acuerdo?* Agreed?"

"Yes," everyone intoned. Yasmine sighed.

"Good. We have"—she checked her watch—"one more hour before lift-off. Shower, eat, whatever you have to do—do it now. We can't be late to our first gig of the tour."

As the band got up and went their separate ways, my phone rang. I looked down at the caller ID and sighed. Immediately snapping into fiancée mode, I pasted a smile on my face. "Hey."

"Babe, why haven't you called?" I could almost see Michael pulling at his silky, blond strands, the way he always did when he was pissed. "It's been several days. I don't even know where you are right now—you disappeared off Google Maps."

I sighed again, barely containing my exasperation. "My location sensor has been acting funny. It's no big deal. And it's only been three days, Michael."

"That counts as several."

"Is there an emergency? What's going on?"

"No, there's no emergency. But I've been waiting for

you to call all week. I want to know where my wife is, that's all."

"Future wife." I frowned, my perfect fiancée mask slipping a little. Andrew looked up curiously, and I turned my back to him. "Are you sure nothing's going on? You sound really stressed out. Did my mom call you?"

"No, everything's fine here," he insisted. "Just…this thing has already changed you. Don't let it change you more, babe."

"Nothing has changed." I felt a little tug of guilt as I recalled my workouts with Yasmine. "I'll be home before you know it."

"Sure," he said, already distracted by something else on the other line. "And then, we can get married."

"Right." Something cold slipped into my body at the thought. "Exactly."

Ten

The closer and closer we got to the venue, the more my palms started to sweat. My stomach and intestines made themselves known with every bump, turn, and stop of the bus. I couldn't focus my eyes on any one thing; the world passed by in a soup of color.

"Nervous?" Andrew folded his long legs into the booth, sitting closer than I've ever sat with anyone except my fiancé.

"Personal space isn't a thing with you, is it?" I tried to push him out of the booth, with no luck. "For someone who used to be so willowy, you're awfully substantial now."

"Depressive overeating will do that to you," he said. "But quit avoiding my questions."

"I'm not nervous," I said as I counted my SD cards once, twice, a third time without really grasping how many I had. I reached for my camera lens and attempted to put it on the body of my camera with shaking hands. I sighed.

Andrew gently took each piece out of my hands and put it on the table. "Ace, this is your dream job. This is what you were meant to do."

"Exactly." I fiddled with my engagement ring. "What if I'm not as good as I think I am? What if they take one look at my photos and decide they've made a mistake?"

"They've seen your work already. They know they haven't made a mistake."

"But what if *these* photos aren't as good as the ones on my site?"

"Then take better ones."

"What if the edits aren't good enough?"

Andrew turned so that we were face to face. "I don't think you're worried about your photos at all. I think you're worried about you."

I frowned. "What does that even mean?"

"Do you feel that you're good enough?" His eyes searched mine. "Do you believe that you can do this?"

I sighed and looked at the table of scattered camera items. "Yes?"

"Is that a question or an answer?"

"Yes," I said firmly. I took a deep breath and let it out in one large gust. "Yes, I believe that I can do this."

"Okay good," he said. He grinned. "Because we're here."

As the band set up their equipment in the café, I set up my equipment on the bus.

Just focus on what's right in front of you. Forget about what has passed, or what is to come. All that matters is this moment. I closed my eyes and breathed deep through my nose, out through my mouth, just like all of those years ago when Dante coached me. I could see his cat-shaped face in my mind, made all the narrower from his sickness. His eyes, like mine, were framed in long, thick lashes, the irises almost black. His easy grin filled my mind, and I both smiled and felt tears welling at the memory. *Dante. I still can't believe you're gone.*

"Alright y'all, let's do this!" Yasmine called onto the bus. Andrew and I rose from our seats, and I grabbed my camera and flash.

Yasmine stopped short of the back entrance to the café. The rest of the band was already there in a semi-circle. "What's going on?" I asked.

"Pre-gig ritual," Jean Lee explained in a whisper. "We never start a gig without it."

"Okay, *mi gente*," Yasmine said to all of us. "It's our first gig of the tour." Quiet cheers went up all around. "I am so proud of all of you for being here, *y estoy muy emocionada* about our two new people. Let's give them a round of applause for putting up with our crazy asses so far." More cheers and pats on the back went to me and Andrew.

"Y'all know what it took to get here," Yasmine continued. "We've been through a lot together, but still, we have persisted. There have been many tragedies in our midst, but you all have shown up, spirit intact, chins up. We may be an all-black rock band, and one of the only of our kind, but that has never stopped any of you from pursuing our collective dream: to tour the nation.

"I want to close in prayer." My eyebrows shot up in surprise, and Yasmine nodded at me. "Yes, *manita*, we are a prayerful band. You don't have to participate; you can just stand there if you need to. But we're gonna pray to God, who has watched over this band from Day 1. I'll start us off." She linked hands with Jean Lee and Philip; Andrew and Danny grabbed my hands. For a moment, I marveled at how perfectly my hand fit into Andrew's, how right it felt to have it there. As if he sensed I was looking at him, Andrew gave my hand a gentle squeeze. Butterflies, like soft kisses, rustled in my stomach.

"*Padre, que siempre está con nosotros*, we thank you. You have always ordered our steps, always protected the very core of each and every one of us. You are our guiding body, the way, the truth, and the light. Nothing that exists can exist without You.

"We come to You today with humble hearts and spirits. We need Your divine intervention, *Padre*. Help us to bring the music to the people in the best way we know how. Let them see You through our music. Help them to see Your mercy and grace through us."

There was a second of silence before Jean Lee picked it up. "God, be our Heavenly protector. Help me to do my very best on the beats. Amen."

Philip soon followed with a murmured, "Protect my guitar; help us follow Your will. Amen."

"Let Your will be done," Danny intoned. "Amen."

"You're the one, the only," Kevin murmured. "Thank You."

"Grant us Thy peace," Andrew said. He squeezed my hand again, and my breath caught in my throat. *Grant us Thy peace, indeed.* "In Jesus' name."

There was a long silence before I realized that everyone was waiting to see if I would contribute. Finally, I muttered, "In Jesus' name we pray. Amen."

"Amen," they all echoed. Yasmine clapped her hands twice.

"Alright, you saps," she said and grinned. "Showtime."

As the band continued to get ready for showtime, I paced at the back door of the café. Andrew watched me with a calm alertness. "You okay?"

"No bullshit? I hate the pre-gig ritual." I picked at the skin around my fingernails, stopping only when I remembered about the bacteria. "Why pray to a God that doesn't care or exist?"

"He doesn't care *or* exist? How can it be both?"

"It's not. Either he doesn't exist, or if he does, he doesn't care."

"Wow. Okay."

I stopped in my tracks, now watching Andrew as carefully as he was watching me previously. "What?"

"When you get into godless mode, you're a bit... intense." He frowned. "You could tone it down a notch. Some of us still believe, you know." Suddenly, he couldn't look at me. He adopted an almost-bored look that I knew was his precursor to anger. I suddenly had the urge to freeze in place and not make any sudden movements.

"Why does that bother you so much?" I blurted. "Why do you care whether I believe in God or not?"

"Why?" he repeated.

"Yes, Andrew, why?"

"Because it's hopeless. It makes it seem that you don't have faith in anything. That's not agnosticism or even atheism. That's just sad."

"No, that's not only it, though." I squinted, the feeling of something being right outside my grasp. "It's something else, too. What is it?"

Before I could hammer in my point, Kevin stuck his head out from behind the café door. "Hey," he said. "You two ready?"

I cast one more look at Andrew, who was now frowning in earnest. I, too, frowned for a moment before wiping it away and pasting a smile in its place. "Yes," I said. "We'll be in in a moment."

This whole thing with Andrew would just have to wait.

The band walked in as a unit: Jean Lee and Kevin were laughing quietly and fake-punching each other; Philip strode with purpose in front of them, eyes scanning the room; Danny strummed his air guitar and nodded to a rhythm only held in his head; and Yasmine, our fearless leader, was at the front of the pack, a ready smile on her face. Andrew and I brought up the rear.

As we reached the middle of the room, the band went ahead to the shallow stage, and I walked toward the front right-hand side of the stage. Andrew squeezed my shoulder and murmured, "Break a leg."

"But that's only for—" He was gone before I could finish. I let my breath out slowly, counting to ten before I ran out of air. My diaphragm quickly filled with air again. *It's like a metronome,* I could hear Dante say. *What swings one way must swing back the other way. What air is emptied from your body somehow finds its way back in.*

Suddenly, the room's ambient noise faded into the background, and it was just me in a quiet room. Warmth spread throughout my body, and a sense of calm settled itself over my shoulders.

I looked down at my camera. Nothing was out of the ordinary, as far as I could tell.

I clicked the main button to the **ON** position, and my camera sprang to life. The metering icon flickered, but otherwise, my camera was as still and calm as my body had become. I checked all of my settings—the ISO, the picture mode, the photo type—and everything seemed to be in place. As if it had set itself. *Strange.*

Just focus on what's in front of you.

I looked toward the stage, and the noise of the room came rushing back to me.

"…are The Leroys," I heard Yasmine say. "Thank you for joining us this afternoon. If you like what you hear, we will be playing at the Gator Lounge tomorrow night, about ten minutes from here. We go on at 8 p.m.

"This first song is a personal favorite of mine called 'Come for Me.'" Yasmine grinned at the audience; some of them whooped and cheered. "I hope you enjoy it." She stepped back from the mic and turned to Jean Lee. She nodded in the affirmative.

Knocking her drumsticks together at the same time, Jean Lee shouted, "*THREE, TWO, ONE.*"

As if hearing the voice outside of my body, I thought, *Lift the camera to your eye. Do it now.* I quickly lifted the camera to look through the viewfinder and snapped the photo. I didn't bother to look at the display to see how it came out; I simply snapped another one.

Move to the other side of the stage. Get down on one knee and shoot from below.

I followed the voice and did exactly that. I quickly moved out of that position to take another photo.

It's what you're made to do, I heard in my head. And then, I realized: the voice I was hearing, my inner voice, sounded just like Andrew.

Shit, I thought.

Admittedly, the crowd wasn't very lively. I had plenty of time to sit and enjoy the music myself, while also earning my keep.

The band, however, gave one of the best performances I've ever seen them give.

It was as if the lackluster crowd spurred them on. Yasmine's velvety voice flowed into the mic and out into the crowd. All but Jean Lee served as backup singers, their voices melding into one sound. Jean Lee held her own on the drums, breaking into epic solos toward the hook of a song and inciting the rest toward the end. Danny, cool and unaffected as ever, kept the baseline steady. And Philip remained remarkably self-contained and upbeat throughout their set.

It was magical.

When their set ended, a few people in the crowd

clapped enthusiastically while others followed halfheart-
edly. "Thank you," Yasmine said, nodding her head
toward the crowd. "We appreciate you listening today. You
can find us on Facebook, Twitter, and Instagram, @The-
Leroys. We'll see you next time."

Immediately, canned elevator music dribbled through
the café's speaker system. Kevin unplugged his amp, as did
Danny and Philip. Jean Lee started packing up the
drum set.

I looked around for Andrew but couldn't find him at
first. Finally, as if my eyes were pulled to him, I found him
at the back of the room. He was still sitting, looking as if
he didn't even realize that the set was over. He leaned in to
say something to the woman sitting with him. She flicked
her shiny, wavy, black hair from her face as she laughed
and casually rested one hand right above his elbow. Even
from this distance, I could see her give his arm a flirty
squeeze and see her breasts on display as she leaned closer
to him.

"Get some good shots?" I started as I realized that Jean
Lee had sidled up next to me.

I sighed as I continued to watch Andrew's weekly
mating ritual. "Yes, I think I got some pretty good ones."

"Good," she said. She tilted her head a little and
smiled mock-innocently. "Watching your boo talk to
another girl must be interestin', I 'spect."

I glared at her but said nothing.

She smiled wider and held up her hands. "I forgot, he
ain't your boo." She shrugged as she turned to walk away.
"But you watchin' him awful close for somebody who's not
datin' him."

Damn it, but she was right.

The image of Andrew talking to that unnamed girl
stayed in my mind for the rest of the day. I saw it as I

edited the photos from the gig; it burned in my retinas as I grabbed something for lunch. The worst part about it was that my mind got stuck on his body's response to her: he looked into her eyes, gave her a sly grin, laughed his murmur of a laugh. It was probably the laugh he used when he knew that he had some girl's attention. I wanted to hate that laugh. I wanted to hate him for using the same laugh on his flavor of the week as he used on me. I wanted to be upset with him for hooking up with some nameless girl while we were on tour.

But why did I care, anyway?

He didn't come back until sometime before dinnertime. The band decided to get something to eat at the local diner, something that didn't cost an arm and a leg. The café had paid the band a decent wage, but "we can't go crazy," Yasmine warned.

The sun fell on Andrew's shoulders as he walked onto the bus. I glared at him as he inched up to the table where I was editing. "Hey."

"Hey," I grumbled, returning my eyes to the screen. "Find another conquest to put under your belt?"

"Conquest?"

"Yes." I brightened up the photo I was working on without looking at him. "I saw the girl you were talking to as we were leaving."

"Harmony?"

"I don't know her name, Andrew. Whatever-the-fuck her name is."

"Harmony's cool. We hung out for a little bit." He shrugged as he looked over my shoulder at my screen. "I like this shot."

I closed my laptop and shot daggers through my eyes. "What gives, Parker? We're supposed to be on tour, with the band, and you're hooking up with random girls?"

"Not that it's any of your business, but we didn't hook up." He slid into the booth on the other side. "We hung out at the beach."

"Where the fuck is there a beach around here?"

"It's a couple hours away, off the highway." He smiled, shrugging again. "It was kinda nice, to get away and do something different. To be around someone who appreciated me for a change."

In his typical Andrew fashion, he hadn't said that he was talking about our relationship, but I knew. "If you got something to say to me, Andrew, spit it out."

"I just wanna know what business is it of yours? Why do you care who I spend my free time with?"

"I don't care." I sniffed. "It's just irresponsible to go gallivanting with some road ho when you have a job to do here."

"Road ho? That's low, even for you." I narrowed my eyes. "And anyway, I did my job," he shot. "The Leroys got more clicks on social media posts than they ever have before, and the place was packed today. But judging from the photo you stopped on, you haven't done your job completely. Maybe worry about that."

"Did the band even know you were leaving? Did you at least tell them that?"

"Yeah, Yasmine gave me the go-ahead. With her blessing, unlike some people. Again, I don't know what my free time has to do with you." Andrew stood up. "Matter of fact, I think we're done here."

"Guess so," I shot back. "See you later."

"Oh, that you will. Considering we're on tour together."

I grit my teeth.

"I don't understand why you're with her."

We had stopped in the mall at this nicknacks store. Andrew needed a gag gift for his dorm building White Elephant gift swap, and I was along for the ride. As I grumbled about his latest "girlfriend," he turned to me with a snow globe in his hands, eyebrows raised.

I blushed and lowered my voice a notch. "You don't even seem to like her."

"She's great." He put the snow globe down to trace the flowers on a necklace. He picked it up, turned it over his long, gentle fingers. I watched his thumb dip into each ridge of the flower petals, circling. My breath got trapped in my chest as I watched. I imagined those long, gentle fingers dipping into me in the same way and had to squeeze my legs against the budding desire in me.

"She's open, and honest, and she likes me," he continues. "We have an understanding—we're both sophomores in college and just trying to have fun. It's easy."

"Easy shouldn't be a qualification for a relationship. Relationships take work."

"And?"

"Easy is a shallow reason to want to be with someone. There's no depth to it."

"Funny, coming from you."

It was my turn to raise my eyebrows at him. He returned my look with a frown of his own.

"Ace, come on. Most of your relationships are only about doing what is traditional. You date because you know it's what you're expected to do. You're just going through the motions but your heart's not in it. You haven't truly made a connection with any one guy since Dante got sick. How is that any less shallow than being with someone because it's

fun? Maybe I want to be with someone who's easy to be around. It'd be a welcome change."

His words hit my chest like hot tar. Though Andrew often said things without saying them, his message was clearly about our friendship. I reviewed our last several interactions in my mind and grimaced. I couldn't remember giving him a single compliment or word of gratitude for being my rock through everything.

"Minnie." I tried again. "Andrew. You're right. I've been unkind lately, especially in light of Dante being sick." I cleared my throat once, twice, fighting the impending tears that always seemed at the ready these days. Andrew, watchful as ever, looked at me with soft eyes. "Anyway, you don't deserve that. I'm blessed to call you my friend, and I appreciate you being a part of my life. What can I do to make it up to you?"

"You can buy me a sandwich." Though he grumbled, he pressed his lips between his teeth to keep from smiling. I tried to ignore the beeping from my watch as Andrew wrapped his arms around my shoulders. I buried my nose deep into the soft muscle, comforted by the body that was almost as familiar as my own. The woodsmoke smell that characterized Andrew invaded all of my senses until there was nothing left but him. My heart pounded frantically at such close contact and my watch, snitch that it is, beeped again. Take a breath.

"Forgiven?" I asked.

"Always," he said.

A storm cloud hung over me and Andrew through most of dinner that night. I think the band felt it because even though they laughed and talked amongst themselves, they didn't bother trying to interact with either of us.

I picked at my fries, trying not to look at Andrew, sitting right next to me. I could feel the warmth of his irritation coming off of him like a cheap space heater. Finally, after twenty minutes of being ostracized from the band's friendly conversation, I turned to him. "I'm sorry."

His eyes flicked to mine then back down to his plate. "For what?"

"You were right; it *isn't* any of my business who you spend your free time with." I poked at a fry with my fork. "And I don't know why it bugged me so much."

A ghost of a smile lit up his face. A spark of mischief curled the edges of his mouth.

Not that I was looking at his mouth.

"You're nosy—that's why it bugged you," he said. He nudged my foot with his own. "It's okay to admit that you're nosy. I already knew that about you."

"Shut up," I said though I laughed. "I'm not nosy."

"You're nosier than a bored housewife, Ace. And terrible at hiding it."

"I will not have you lie on my name like this." I pretended to look away and crossed my arms.

"It's okay to admit it, Ace," he said, leaning toward me in a way that made the room spin a bit. "Go on, say it. 'Andrew, I like to be all up in your business.'"

"Nope."

He rolled his eyes. "Say it. It's the only way I'll forgive you for your gross miscalculation of my character."

I sighed. "Fine, fine. Andrew, I like to be all up in your business."

He grinned. "See, now was that so hard?"

I pushed his arm and laughed. "Whatever. Are you gonna eat that pickle?"

"I always save my pickle for you." I blushed, and his grin grew decidedly sly. He snagged a fry from my plate and replaced it with the pickle. I looked at him as he munched happily.

"So, am I forgiven?" I asked.

His eyes danced as they flashed to mine. "Always," he said.

Eleven

The rest of the week passed by in a blur of gigs, waking up early to go to the gym, and hanging out with Andrew—reluctantly at first, then more willingly. We traveled across three states in five days, and it was then that I realized that I actually hated watching the world pass me by while on a bus.

About a week into our tour, I realized that I wasn't the only one. Andrew and I were doing our nightly routine of catching up with each other's lives when Jean Lee plopped between us in a flurry of wayward arms and legs. She wrapped her arms around our shoulders and looked at us in turn. "Andrew, Alicia. How's my favorite couple doing?"

I rolled my eyes as Andrew chuckled. "We're not a couple, Jean Lee. Never have been, never will be."

"Could've fooled me," she said. "Y'all bicker like my grandparents, and they been happily married and in love for the last fifty years." Andrew pressed a smile from his lips as I growled. "Anyway, that's not why I'm here. I have a preposition. Y'all ready?"

I frowned. "Do you mean a *proposition?*"

"Same thing." She grinned. "Y'all ready?"

"Ready," Andrew said.

"K, so I wanna sleep in a real bed. Not these lofted pieces of shit that Yas has us sleeping in all the time. A real mufuggin *bed*, ya heard. So my preposition is that we all vote on it in a few minutes, at supper. I know Yas is gon' vote against it, and so will Philip because he's stingier than a friend collectin' on a five-dollar loan. But if y'all vote yes, Kevin'll do it, and Danny can sleep anywhere but is a fancy-ass dude, na mean? So, what do y'all say?"

"I'm not entirely convinced that you didn't say all of that in one breath," I said. "I'm impressed."

"You in or what, AJ?"

"I'm in."

Jean Lee whooped and clapped me on the shoulder. "My girl! Andrew?"

His eyes found mine again and I shrugged. He looked toward the rest of the band, assessing. Finally, he looked at Jean Lee. "I'm in."

Jean Lee grinned and kissed him on the cheek. I frowned as a spike of jealousy hit me square between my shoulder blades. *Calm down, Ace. He's not yours.*

"I knew y'all were my favorite couple," she said. I groaned as Andrew laughed. She stood up and stretched. "Let's get ourselves some real beds!"

As Jean Lee predicted, she won the vote. Danny grunted in approval. "Praise Jesus," he muttered. "A real bed."

"You all are whining about not sleeping in a 'real bed' and we've only been on the road for a week," Philip said. "What's gonna happen when we've been on tour for a month?"

"We'll think about that when we get there," Jean Lee

said. "Or when we get to the hotel and are snug as a bug in a rug in our nice, comfortable beds."

Yasmine sighed and pinched the bridge of her nose. "I hope for your sakes that this doesn't cost too much. It'll cut into our profits, *entienden?* The more we spend on hotels and fancy meals and shit, the less money we all make at the end of the night." I could barely hear her over the chants of, "Bed! Bed! Bed! Bed!" Philip shook his head and sighed. Andrew smiled.

"Alright, alright," Yasmine said. "Let's find a hotel."

Three hours and several booked hotels later, we came to a motel with a bright red neon sign. *Manny's,* the sign read. *$60 a night, no hidden fees.*

"Do motels usually have hidden fees?" Kevin wondered. "What are the fees for?"

"Who knows?" Danny grumbled. "That's why they're hidden."

"Cool it, bro," Kevin responded. He held up his hands. "We get beds tonight; isn't that all that matters?"

"Exactly," Jean Lee chimed in. She pumped a fist in the air. "Bed! Bed! Bed! Bed!"

"Well hopefully, these beds that you're so looking forward to don't have bed *bugs,*" Philip said over the din. "I don't want any of that shit on the bus."

"So optimistic," Jean Lee said.

"Maybe once you have your head on a real pillow, you'll relax," Kevin chimed in.

"He needs something else to relax." Danny smirked. Hoots and lewd gestures went up all around. Jean Lee made a thrusting motion with her hips and stuck her tongue out of the side of her mouth. Philip rolled his eyes; Andrew's shoulders shook with silent laughter.

"*Por favor*," Yasmine shouted. "Jesus, I can't take y'all anywhere!"

When we got to the counter, we were greeted by a bored-looking, middle-aged white man. He looked at us from under a droopy brow. "Yes?"

"We're hoping to book some rooms for the night," Yasmine said. "Do you have any vacancies?"

The man regarded all of us in turn. "How many?"

"As long as each room has two beds, we can do four rooms."

The man looked away to jiggle his computer mouse. As his face became awash in blue light, he tapped some of the keys. Eyes moving back and forth, he said finally, "we have two rooms: one is a suite with two bedrooms, four beds, and the option for a cot. The other has a king-sized bed. Do you want both?"

Yasmine shrugged. "Sure, that works. How much?"

"$120. Two rooms, $60 each."

"Oh," she said, grinning sheepishly. "Right. Philip, do you have the card?"

Philip handed the desk attendant a card. Jean Lee whispered, "Who's stayin' in the king-sized bed? I mean, I'm willin' to take one for the team if—"

"Can you be quiet for a minute?" Yasmine said through gritted teeth. "We'll figure it out in a minute."

The man sighed and ran five hotel key cards through a machine, then another two through. He handed the cards to Yasmine and said, "These five are for Room 7. These two are for Room 12. Someone will come by with the cot for Room 7."

Yasmine nodded.

The man tapped his finger against the desk as the receipt printed. Face still holding his bored look, he handed it to Philip. "Sign, please."

Philip signed.

"You're all set," the man said. He opened his newspaper. "Have a good stay."

As we gathered all of our stuff, Jean Lee said again, "So who gets the king-sized bed?"

Yasmine turned to the group and adopted her Official Group Leader look. "You know the rules," she said.

I grumbled the whole way to Room 12, with Andrew surprisingly chipper behind me. "Can't believe they stuck us in a room together. *With one fuckin' bed.*"

"We drew the short straws, and, as a reward, you get to sleep with me." I grit my teeth, the grinding doing little to soothe my nerves. The look on Yasmine's face—a tiny smirk of satisfaction quickly brushing her lips before she stowed it behind a more stoic look—made me wonder if we'd been set up.

"Anyway," Andrew continued, "the room has a king-sized bed, Jones. Don't get all riled up." I could hear the little-brother syndrome creeping in his voice. "I know you like to get handsy but remember: you're spoken for."

I glared at him over my shoulder.

"Don't worry. If you forget, I can remind you. In fact, I think we should tape a picture of your fiancé above our bed, just to make sure."

"Andrew, if you don't stop talking *right fucking now*—"

"Okay, shutting up now." Even still, I could tell he was grinning behind me.

When we finally reached Room 12, I tapped the card against the reader. A friendly green light appeared, and the door opened with an annoyingly chipper *click!* I grit my teeth again and shoved my bags through the door.

"Ah yes. The illustrious motel room." Andrew adopted

a snooty-rich voice, complete with his best English-butler accent. "Here, we have our functional coffeemaker. Or, from the looks of it, nonfunctional." I snickered.

Walking over to the bed, he placed his hands on the side and did a front flip with his legs splayed out in front of him. "Comfy enough, I guess," he said in his normal voice. He patted the space beside him. "Come try it out, Ace."

I shook my head, dropping the key card on the tiny desk below the window. "I'm good, thanks. Don't want to spend any more time on a joint bed with you than I have to."

He rolled his eyes. "Seriously? What, you think I'm gonna petition you for sex or something?"

"Gross. But no." I met his eyes though my cheeks felt like they were on fire. "I just don't care to do it."

"Do what, exactly?" Andrew's eyes took on a predatory look, and I knew what was coming.

"Andrew Parker," I warned. "Don't you fucking do it."

"Do what?"

"Andrew, I mean it!"

"Why is it that you're always accusing me of something even though I haven't done anything yet?" he asked, his voice deceptively silky. I backed up against the door and held onto the handle. He smiled a wolfish grin and my arms started to shake. As he came closer, I could feel my breath quicken and my heart race. He stopped a foot away from me. I frowned at my body's reaction to Andrew. *Is it just because we're in a motel room alone? Or is it because I haven't seen or been around Michael in over a week?*

"Last chance," Andrew murmured. I held onto the door handle behind me with both hands to keep myself upright. My legs weren't up to the challenge. *When did Andrew's voice get so irresistible?*

He pressed closer into my space, watching my breath

escape from between my parted lips. There was something ferocious about the way he looked at them. Something purposeful. No one, not even Michael, had ever looked at my face with such intent. I caught his eye just as he looked into mine.

"Three," he murmured. "Two…"

I closed my eyes, or maybe blinked too long. Whatever the case, I suddenly found myself upside-down and staring at Andrew's backside.

"Let me go!" I exclaimed as he walked toward the bed.

I could feel him shrug, stopping at the foot of the bed. "As you wish," he said.

He gently dropped me to the bed and proceeded to wiggle his fingers in my armpits.

Up until this moment, I had completely forgotten that, in a moment of weakness several years ago, I admitted to Andrew that I was impossibly ticklish on every square inch of my body. I also forgot that Andrew collected useless facts about people the way hoarders collect newspapers. I imagined the inside of his mind looked like a magical underground bank, complete with winding tunnels and minions keeping track of everything.

None of that mattered in this moment, though, as I fought to the death to gain purchase.

"Get off of me!" I screeched, somehow rolling and bucking him off of me. I struggled to get on top of him, but he was able to resist. Still, his fingers wiggled in a come-hither motion in my armpits.

"If you don't stop, I will pee on myself." I screamed with laughter, completely at odds with my body. There's nothing funny about being tickled.

"I will take mercy on you under one condition," Andrew said. I marveled at how calm he sounded, given that he was holding down a 160-pound woman. "You must say this: 'Andrew is the knower of many things. I am perpetually sullen.'"

"I am *not* perpetually sullen, and you know nothing, Andrew Parker!"

"Say it," he demanded. One finger moved from my armpit to the back of my knee. "Do it or I will tickle you *until* you pee."

"Fine, fine!" I panted, annoyed that I gave in so easily. "Andrew, you are a knower of many things and I am perpetually sullen. Now get the fuck *off of me!*"

He stopped tickling immediately but held himself suspended above me. As I came back to my senses, I noticed that Andrew's eyes were alight with mirth. *Figures.*

But there was something else there, too. His light brown eyes searched mine, caressing my face, probing it. Though this look was gentler than the previous one, it was no less intense. His shirt was slightly disheveled, and his eyebrow hairs were out of place. I reached up with one finger to smooth them back into place.

"Ace," he said. I could hear the longing, so much like mine, in the timbre of his voice. This thing between us grew until it pressed against my chest, rested between my thighs. I knew I should move away, but I was paralyzed. Andrew leaned on one elbow and wrapped one of my tight curls around his finger. The only sounds in the room were my frantic breaths and the gentle clanking of the AC unit in the background. My gaze zeroed in on his lips, and I wondered: *are they as soft as they look?*

Someone knocked.

Andrew cut his eyes to the door and frowned at the interruption. Interruption of what, I couldn't be sure. "Coming," he said, swiveling his eyes back to mine. I nodded curtly, sitting up as he moved toward the door.

I fixed my shirt and silently cursed myself in my head.

What were you thinking? Why didn't you move? It was unaccept-
able. I had come too close to breaking a commitment to
my future husband and, given my history with Andrew,
sleeping in the same bed with him would be even more
temptation.

No matter how cautious I was.

I was a brazen hussy and couldn't trust myself to be alone
with Andrew. Luckily, fate gave me a break and sent
Andrew's flavor of the month from three states over.
Helvetica, or whatever her name was. By the time Andrew
opened the door and introduced her to me, I was already
planning my escape. I flew to the band's room at the first
opportunity. When I got there, they all looked up.

"You look flushed," Yasmine noted.

"Had fun with Andrew?" Jean Lee piped up.

I glared at the both of them and sat on the edge of the
couch. Danny snickered as Philip had to draw two in their
Uno game. "I don't know what kind of fun you're referring
to, but no, we didn't *have fun*. Deal me in."

Yasmine took the deck and dealt me seven cards. "*Está
bien, manita.* You act like someone accused you of stealing."

"But you might as well," Jean Lee said. She frowned at
her cards. "Your relationship with Andrew is like a gift
from God. Bein' with anyone else can't compare."

"How would you know?" I challenged. I put down a
blue two—a nice, neutral card. "You've never even met
Michael. Besides, what does God have to do with my love
life? Your God doesn't care about my love life. He hasn't
until this point, anyway."

"'Your God'?" Danny repeated. "The fuck does that
mean?"

"She doesn't believe in God," Yasmine said absentmindedly, studying her cards. "And anyway, God has everything to do with your love life. Trying to keep God out of it is probably why you're in that shit relationship you're in now."

"It's not a shit relationship," I said. "Why's everyone so hard on my fiancé? He's a great guy."

"Oh, I don't doubt that. I met him." Yasmine shrugged. "Doesn't mean he's the *right* guy. And it doesn't stop you from being in a shit relationship with him."

"But you and Andrew? That's that thing damn near everyone's lookin' for," Jean Lee put in. She crowed in triumph as she made Kevin draw four. "Why you waste your time on a man who clearly does nothin' for you in bed is beyond me."

"Andrew is *not* what everyone's looking for," I retorted. "At the very least, he's not what *I'm* looking for. And I'm not what he's looking for. He's always trying to change me, instead of taking me just as I am. And he's flaky. Also, I haven't had sex with him," I said quickly, blushing at the thought of doing…that…with Andrew. "And I've haven't had sex with Michael yet, either."

"But you're mighty tempted," Jean Lee said. "You and Andrew look at each other like nobody else's in the room. He touches you every chance he gets. And you put up a helluva fight, but anyone in seein' distance can see that you've got a thing for him, too."

My face was engulfed in flames.

"Can we move on?" Philip interjected. "I'd rather not sit here and gossip like a bunch of females." Danny nodded his agreement.

"Where is Andrew, anyway?" Jean Lee asked, as if Philip hadn't even spoken.

"Dunno," I said, studiously avoiding their eyes. "I'm not his keeper." I didn't want to mention that I was trying to outrun my sexual attraction for Andrew. I figured it would completely undermine everything I had just said.

"But you two share a room," Yasmine said. "Where'd he go?"

"Hennessey showed up at our door," I muttered. "I'm guessing he went with her. Or they stayed in. Whatever."

"Who's Hennessey?" Kevin asked.

"She means Harmony," Yasmine corrected. She frowned. "And that can't be right. Harmony lives three states over."

I shrugged. "It was the same chick he was talking to at your first gig."

Yasmine raised her eyebrows. "Wow, that's dedication."

I sighed. "I agree with the guys. Can we talk about something else?"

Jean Lee looked like she was about to argue, but Yasmine sent her a pointed look. Jean Lee shrugged. "Bet." She grinned as she looked at her cards. "I'mma need all the concentration I can get anyway." She threw down a wild card and shouted, "UNO!!"

Andrew didn't come back to the room until late that night. By that time, I had played and lost several rounds of Uno with the band, showered, chosen my side of the bed, and tossed and turned for twenty minutes. I couldn't get this weight off of my chest, an anxiety I hadn't felt since Dante was alive. Dread seeped into the very marrow of my bones, taking up space in my body, inhabiting it like an infection.

As soon as I heard the lock click open, I let out a long sigh. The weight lifted from my chest, though my heart squeezed in a semi-painful way. *Strange,* I thought.

"I know you're still awake, Alicia. Don't pretend you're sleeping."

I rolled my eyes in the dark and turned toward Andrew's phone flashlight. "I wasn't pretending," I said.

He tilted his head with a small smile.

"I wasn't," I insisted. "I was taking a deep breath."

"Okay," he said. He unbuttoned his jeans. "Sure."

"Can I turn around now? Or would you like me to watch you undress like a perv?"

"You want to watch me undress; don't try to pretend."

I let out a grumble of frustration as I turned away from him. "You're such an asshat, Parker."

"Am I?" I heard fabric drop to the floor. "Or am I too close to the truth?"

I felt him slide into the bed. I closed my eyes, tried to slow down my breathing by counting to ten. *He's in bed with almost no clothes on. He's so close, I can feel his body heat.* My heart pounding still, I leaned toward the floor and picked up the extra pillows. I threw them onto the bed. "Put these in between us," I ordered. My voice sounded sharper than I intended. I tried not to think about why that was.

"Ah, yes," he said. "The pillow barrier. Classic."

"I don't want to feel anything funny in the night."

"Who said I'd be the one acting funny? You're the one all hot and bothered."

"Must you engage in Little Brother Syndrome all the time?"

"Must you be prissy all the time?"

"I'm not." I paused as a wave of sadness overtook me. We lay in silence for a while before I turned to him. "I wasn't always this way, you know."

Andrew stilled as I bit my top lip. He waited.

"I'm not a virgin." I flipped to stare at the ceiling. "I lost it a while ago."

And still, he waited.

"Why are you so quiet?" I snapped.

"Seems like you have more to say."

"There's nothing else to say. That's it."

"Is it?"

"Why are you so pushy, Parker? Let it go."

"Okay." He let out a long breath. "'Night, Ace."

"That's it? You're going to sleep?"

"Alicia," he said, his gentle voice lined with irritation. "Either you do want to talk or you don't, but you gotta pick one."

"It was with Nicholas," I blurted. I bit my lip so hard that it hurt. "The night that we broke up."

I heard him shift closer to me, felt his hand resting on my upper arm above the pillow barrier. "Tell me about it."

"Tell you about the sex?"

"Ace."

I sighed.

"We had been talking about it for a while," I said finally. "We would go back and forth on it. I pushed for it to happen. I figured that it was the next step in our relationship. We had done everything else by that point. Besides, I just wanted to get it over with, just be done with the pain part. Who better to lose it to?" Though I knew he couldn't see my blush in the dark, I turned my face away from Andrew. His hand moved from my arm to my chin, tilting it toward him, his thumb lightly pressing into it. I gave up and turned back toward him.

"When it finally happened, I knew we had made the wrong choice. I told him that I regretted it." I paused, weighing my options. Finally, I decided to tell him a half-truth – what I told Nicholas, but not the whole story. "I told him that I thought I was ready but I wasn't. When I left his apartment that night, I didn't realize we would break up, but apparently, life had other plans.

"Regardless, that was the true end of our relationship.

We had sex once and that was it." I scrunched the end of the blanket in my fist. "I haven't done it since."

"Wow, Ace," Andrew said. "That's tough."

"You don't even know the half of it." Which was true —Andrew could not possibly know the half of it.

What I didn't tell Andrew was that I had broken up with Nicholas because I had feelings for Andrew. It took about five minutes and one conversation with my neighbor, Thalia James, before I rushed to Nicholas's place to tell him the truth.

The funny thing was, Nicholas didn't seem surprised. It was as if he knew he wasn't number one in my life. *Why do you think you haven't met my parents yet?* He raised an eyebrow and I had laughed.

Still, the events that followed were heartbreaking. Nicholas may have taken our breakup well, but he was the only one.

I sniffled and felt Andrew stiffen next to me. "Ace, are you crying?" He asked, voice lined with dismay.

"Nope." I tried to suck the mucus back into my nasal passage as quietly as possible. Andrew had hearing like a bat, so any noise was bound to confirm his suspicion. I couldn't figure out why I was crying. Maybe it was the loss of opportunity; maybe it was that I knew how that night ended. It could have been my body remembering what my mind didn't want to.

Regardless, my tears set off Andrew's sonar. Before I could stop him, I heard the pillows drop to the ground, one by one. Then, he crept to my side of the bed.

"Alicia," he said. "You know what time it is."

"Don't say it," I sniffled.

"You've avoided it long enough. It is time."

"Can't you just leave me in peace for once?"

"No can do," he said. "It's time to"—I sighed—"bring it in."

"Are you really still using the phrase? Can't you just say "let's hug" like a regular person?"

"Nope."

"Must I hug you? Is this a requirement?"

"Nope."

I rolled my eyes. I knew where this was going. Other than tickling me, Andrew always let me choose. His level of patience as I vacillated between choices was unmatched. A thought, unbidden, came to mind: *I bet he lets all of his conquests cum first.* The very thought set my body on fire.

"You're not gonna let this go, are you?"

"I will, but will you?"

I paused as I weighed my options. *Might as well get it over with,* I thought. Despite my reluctance, a small part of me yearned to be in Andrew's arms. "Fine," I said. I tried to inject my voice with warning and failed. "But don't let this become a habit."

"Sure," he said. "Okay."

Slowly, I scooted the additional foot toward him. As I did, he repositioned his arms, so they wrapped around my body. As if finding a familiar home, my head dipped to rest in that space between his neck and the outer edge of his shoulder. Already, even though he had been in bed less than twenty minutes, he smelled like sleep and warmth. Between that and his usual bonfire scent, the combination was positively heady. I breathed in deep and gave an inadvertent sniff. I could feel Andrew's smile in the dark.

"Still sniffing me, I see."

"Andrew Parker, shut up before I pummel you."

"You wouldn't."

"I would," I mumbled, but we both knew I wouldn't.

It felt different, somehow. Despite the fact that

Andrew and I had hugged often in our earlier days—
something that started happening around the time that I
found out about Dante's illness—this hug felt weightier.
As if we both had more to lose. His arms held me firmly.
My hands went under his arms and up his back to clasp
his shoulders, bringing my body close to his. I resisted the
urge to tangle my legs with his, to fully press my front to
his and relieve the mounting urge between my legs.
Instead, I rested my forehead on his chest. It was as if I
couldn't get close enough, couldn't burrow myself deep
enough. I held on for dear life. Soon, his shirt felt damp
to the touch and it was then that I realized I was
sobbing.

"Let it out," he murmured. "It's okay, I'm here and I'm
not leaving."

"I'm fine," I sobbed.

His laugh rumbled through his body and shook my
own in a way that made my body stand up at attention. He
pressed his cheek to the top of my head. "Alicia, you are
the worst liar I've ever met. You are *not* fine. And you
haven't been for a while."

He smoothed his hand down my back. "But it's okay.
I've got you."

---

*I knew something was wrong when Ana called. She never
calls anyone if she can help it. Something about the
government always monitoring our phones.*

*"It's Dante," she said. "I went to the doctor with him
today because the doctor said he had some news for him. He's
sick."*

"Who's sick?"

"Dante." I heard her shift the phone, and I thought

maybe I misheard her. Dante never got sick—it was one of the side effects of his particular brand of OCD.

"With what?"

"Cancer."

People say that news like that always hits them like a ton of bricks or something equally heavy. On the contrary, the news seeped into my very pores. It wasn't a hit; instead, it poisoned me slowly.

Tears blurred my vision and I asked, "Is he okay? What can I do?"

"Nothing," she replied solemnly.

I could hear my mother in the background. "Is she crying?" She called out. "Tell her to stop all that crying. This is not an emotional thing, it's a life thing. Everything will be fine."

I felt more than heard Ana's long sigh. Mother couldn't be more opposite than Ana, and Mother tended to wear on her nerves. "I'll call you when we know more. Stay strong, Alicia." With that, she hung up.

I stood waiting for the after-school bus, taking deep breaths to push the tears down further and further. I could almost feel it colliding with the other painful memories that I had no time to indulge.

"Well, look who it is," I heard behind me. "My favorite card."

"Not today, Minnie." I leaned my head back and looked up at the dark sky. A raindrop fell directly into my eye.

"What's wrong?" he asked. His feet rustled through the rocks on the pavement.

"Nothing," I sighed. "Just a bad day."

"Tell me about it."

"It's nothing. I'm not in the mood for jokes today, is all."

"I can be serious. Tell me."

"My brother is sick." I turned to him. Tears threatened

to fall, and I could feel my throat closing. "Cancer. We're waiting to hear more from the doctors."

"How serious is it?"

"Not sure yet. But he'll be fine. Everything will be fine."

I remember that he was silent for a long time, to the point where I didn't know if he would respond. Finally, he said, "Wow, Ace, that's tough."

"Not tough." *I could feel my vision swimming, and I felt unsteady on my feet. I took a deep breath, anticipating my watch's command.* "It'll be fine. It could be worse. We just have to make sure to follow the doctor's regimen so that he gets better."

"What's your brother's name?"

"Dante." *The answer came on a whisper. I could feel the tears making their reentrance; my throat felt like it was on fire. I walked away from Andrew.*

"Alright, that's my cue. Time to bring it in."

"'Bring it in'? What's that?"

"A hug," *he said.* "Let me hug you, Ace."

"I'm not a hugger. Besides, we don't even know each other like that."

"We don't know each other like that, despite hanging out together every day for months and talking about anything and everything?" *The wry disbelief in his voice could've peeled paint off the walls.* "You can do better than that."

"Why is it that you must foist your opinions on me at every turn?"

"Fine, fine. You're right, I do foist my opinion on you quite a bit." *He hopped up and sat on the ledge.* "Then, it's your choice. You can hug me, or you cannot."

We sat and stood there in silence for what felt like an eternity. He looked at me steadily, and I at him. Finally, I sighed.

"Fine, I'll accept the hug. Whatever." *Though I*

shrugged, my heart stuttered at the thought of being that close to Andrew. I already felt a strange connection to this boy, despite only knowing him for a few months. He provided a respite, the likes of which I had never known, and it made me think all these crazy thoughts. Thoughts about how maybe not all boys and men were alike, and that maybe, maybe there is someone safe to love.

I stepped tentatively toward him as he hopped off the ledge and opened his arms again. As our bodies made contact, he wrapped his arms around my shoulders. I could feel the tension slip from my back and I almost gasped with relief. It was as wonderful and terrible as I had imagined.

I couldn't remember the last time I had a regular hug, let alone a hug in a time like this. Hugs are for hellos and goodbyes, *Mother was fond of saying. Not in-betweens.*

I squeezed my eyes shut against the surprising upsurge of tears. Being in his arms made it more difficult to hold them in. I buried my face in his shoulder and wrapped my arms around his thin frame. He smelled like some combination of the earthy, comforting woodsmoke from a bonfire, and mint.

"Do you want to know the best thing about this?" he murmured in my ear.

"Okay." I tried to swallow the sound of my tears.

"I'll never know if you're crying or if your face is wet because of the rain, so you have the freedom to cry without shame."

And so, I did.

Twelve

T he next morning, I woke to the early morning light streaming through the sheer curtains. I blinked and felt as if my eyes were swollen. My head also felt like it weighed a metric ton.

Andrew was nowhere to be found.

My stone of a heart dropped to my stomach. *Of course, the one moment I show vulnerability, he leaves.* A small flutter of panic, at the thought of my vulnerabilities on display, caught in my chest, but I tamped it down. *No. Everything is fine. If he leaves, it doesn't matter. I still have Michael. I don't need Andrew.*

As my mind raced, the bathroom door opened, and Andrew stepped out in a towel and cloud of steam. My eyes widened before I quickly shut them and cursed under my breath. I hadn't closed my eyes quick enough to stamp out the memory of his muscles rippling in the daylight, the shape of his lean arms and chiseled abs made more prominent by his damp skin. *And those eyes…was that look meant for me?* Any straight woman who saw that look would do anything he asked. *Except me,* I tried to convince myself.

"Can't you ever stay dressed, Parker?" I snapped.

I could hear the smirk in his voice. "What? Liked what you saw?"

"Get dressed."

"Maybe if you ask nicely."

"*Andrew.*"

I heard some rustling and a zipper being zipped. "Okay, okay, you can open your eyes, prissy. I'm dressed."

I slowly opened one eye then the other. Andrew stood three feet away, jeans and a T-shirt on, a smug smile plastered to his stupid face. Meanwhile, I felt like a five-year-old for even thinking the words *stupid face,* in that order, in a sentence.

I couldn't help noticing that his clothes didn't cover up all the muscles in his arms. It was a slippery slope to imagining what he had been concealing with his towel.

"Better?"

"Yep," I said. I bent my knees and lay my head on them. "My head is killing me."

"Well, your face is killing me, so I guess it fits."

"Wow. We can now graduate to second grade."

"You liked it." The bed sunk down under Andrew's weight. "No bullshit, though, you okay?"

I shrugged, my head still on my knees. "I'm alright."

"It took you a while to go to sleep last night."

"Yeah, I don't wanna talk about it."

Andrew was so silent that I lifted my head. He regarded me with inquisitive eyes.

"I'm just tired of crying around you," I admitted. I gave a small chuff of a laugh. "I cried for what felt like years."

Andrew shrugged back. "Ace, you know me. It doesn't matter how many times a day, a week, a month, or a year you cry. I'll still be here."

I bit my lip but didn't say anything.

He stood up and stretched his hands to the ceiling. He walked toward his side of the bed, gathering the things he had in his jeans last night. As he stuffed things in different pockets, he said, "Yasmine stopped by and said that she'd let you sleep in. Something about a rest day?"

I looked up, eyes wide. "You didn't tell her I was crying, did you?"

"No." Andrew looked at me as if I told him I thought he ran in the streets naked. "Why would I do that?"

"I don't know." Something about having all of my vulnerabilities on display for him the night before made me blurt, "Knowing you, you would think it's a good idea."

His hands froze in midair over his front pocket, keys in hand. "In what world?"

I shrugged and picked at the skin on my fingers to avoid his eyes. I could feel that heat of his impending rage radiating in the air, hovering around the both of us.

"When have I ever broken your confidence? Think about that before answering," he answered, voice low and hard. My watched beeped and I took a breath. *I forgot how quickly he loses his shit over this kind of stuff.*

"Minnie, don't hulk out on me," I said, holding my hands in a conciliatory gesture. "I'm sorry, okay? I didn't mean it. You're right, you're a good secret keeper. Forgive me?"

He was quiet for a moment as he continued putting things in his pockets. *Please forgive me*, I thought with an edge of desperation I couldn't explain. Though we stopped being friends, though he seemed determined to change me, I could always count on him to forgive me no matter what. *There is nothing unfixable*, he said. *There is always opportunity for grace and forgiveness.*

After a long moment of hesitation, he sighed. Finally, he said, "Forgiven." He added roughly, "Always."

When Andrew finally finished getting ready, and I looked decent enough to leave the room, we packed up our stuff and headed toward the bus. Yasmine was giving someone orders when we got to her. She looked at Andrew then at me. "Sleep well?"

My face burned but Andrew replied smoothly, "Yep. Slept like the dead."

Her mouth tightened a little bit but she kept her face neutral otherwise. "Good." She turned back to the clipboard she held in her hand and made a note. "Head onto the bus. We have some things to talk about."

Andrew and I looked at each other in surprise. Yasmine's voice caught at the end of her sentence, and she looked like she was about to cry. We bumbled onto the bus, me behind Andrew, and waited to hear what was going on.

Yasmine joined us all on the bus about five minutes later. The others were strangely quiet. Usually, the band roasted each other while we waited, loudly bantering back and forth. Today, the air held a subtle vibration to it, like a rubber band pulled taut after being plucked. I started to pick the skin around my nails while keeping my hands under the table. Soon, I felt strong, long fingers grasp my own. He smiled at me with understanding in his eyes.

"So, as some of you may have heard, *mi abuela se murió*," Yasmine said without preamble. I looked to Jean Lee curiously. *Grandma died*, she mouthed. My eyes widened as I dragged my eyes back to Yasmine.

Yasmine flicked a few tears from her face, sniffled, and continued, "My grandmother raised me when my parents weren't fit to do the job," she said to me and Andrew. "*Familia* was never at the top of my mother's list of concerns, and my dad wasn't too much better than her. My grandmother raised all four of their children, on one income, in the hood. She was my rock, and I can't imagine my life without her." She stopped again, lips quivering, her face scrunched in a painful grimace. She took a deep breath and continued.

"We will have to postpone our next couple of gigs as I do funeral arrangements and then bury her," she said. "I'm the oldest of my siblings so it is *mi responsibilidad*. My duty. So I will do that, and then we will continue on. Does anyone have any questions or concerns?"

"Let's split up the responsibilities," Philip said, coming up to stand beside Yasmine. He put a hand on her shoulder as she blew her nose into a tissue.

"I'll call the venues and let them know what's going on," Kevin volunteered.

"I'll reach out to our friends and let them know when the funeral is," Danny intoned.

"I've got the social media accounts," Andrew said.

"I'll talk to the funeral home about the arrangements," Jean Lee put in.

"And I'll be there for you, whatever you need," Philip murmured to her. As she nodded, he squeezed her shoulder and pressed a kiss to her temple. My eyebrows shot up and I looked at Andrew again. He watched them, unsurprised and unfazed. *Did he already know that they were together?*

Philip turned to all of us again. "Alright," he said, "it's gonna take some time to get home. Let's get going."

The drive back to our hometown was long and arduous. The cloud of tension hovered around all of us, and Yasmine was almost mute the whole way. Andrew was also characteristically silent and didn't mention our night in the hotel room at all. Despite this, we coexisted in a friendly quiet, as if my uncontrollable sobbing resolved something, somehow.

The friendly, comfortable vibe shattered in one moment toward the end of the journey home. Andrew was sitting on a bottom bunk, sifting through a small notebook when I came into the sleeping area. I looked on curiously until he flapped the notebook shut. "Need something, nosey?" he asked.

I grinned slyly. "Whatcha got there, Minnie?"

"A notebook full of none of your business."

"Why so secretive?" I sidled closer. "Is it erotica? Your diary? A love letter?"

He shifted slightly to move the notebook on the other side of his body, away from me. "None of the above. Why are you so interested? I've had this notebook since we started on tour."

I looked past him, judging the distance between me and the notebook. "You seemed deep in thought. Figured it was a good time to ask you about it."

"Well, it's not. Problem solved."

As he looked away and toward the notebook, I lifted it deftly from his grasp. I grinned. "Thanks, nerd. Since you won't answer my question, I can just see for myself."

"Not if I have anything to do with it." He reached for it, but I kept it just outside of his grasp. He got up and backed me into a corner. "Nowhere to go now, Jones. Hand it over."

"Not a chance."

"Hand it over."

"I will guard it with my life."

"Alicia Jones."

Inwardly, I shivered at the command in his voice. My

alter ego, Ace, was ready to do anything he wanted when he used that voice on me.

Outwardly, I smirked. "Nope."

"Not gonna give it up so easily, huh." Andrew's eyes lit with mischief, and I knew I was in for it. "That can be resolved."

He stuck both of his forefingers in my armpits.

"Not fair!" I shrieked. He wiggled his fingers with little sign of stopping, but I kept a tight hold on the notebook. "You shouldn't be able to use my weaknesses against me, so close to the last time."

"Isn't that the point of knowing someone's weaknesses? To utilize them?" The tickling intensified. "Hand it over."

"Never!"

"Never?"

"You heard me!"

"So you want this to continue for the rest of our trip, then?"

I looked at him, accusation bright in my eyes and cheeks. "You wouldn't."

"I would."

"Timeout, timeout. Let's discuss our terms." Andrew stopped tickling, and I held the notebook behind me as I looked at him defiantly. "What do I get in return for giving this back?"

He raised an eyebrow. "Do you really think you have the ability to bargain in this?" he asked. "I hold all the chips. All you have is a notebook—which I can easily get back from you. What's in it for me?"

"My friendship." I smirked. "And I will continue to keep all of your deepest, darkest secrets."

"What secrets?"

"That thing that you told me about third grade." His face remained blank. "And your first crush."

Understanding set a fire ablaze in his eyes. "You wouldn't."

"I would." I wiggled the notebook in between us. "What do I get in return for my silence?"

Andrew sighed and rolled his eyes. "It's my writing notebook," he said finally. "I'm working on the novel."

I raised my eyebrows. "Yeah?" I asked. "You figured out the love scene?"

He shrugged. "Yeah."

"So what happens?"

"The main character falls in love with a girl he knows is unattainable." He moved closer and reached for the notebook. Gently, he pried it loose from my hand but stayed close. His eyes were fastened to my lips, making my mouth tingle at the possibility. I could imagine it now: Andrew pinning me up against the wall, running his hands down my sides, squeezing my hips, murmuring his approval at my curves. His kisses would rain down my neck, just a whisper of his tongue to my skin as I clutched his arms. He would nuzzle me at the base of my neck, right at the collarbone. My heart would race in anticipation of what could come next; the world would stop spinning on its axis as he tracked my breath passing through my lips, tasting my skin, gently biting the soft lobe of my ear. And then finally, finally, his mouth would consume mine. Possess it.

My heart, finally slowing down after being tickled, picked up its rhythm again at the possibility of being kissed like I was revered. My watch beeped, but I ignored it. "She's getting married, but he's been captivated by her since they were younger. It was never the right time for them. Until now."

"Oh?" I said, my voice muddled with panic and unexplainable longing. "Why now? After all those years?"

"Well, that's kinda the guy's fault." Andrew traced an

imaginary pattern on my arm and I shivered, unable to shake the vision of him pressed against me. My back arched slightly, and I hoped Andrew didn't notice. "He might have tried to dissuade her a while back. He didn't trust that she was what he was looking for. So she moved on."

"How does she find out about all this?"

"See, it's a funny thing," Andrew murmured to my lips. "She can't just *find out*. That would bore the reader. She has to come to that conclusion, and the readers have to see it unfold. It has to be part of their journey together. As friends, but also as something more." When he paused, still watching my mouth as if it held a secret, heat pooled between my legs. "So while they're off on their quest, he does some things to help her along. Because she's kinda dense about this stuff."

"What does he do?" I breathed. I could see my own chest in my peripheral vision, rising and falling rapidly with the quick pace of my breath. Andrew's eyes flicked downward, made a leisurely stroll past my lips, and then up to my eyes. I braced myself against the wall.

"He seduces her, of course."

"Of course," I squeaked.

"I could let you read the book, if you want. So you can see what I mean." Andrew's face was so close to mine that I could feel his breath mingling with my own. One of his forearms bracketed my body; the other rested on my shoulder as he played with the curls around my face. I wholeheartedly wished for Andrew to develop telepathy so that he would know how much I wanted him to sink his hands in my hair and consume me. Somehow, the notebook disappeared. I didn't know how, nor did I care. "But I have a feeling that you already know what that's like. An unexplainable longing." He bit his bottom lip as he whispered this in my ear. I sighed like the hussy I was. "Missed opportunities realized."

"I don't think I need to read the book for that," I whispered. My mind blinked off-line, overwhelmed by Andrew, but some part of me registered that we were too close. And definitely not talking about fictional characters. And definitely in the danger zone. Despite this, doubt flooded my body, whispered in the ear that Andrew's voice didn't occupy. *There's no way that he feels that way about you. Especially not after all that has happened. It's been too long, and you're so different now.*

But as I looked past Andrew's lips, so close to mine, and looked up into his eyes, I saw it. Unbridled desire stampeded across his face, made it an open book. Like mine. His lips were so close. I closed my eyes and tilted my face up, ready to let the chips fall where they may.

"Y'all look mighty cozy back here." Jean Lee sidled up to us with a sly grin, and I fought to move away so fast that I bumped my head on the wall. To his credit, Andrew stepped away from me much more smoothly. I scowled at him for showing so much grace.

"We're no cozier than we usually are," I snapped. I brushed my sweaty hands against my legs. I saw, from the corner of my eye, Andrew subtly adjust himself. *Jesus.* "Andrew was just—"

"Examinin' your face to make sure everythin' was okay?" Skepticism thickened her Louisiana drawl. "I can see why he'd wanna check. Your eyes do look a little dilated."

Andrew chuckled as my face burned brighter. "Nothing is wrong with my face." I straightened to my full height. "Everything is fine, thanks."

"I bet it is," Jean Lee said. She chuckled, too. "I bet it is."

. . .

I stayed away from Andrew for the rest of the day. I needed time to process what happened, and being near him suddenly scrambled my brain.

And what did he mean, anyway? I thought angrily. *I could let you read the book, if you want. So you can see what I mean,* he had said. *But I have a feeling that you already know what that's like. An unexplainable longing. Missed opportunities realized.*

I don't *want to read it,* I thought. *I have Michael, and he fulfills my needs just fine. And who does Andrew think he is, anyway?*

When we stopped for a stretch break, the band and I clamored out of the bus, with me at the front of the pack. Anything to put some distance between me and Andrew. *Fresh air will help me,* I thought. Or, at the very least, it would give me the space I so desired.

I walked around, stretching my legs, before I found a clearing with picnic benches. Yasmine and Philip were sitting at one of them, away from the bathrooms and the happy sounds of Jean Lee and Kevin throwing a football. Despair and defeat wrapped itself taut around Yasmine. Her body shook with silent sobs and small gasps of air. I could see their hands interlinked on Yasmine's lap, Philip making soothing *shh* noises and murmured encouragement as Yasmine tried to contain the enormity of her grief. His thumb made small circles on the back of her hand.

I looked down at my phone and pretended to check it, hoping to avoid being caught ear-hustling on such an intimate and profound moment. Despite this, I couldn't stop myself from listening in.

"*Mi amor,*" Philip said, his words the tender caress of a lover. "You know you don't have to pretend to be strong with them. They get it. They all met her."

"But who will lead them?" She hiccuped. "I'm

supposed to be the fearless leader. I'm supposed to keep everything together, *verdad?* What do they do if I can't keep it together?"

"We've been through a lot together, including death. Remember Leroy?"

"I know but this is different. She was like a mother to me."

"I know, *mi cielo*, I know."

They were both quiet for a moment. Finally, Yasmine broke the silence.

"I wish I had been there when she died. She died alone, probably worried for all of us kids, probably praying to *Padre* for everyone but herself."

"She didn't die alone. Your sister was there with her."

There was a brief pause in which I imagined Yasmine giving Philip a sidelong look. He chuckled. "That *pendeja* couldn't function without *abuela;* she was probably no comfort at all." She sighed. "I should've been there."

"Yasmine, she died peacefully in her bed. They said that she didn't feel any pain at the end, right? Isn't that the best way to go?" His voice took on a dark timbre. "It's definitely better than the way Leroy went, wouldn't you say?"

Yasmine nodded and sighed again. "*Claro.* It doesn't stop the pain that I feel."

"Of course not. But what is it you always say?"

"What? Better out than in?"

"That's the one." His voice rang with warmth. "Yas, you know better than any one of us what it does to the body when you keep that shit in. So let us support you for once. Let *me* support you. We can weather whatever storm is coming, together."

Yasmine nodded slowly, wiping her face. "Yes, okay," she said finally. She took a shaky breath. "I'm so scared, Phil. How do I survive it?"

"Through your faith," he said. "With God and through God, you can make it through anything."

Seeing Yasmine and Philip together left more questions than answers. Leroy was their sixth band member who died some time ago; he was the original leader of the band before Yasmine had to take over. But what happened to him? And why did that leave Yasmine so broken?

Outside of that, though, a thought occurred to me. Yasmine was the strongest woman I knew, both physically and—seemingly—emotionally. Could it be because she leaned on others for support?

It reminded me of Dante's tattoos. I always thought that it was ironic, given his adherence to the Bible and his propensity for fastidiousness, to have tattoos. I mean, didn't he worry about how many people had been under the same needle? But the two that he deemed important enough to risk it talked about faith, and about leaning on God's understanding, instead of our own. I frowned at the memory of this, feeling like there was a message that was just outside of my reach.

By the time I worked up the nerve to ask Yasmine anything, we were home. Though I loved being on the road with the band, it would be nice to have some relaxation time with Michael. When I called him, however, he didn't seem that thrilled.

"Yeah?" He gave someone a quiet order, and I heard acquiescence in the background. "Nice."

"Are you sure?" I frowned. "You don't seem too excited."

"Oh, I am, babe." To his credit, his voice brightened a hair. "I've missed you. It's been lonely without you."

"I've missed you, too," I said, instantly melting. Despite his bro-like attitude, Michael could be incredibly sweet. "I can't wait to see you."

"You too." He sighed. "It'll be good to have you home again. Your mom is a handful to handle by myself."

I stiffened. "Do you miss me because you want me to handle my mom, or do you miss me because you miss *me*, Michael?"

"Hey, let's not fight." He shifted the phone from one ear to another as he spoke. "Just come home soon, okay? I love you."

"I love you, too," I grumbled.

Talking to Michael left me with questions, too, and an uneasy, molten lava burn in my gut. Something wasn't right, but the only thing I had to go on was his unaffected tone and Ace, my hypervigilant alter ego. She shook her head back and forth in my mind. *Something happened. Something's about to go terribly, terribly wrong.*

"Hey, squirt."

I rolled my eyes. "Squirt, huh. You know, with everything that's been going on, you would think that you would be less of a nuisance."

"Gotta keep it consistent." Andrew smirked. He stopped to squint at me. Following the line of my restless hands, down to my jiggling legs, he said, "Something happened."

"Nothing happened." I made a conscious effort to stop my legs from jiggling, but I couldn't keep a wrap on my hands. Andrew put his hands over mine and looked at me. I figured I was imagining it, but I felt a tiny spark between our skin. I snatched my hands away. The memory of his lips so close to mine hadn't faded entirely.

"Nothing happened," I insisted. I stood up quickly, stomping down the stairs. Andrew followed me with an easy, enviable grace. To stop myself from thinking about it too much, I bent down to grab my bags from under the bus and felt a twinge in my left calf muscle. I ignored it. "I'm just feeling sad for Yasmine, is all."

"Right." He loped by my side as I huffed and puffed with all of my bags. "So you didn't have an unpleasant conversation with Muscle Head?"

"Nope."

"And he's thrilled that you're home early?"

"Sure is."

"Sure," Andrew said. "Okay." I felt more than saw him come to a stop. He placed a gentle hand at the small of my back, and I froze.

Unfortunately, so did my damn left calf.

My calf muscles had always given me trouble in high school. My coach would just roll her eyes as my toes froze painfully in place and my calf seized up. "Ace," she would say, "I told you to drink more water. Now look what's happening."

Andrew crouched next to me as I sat on the ground, concern etched in the lines of his face. "Are you okay?"

I bared my teeth at him as fingernails of pain shot up my leg. "Yup. Just casually sitting in the middle of the sidewalk. No big deal."

"What can I do?" His hands hovered over my leg, my pain reflected in his eyes. "What do you need?"

"Grab the Gatorade from my backpack and give it to me." Andrew quickly unzipped the bag and handed me the drink. I gulped it greedily, hoping for a miracle. The last time I got a cramp in my leg, I could barely walk for the whole day. If I caught it early enough, though, chances are I'd be okay within a few hours.

This time, I was lucky. I felt the pain ease after a few minutes, and I breathed a sigh of relief. After watching me for what felt like eternity, Andrew stood up and offered me a hand. I looked at it with narrowed eyes.

"Let's go back to my parents' place," he said, wiggling his fingers for emphasis. "It's closer than your place or mine, so you can rest there, and then head back to Muscle Head."

"Don't call him that," I said, but took his hand anyway.

By the time we got back to Andrew's parents' house, the pain had eased even more, to the point where I could (slowly) limp. Even still, when I looked at the twenty-five steps up to the house, a sense of dread draped itself over my shoulders. Andrew glanced at me then at the stairs.

"Guess I'll have to carry you," he said.

I tensed automatically then instantly regretted it as my leg also tensed up. "Absolutely not."

"How else are you gonna get up the stairs? Don't be such a priss. I promise I won't come onto you."

I rolled my eyes. "It's not that."

"Then what?"

I sighed. "I want to keep at least one modicum of dignity. I feel like I have none left, dealing with you."

Andrew's murmur of a laugh surrounded us, made my face heat up with embarrassment. "C'mon, Jones, don't suffer just to keep your dignity."

"I can make it up the stairs, thanks."

As I started my slow ascent, Andrew loped up the stairs two at a time, dropped our bags on the porch then came back to watch me get to stair three. He raised an eyebrow, and I held up a hand. "Don't fucking say it."

"I'm going to carry you upstairs, Ace. Your face is killing me."

"Really? You want to make jokes right now?" I gasped for air as I tried to move away from him.

He looked up toward the sky as if to say, *Lord, why.* Finally, without saying a word, he scooped me up into his arms. Though I initially protested, I couldn't help but notice that my leg thanked me for relieving the pressure. *Great*, I thought. *Even my body is working against me.*

"Put me down, Parker," I said, the fight going out of me instantly. I tried not to be a creep and sniff his shoulder, where my head was. "I'm fine now. I think I just needed a minute to take the weight off my leg."

"Cool. So this will be more enjoyable, then." He walked slowly up the stairs, being careful not to hit my legs on the handrails. "Be quiet and enjoy the ride, squirt."

I rolled my eyes but stayed silent.

Honestly, the "lift" was quite enjoyable, despite all my complaints. I couldn't think of a time where anyone had held me like this, and it felt nice. Andrew's steady heartbeat against my shoulder helped my own heart rate to follow suit.

Once we were inside, I took the two minutes to look around. Nothing much had changed in the last two years since I had been here. The lower level was dark, cool, and silent. Nobody was home, I supposed. Family photos lined the walls, displaying each family member at different stages of life. There was a photo of a toothless Andrew—I could tell by the baby's smile—and a photo of Mr. and Mrs. Parker on their wedding day, right next to it.

The air in the house held the smoky, bonfire smell that was Andrew's signature. I breathed in the familiarity, feeling it wrap around me like Andrew's arms. I marveled at how everything felt like it was welcoming me home.

When we finally made it to the second floor, Andrew moved toward the upper level family room. He placed me on the couch and smoothed some of the curls away from my face. "You doing okay?"

I tested my leg by gingerly moving to and fro. "Seems to be holding. I feel strangely peaceful, actually."

"Endorphins." Andrew's eyes flitted the length of my

body, taking inventory, and I flushed. "But you already knew that."

"Yeah." I cleared my throat and his eyes flashed up to my face. "I'll nap for a bit then head home."

Andrew raised an eyebrow.

"I'll be fine. I'll call a Lyft." He continued to look, eyebrows raised. "Seriously. Stop hovering." I flapped my hands at him.

He sighed. "Okay, fine. But I'll be downstairs if you need anything."

At first, I thought I was dreaming. Andrew was talking to someone, pausing, and then speaking again. As my mind tried to cut through the fog of sleep, I realized that he must be speaking to someone on the phone. And what I heard perked me up immediately.

"Michael, she's been sleeping on my couch for the last two hours as if she's been drugged." He paused. "No, she hasn't *actually* been drugged. She got a charley horse. I just barely got her in the door before she fell asleep." I could almost feel the hardening of his voice, as if being exposed to too much sun left him leathery and weathered. "She's your fiancée; you're not gonna come get her?"

Andrew listened for a moment longer before he said, "No, don't worry. I'll take care of her." Though I couldn't really see him, I got the sense that the conversation ended. A long sigh followed.

I struggled to sit up, which Andrew's sonar picked up, of course. He bounded over to the couch and held a hand out. I ignored it and pushed myself to an upright position. "How are you feeling?"

"I take it your conversation with Michael went well?"

He sighed again, running a hand over his head. "He said he's stuck at the store."

I looked at my watch. "Sounds about right."

"His fiancée is in pain. I can't imagine anything more important than that."

I shrugged, relieved to find that my leg only hurt a little. "He's a manager, Minnie. I'm used to it."

"See, that's the thing. You shouldn't be."

I stared back at him, feeling the fires of rage and indignation spiking in my blood. Despite this, I said nothing for a while. *Give vulnerability a chance,* something within me said. *Tell him how you're feeling.*

Fuck it, I thought. *Why not?*

I sighed. "Honestly, I got a less-than-welcome-home response from Michael." I willed myself to stop fidgeting. "He didn't seem very happy that I was home."

Andrew tilted his head a little bit, frowning. "What made you think that?"

I shrugged, a blush blooming in my cheeks. "I told him I was home and he was like, 'oh, okay.' After I mentioned to him that it didn't seem like he was happy about it, he perked up a little, but not much."

Andrew nodded, lips tight. "I'm sorry, Ace."

I laughed, a humorless little *hmph* of a noise. "What are you sorry for? You're not my fiancé who's not even excited to see me." I shook my head, the words spilling out of my mouth before I could stop them. "What if I'm not good enough for him?"

"Not good enough for him?" Andrew's voice hardened. "In what way?"

"What if he thinks I'm too needy? Or what if he's not attracted to me anymore?" I looked down at my interlinked fingers. "What if I made him wait too long, and now he's given up?"

"If he has suddenly lost his attraction or love for you because you made him 'wait too long,' whatever the hell that means, then maybe it's a good thing you two aren't married yet."

I looked at Andrew, the connection between our eyes staving off the impending loneliness. "What do you mean?"

"Ace, you're worth waiting for." He met my eyes, jaw clenched and eyes tight. "You're worth loving. You know that, right?"

"Sure," I said, though my stomach flip-flopped.

"Are you saying sure because you believe it, or because you want me to believe that you believe it?"

I shrugged. "Both."

He sighed, long and low in the way that he did when he was impatient. "Ace."

"What? Just being honest."

"Good. Be honest with Michael, too."

"What does one have to do with the other?"

"Did you tell him how you felt about his lack of enthusiasm?" Andrew crossed his arms, lips drawn in a tight line.

"Yeah, I told him it didn't seem like he was too excited for me to be home."

"That's not what I asked. Did you tell him how you *felt* about it?"

I couldn't think of anything to say. Andrew nodded, his mouth forming an even more grim line, as if my silence said everything. "Exactly. You have no problem telling me just how you feel about me. If he is truly the one you want to spend the rest of your life with, don't you think you should do the same with him?"

"I guess."

"You guess?"

"Okay, fine, yes."

"Don't you want to grow into a more vulnerable person?"

I snorted. "No." Andrew raised one eyebrow. I rolled my eyes and sighed. "Okay, fine, maybe I need to work on being more vulnerable with Michael, at least."

"Yes, Ace, you do." He pulled on his face with his fingers and let out an even longer sigh. "Listen, what you do within your own romantic relationships is, ultimately, your business. But delve deep. Ask yourself: do I feel better when I share my true self with Michael, or when I keep it locked away? Then, you'll know what to do."

I hated to admit it, but I knew he was right.

Thirteen

Even in high school, one of the reasons why Andrew and I got along so well is that we hated talking for long periods of time. We spent hours upon hours playing video games in silence, and then, in college, we graduated to cartoons and superhero movies.

Andrew went to scavenge for sugary cereal while I set up the movie. When he came back, Lucky Charms in hand, he looked at the TV and grinned. "Classic," he said. "*Superman*. Still a fan favorite, I see."

"Superman is the all-American. Charming, good looks, fights crime. What more can you ask for?"

"You do realize that Superman is an alien, right? It seems ironic that you view him as the all-American."

"But he's a lovable kind of alien. The cool kind of alien."

We grinned at each other. We had been having this conversation since the beginning. It had a nice rhythm to it.

"You know," Andrew said as he passed me the box of Lucky Charms, "one day, you'll get tired of Superman."

I snorted. "Heresy."

"You can't love the same person forever." A jug of milk appeared in his hand, and I marveled that I hadn't seen it before; it was so large. "It's impossible."

I frowned and stopped picking through the cereal. "Wow. That took a turn. Cynical much?"

"Seriously though." He folded the cereal into the milk at a pace that was a hair less than furious. "Everything dies, including love. Even people's relationships don't last more than a few years nowadays. What makes you think that your love of Superman will outlast that?"

My heart picked up a pace more frantic than Andrew's cereal folding, but I breathed around it. "Andrew, you can't seriously believe that love can't last forever."

"I can, and I do." He stopped swirling and stared at me. "I'm surprised that you *don't*."

I blushed. "My parents have been together for thirty years. There must be something to it."

"Sure, people stay together for a while," he conceded. "But love? Do you really think they love each other still?"

"I do. Your parents are still together; do you think they're any less in love than they were when they met?"

"I do, actually." He shrugged. "Lately, they've become…distant from each other."

"They have three kids in college. That can cause money issues, tension."

"It's more than that." He sighed and picked up his spoon again. "It's not like I'm not looking for love. I just don't think it'll last that long."

The Ace inside me looked on as my heart ripped itself into several thousand tiny, unfixable pieces. I pressed my fingers together, the numbness spreading throughout my body. "So you really don't believe in a love that lasts forever?"

"I really don't." He pressed play on the movie. "And neither should you."

That numb feeling stuck with me for the rest of the day. There was something about our conversation that I couldn't shake. In a way, I felt betrayed, as if the boy I grew up with somehow became a man that I didn't recognize. *Or was he always this way?*

Despite my efforts to think differently, I couldn't help but think of it as a character flaw. I was cynical at times, sure, but not believing in *love?* What kind of psychopath didn't believe in *love?*

"It doesn't make him a psychopath," Cat said later that day. Jeremiah murmured something to her on the other end of the phone line, and she giggled. "Cynical, sure, but not a psychopath."

"But you know what I mean." I wrapped the headphones wire around my finger. "What do you think it means?"

"I think it means that Andrew needs to be with someone that makes him believe in eternal love again." I could almost hear her shrug and see her sly smile. "Maybe that person is you."

I snorted even as the seed planted itself in the soil of my mind. "Please. I'm not leaving Michael for Andrew. I wish everyone would stop trying to get me to break up with Michael."

I stopped winding the phone cord as an idea popped into my head. "Wait. Here's a thought."

"Ace, don't," Cat begged. "Nothing good comes of it when you say that—"

"How about this," I continued as if Cat hadn't spoken. "Let's all hang out together. You and Jeremiah, me and Michael, and Andrew. I bet you I can show you how little affect Andrew has on me, and how in love with Michael I am. If I win, you have to stop trying to hook me up with Andrew."

"And if I win?"

The rock of the suggestion weighed heavily in my stomach, but I said it anyway. "If you win, I'll consider breaking up with Michael. But I have to have time to consider it," I cautioned.

"That's all I ask," Cat said. "Fine, then; it's a deal."

I had a bad feeling about this. Much like Andrew, Cat was intuitive in this sense. And she never took a bet she wasn't sure to win. I just hoped I didn't lose my heart in the process.

We set the day and time for the next day around 6 p.m. Neither Andrew nor Michael knew about mine and Catalina's bet, and I wasn't about to tell them. Michael agreed to hang out with everyone easily enough, and Andrew, less so. "Seems like a fifth-wheel type of situation," he said.

"It'll be fun," I said. "Don't worry, you'll see."

"Sure," he said. "Okay."

He didn't sound convinced.

I walked up to Cat's with my heart fluttering like wild bats caught in a girl's hair. *I hope this was a good idea.* I also hoped that Andrew lived up to his true nature of always being late. Michael had to work late at the store, but I was convinced it wouldn't take Catalina long to see what I saw: that Andrew and I may be cool, but my feelings for him were solidly in the past. I may have fallen in love with him in high school and nurtured that love in college, but he rejected me. There was no way I would give him a second chance to dismiss my feelings for him. I couldn't watch him go from girl to girl and hold out hope that we could be together. We would be friends, nothing more.

I put my hand up to knock on the door, forming a fist and knocking heartily. I tapped my foot, fidgeted with the neck hole of my shirt.

"Nervous about something?"

I almost peed my pants a little. As I turned to face Andrew, I glared. "No," I snapped. "Can you make even just a little noise when you move?"

"What would be the fun in that?" He grinned as he brushed his hands against my fidgeting ones. "Down, girl."

Before I could open my mouth to retort, the door swung open before us. Cat stood in the doorway, smiling at first then smirking when she saw Andrew's hand over mine. I snatched mine away quickly and blushed.

"Welcome to our humble abode," Cat said, sweeping her hand out to the side and stepping away from the doorway. "Andrew, have you been here since we moved back?"

"Nope." He stepped through first, looking around. "Nice place. Good vibes."

"Thanks," Cat said, preening a little. She looked up toward the stairs. "Jer! Andrew and Ace are here!"

"Just them two?" Came the answer.

"Yup." Cat smirked again. I rolled my eyes.

Jeremiah came bounding down the stairs in socked feet. He and Andrew embraced, then he bussed a kiss to my cheek. "Good to see you both. Where's Michael?"

"Working," I said quickly. Cat gave me a shrewd look. "He should be on his way soon."

"Okay." Cat clapped her hands twice. "Well, we've got pizza. Ballin' on a budget and all that."

"Of course," Andrew and I said at the same time. We looked at each other and laughed. Cat was *always* "ballin' on a budget." For someone who seemed to love the finer things in life, she knew how to find a deal or cut back expenses. Food was one of those expenses—ironic, given that her husband was practically a chef.

"One day, everyone will appreciate my ability to find a good deal." Cat *hmphed*, nose stuck in the air. "Until then, eat your free pizza and like it."

"How many toppings does it have?" I asked. "Or did the coupon say you could only get cheese?"

"Bet you it's just cheese."

"Who knows, maybe there's half a pepperoni on one of them."

"Okay, *don't* eat," she sniffed. She opened a box and mouthwatering flavors seeped out. "These pizzas will last us at least three days. I'm perfectly okay with having y'all starve."

"Please, please eat the pizza," Jeremiah grumbled. "I don't want to eat pizza for the rest of the week."

I rolled my eyes at Andrew, and he snickered. "Fine, fine," I said. "We'll take one for the team, but only because Jeremiah begged."

As we all picked our slices, Andrew said, "So, Muscle Head is working late, huh?" Though his voice was light, casual, that erratic muscle in his jaw jumped. I could almost hear him grinding his teeth together from the effort of trying to hold back his words.

I felt a muscle tick in my own jaw at the derisive nickname he gave my fiancé. "Don't call him that."

"He calls me Andy, so it's only fair."

I sighed, knowing I wasn't going to win this fight. "I'm sure *Michael* will be on his way soon." I forced a smile to curl my lips. "Something probably happened at the store. He's not usually late."

"Why are you doing that?"

I fought the urge to retort, and my anger finally won

out. "Doing what, Andrew?"

"Being disingenuous." He squared his posture, facing me with narrowed eyes. "You're among friends. Muscle Head isn't here to see what a good little wife you can be."

I heard a low grunt of a cough somewhere behind me. Cat muttered, "Well, shit."

"What the fuck is that supposed to mean?"

"It means exactly what I said." Andrew leaned his hip against the kitchen island, crossing his arms. "Alicia, your whole life right now is disingenuous."

"My whole *life?* Jesus, cut the hyperbole, Andrew."

"Is it hyperbole, though? Think about it." He stepped closer, uncrossing his arms to bracket my body with them. "You spend most of your energy showing Michael what a good catch you are, being the good little fiancée. You use the rest of your energy showing your parents what a good little daughter you can be, following all their rules, even at almost twenty-five. And for what? What does that get you?"

My watch beeped, but I ignored it in favor of feeding my rage. Andrew didn't know shit about me, and frankly, I was tired of hearing his opinions on my life. "Go to hell, Andrew. You don't know the first thing about my relationship with Michael. Or with my parents."

"I don't, huh? So you *do* tell him that it drives you crazy when he doesn't put his bag on the hook." Andrew watched me with defiance blazing in his eyes. I tried to focus on his words and not the delicious place they were coming from. "You stood up to your parents and told them that you don't want a bunch of fake-ass socialites at your wedding. That you regret missing Ana's wedding. That you wish you saw your nephew more. You say all that to them, Alicia? Or do you just think it and hope they get it through osmosis?"

I didn't say anything because fuck me if he wasn't right. "What's your point, Minnie?"

His huff of a laugh rippled through my body. His breath caressed my upper lip. "My point is that you have spent so much of your life covering up all the shit you're dealing with that you don't even know who your real self is. Tell me, Ace, what is it that you're so afraid of? Why can't you just be yourself, with your real feelings?"

"I can, and I am."

"Prove it then." He pushed off the island, crossed his arms again. Challenge burned in his eyes. "I dare you to be your full self, all day, every day, for the next week. No holding back swears, no baby voice, no holding your tongue. Pure, unadulterated Ace. With everyone." He narrowed his eyes. "Including your parents and Michael."

I lifted my chin, the point of it jutting out. "No problem."

He smiled without humor. "Good."

We stared at each other for a few moments, my face burning, his wearing a smug smile, before Catalina almost audibly rolled her eyes.

"Now that we've established that," she said, "can we fucking *eat?*"

Michael didn't show up.

Throughout the movie and conversation with Cat, Jeremiah, and Andrew, I snuck peeks at the door, hoping that anytime, he would ring the doorbell. I sent him multiple *where are you?* texts. And yet, nothing.

Finally, Cat caught onto what I was doing. She put a gentle hand on my shoulder and said, "I don't think he's coming, Ace." I sighed and shook my head. *What store-related emergency could have kept him this long?* I wondered.

Admittedly, though, after I wrenched my eyes from the door that last time, I forgot all about Michael. The conversation flowed, and it was like Andrew and I picked up exactly where we left off years ago. I hadn't realized how much I missed the grounding force of our friendship until he replanted our roots. At one point, I looked over at him while he was mid-laugh. He threw his head back and let it loose to the ceiling, the sound bouncing off the flat surface. His Adam's apple bobbed to its own private symphony, and I closed my eyes to the sliver of skin and muscle of his abs exposed by his long, languid stretch. It was all I could do to stop myself from imagining those muscled, sinewy arms wrapping around my frame and picturing his low-pitched voice vibrating my insides as he thrust into me over and over again.

My watch beeped. *Asshole fucking watch.* I breathed deep, glad that no one could hear my thoughts.

Of course, he caught me mid-breath. He smiled. "You okay, Ace?"

"Doing great, thanks for asking." I let out my breath in a rush of air and mashed-together words.

He tilted his head as he asked, "What is it?"

"It's nothing," I said, blushing as he lifted an inquisitive eyebrow. My eyes slid from his. "It's just nice to hang out with you all again."

"You hang out with me, Jeremiah, and Michael almost every week," Cat pointed out.

"I know, but it's not the same as this." I sighed. I felt the joy and comfort of being among those who knew me seep into my very marrow. "This feels complete, somehow."

All three nodded, too, lost in thought. Finally, Jeremiah spoke up. "It's because we're family. We've been through a lot together."

"A lot of bullshit," Cat agreed. "Do you remember being stuck in detention for being late to school six times?"

"Or when Ace got grounded *again* for not adhering to her parents' commandments?" Jeremiah smirked at this.

"Or when Cat and Jeremiah moved across the country?" I said.

"Or everything that happened with Dante?" I felt my jaw tighten as Jeremiah said this. "That was a weird time."

"Not weird," Andrew murmured. "But definitely tragic."

"Can we talk about that for a minute?" Cat interrupted. "We never talk about Dante, despite the fact that he was a *fixture* in our lives from Kindergarten till he died. I think I saw him more than I saw your parents. Or my parents, really. Now, it's as if he didn't exist."

"I don't pretend that he didn't exist," I protested.

"Other than tonight, when was the last time you even said his name?" Cat looked at me as if waiting to hear an excuse. My fingers tapped out a rhythm on my thighs.

"There's just nothing to say. He's gone, by his own choice. What could I possibly say about him?"

"You know damn well it wasn't by his choice, Ace," Cat shot back. "He had a terminal illness. He was gonna die regardless of whatever hellish treatment they put him through—"

"He could've given us a little more time, but instead, he put his own needs above all else. He could've had months, even *years*, but he decided that it was 'God's plan' for him to die. So he beat Him to the punch."

"He didn't commit suicide. He let nature take its course."

"Really? Was it nature or God that killed him? Because I've heard it both ways, and honestly, I think it's a bullshit-ass excuse to get out of fighting for your life."

The silence yawned before us, becoming its own entity. The shakes that had inhabited my hands grew until my whole body vibrated. Andrew, the closest to me on the couch, reached out to touch me, but I moved away. I stood up and gathered my stuff.

"As fun as this has been," I said, "I should go find out what happened to my fiancé."

I stood at the entrance of the church, feet cemented to the floor. People whose faces I couldn't remember flowed past me. Some were crying, but I couldn't find it in me. I couldn't cry for someone who didn't fight for their life.

Still, it was as if my body knew that once I made my way down the aisle, I couldn't deny that Dante wasn't coming back. I sighed a watery sigh. Death had such finality to it.

"And you said you wouldn't need me." The soft murmur at my ear made me hear sonnets and feel butterflies, but outwardly, I rolled my eyes. Only one person had the confidence and gall to sneak up on me at a funeral.

"I don't need you." I straightened my spine a little more and sniffed. My fingers tapped an impatient beat on my leg. "I'm taking my time."

He gently wrapped his arms around my shoulders and rested his chin against my hair. "Sure," he said. "Okay."

We stood like that for a while, with me sheltered in the warmth of his arms, his chin on my head. Finally, he let go and stepped in front of me. I looked down at his proffered hand. "Ready?"

I stepped around him, ignoring his hand, and walked slowly down the aisle. Heads turned to watch me go. I felt the heat of a hundred gazes on my back as I made my way to the casket. With each step, I kept my back straight and my chin up. I could feel my mother's eyes on me, a warning glance. Don't ever let them see you sweat. Oh, how well you taught me to hide in plain sight, Mother.

I stopped a few feet from Dante's casket. It was closed on account of Dante's wishes to be cremated, but I could only imagine what he would look like at this moment. Silent and still. At peace. My chin wobbled, and my eyes filled with tears. The burning that I had felt in the first days after Dante died sprang up with a vengeance. I choked on it. My fingers, ever moving, tapped out an even more frantic beat. Despite this, my watch stayed silent.

There will never be anyone who can fill this hole you left me with.

A hand gently squeezed my arm and I looked up to find Andrew standing there. His eyes took stock of my face and understanding darkened his eyes. His fingers came up to brush my tears away, like they had so many times before this, and his face leaned toward mine. For a second, I thought he would kiss me. My watch spoke into the silence with one beep then another. Take a breath.

Instead, his breath kissed my ear as he murmured, "Let's pray." His hand slid down to my own and gently tugged me toward the casket. We both kneeled, heads bowed, and Andrew spoke.

"Lord." He paused, reverence reverberating in his voice. I looked over at him and saw tears leaking from his closed eyes. Despite this, he kept as still and steady as always.

"One of Your sons has come home to You. Grant him safe passage. And watch over us here on Earth who mourn this loss but celebrate his life. In Jesus's name we pray."

"Amen," I whispered. Andrew gently pulled me up with him and steadied me on my feet with two hands on my shoulders. I could feel those hundred sets of eyes on us but all

I could see was Andrew. He may have taken me from the oasis of my rage and plunged me into the cold sea of my sorrow, but his eyes kept me from going under.

If the funeral was everything that Dante hated in this world, the repass was a horror show. None of Dante's friends showed up, and it's a miracle that Ana was even invited. Most of the people were "friends" of my parents who knew nothing about Dante, not even his name. They all came up to me at some point to weep about how great Donny or Donald was, and to talk about how they couldn't understand how I could stand the grief. After I almost rolled my eyes for the fifth time, Andrew pulled me into the powder room.

"Hey." I remember looking at him and seeing his eyes dance with mischief. "You should laugh at the next person if you're really trying to get under your parents' skin. I'm sure they would love that."

I huffed out a laugh reluctantly. "These people don't know Dante, and the ones that did weren't invited. He loathed my parents' Black Social Elitist non-friends. Why's it so important that they're here, anyway?"

Andrew didn't answer.

"And anyway," I continued, "this vibe embodies nothing that Dante ever was in this life. There's no authenticity to it, no depth. Is this really what my parents think of Dante's life? This meaningless, shallow shell of a party?"

Andrew raised his eyebrows and turned toward the closed door as someone burst into raucous laughter right outside. He swiveled his eyes back to meet mine. "Say the word and we're out of here."

"The word," I deadpanned. I opened the door and grabbed his wrist. "Let's go."

Andrew and I ended up at our favorite park, as we usually did. I quickly unbuckled my heels and flung them into the sand. I wiggled my toes, the delicious feel of grains sliding across my skin, and sighed. Andrew watched me from a few feet away. My face burned as I felt his eyes trying to connect with mine.

He rested his forearms on his knees and looked at me again. "How are you holding up, Ace?" He asked. "No bullshit."

"No bullshit? I'm fine." I picked at my cuticles and sighed. "Dante didn't want to live this life, so why should I mourn him?"

Andrew, patient person that he is, didn't say anything.

"I mean, what the fuck, right?" I turned to Andrew, feeling my ire burn through my skin. "Who does that? Who gives up on perfectly good medical treatment when he has a family to provide for? Who just throws everything away on the misguided notion that it's God's plan for his life?"

"Maybe he didn't feel like it was his choice anymore." Andrew sat back and placed one arm on the back of the bench. "Dante believed wholeheartedly that God was calling him home. Is that so hard to believe?"

"Yes! Yes, it is. Why would God 'call him home' when Dante has a child who has barely experienced life? Why would God want Dante to leave his wife with that? What kind of God do we serve if He doesn't care about what people leave behind in the wake of the tragedy of death?" I felt tears fall and make their path down to my chin. "How could he just leave me here?"

As Andrew slid closer to me on the bench, and wrapped me in his arms, I couldn't stop the question from repeating in my head. How could he leave me here? How could he just leave?

Soon, it became hard to know which "he" I was talking about: Dante, or God.

Fourteen

I heard a knock on my door almost as soon as I hung my keys on its rung. Looking at my watch and frowning, I opened the door.

"Babe," Michael said. "I'm so sorry." I grimaced but stepped aside to let him in. "Work ran late, and I thought I was going to get there, but I couldn't get there in time. By the time I was done, it was late and I figured we could see the gang another day. Forgiven?"

I don't know if it was the rehashing of painful memories, or Andrew's insistence on vulnerability, but something in me snapped. "No, not forgiven."

"What do you mean?" Michael frowned, too. "You know I couldn't have gotten away."

"I don't know any such thing, Michael. It was important for you to be there tonight. It was important to *me* that you were there. When you didn't show up, I was hurt by that."

"Well, I don't know what you want me to do. I have to make a living for us."

"Yes, I get that." I sighed and ran my hands over my head. "But it's like it's not a big deal for you to hurt me."

"Whoa, where is this coming from?" He moved toward me and put his hands on my shoulders. "Of course it's a big deal if I hurt you. I didn't know this meant so much to you. I thought we were just hanging out with Cat and Jer like we do every week."

"We were, but—" I sighed again, shaking my head. "We're getting married, Michael, and it feels like you're getting more distant instead of less. I need to know that you're committed to showing up when you say you will." I looked up at him. "Sometimes, it feels that you're not really present. I want—I deserve—someone who can be my rock. Can you do that?"

"I can be that," he said. "I *will* be that. It won't happen again, babe, promise."

I sighed, not willing to say it aloud but not quite believing him. Lately, it felt like I saw him less and less. I had already felt like I didn't see a lot of Michael, what with a grueling football schedule and working at his family's store. But now, the distance between us grew into its own entity, maturing from clenched jaws and agitated movements to excuses about working late. While it's true that summer was the second busiest season for Michael's store, and in football, it had never been so busy that he couldn't call me to say he'd be late. A growing sense of dread and suspicion bloomed in my stomach as I started to put a timeline together in my head. *Our distance started happening after Andrew and I reconnected,* I realized. I didn't want to say it aloud, because if it was said, it couldn't be ignored. If it was said, *I* couldn't ignore it. But it had to be said.

"Michael," I said finally. "Do you have a problem with Andrew?"

"What? No, babe." Michael shook his head emphatically and puffed his chest out in the way he does. "Our relationship is strong. I know I'm in love with you and you're in love with me. Nothing will come between us, right?"

I nodded, even as doubt joined dread and suspicion deep in my belly. "Right," I echoed. "Nothing can come between us."

I didn't know whom I believed less: me, or Michael.

"Confronting him is only the first step. Now, you have to learn how to deal with your hurt feelings."

I rolled my eyes as I broke off another piece of my cinnamon roll. "Okay, Brené Brown."

Andrew and I decided to meet up at "our" coffee shop the next day. Even though now I could see how uncomfortable Michael was with my relationship with Andrew, I needed validation that I wasn't completely crazy, that I wasn't imagining it. Cat was busy—with what, I couldn't be sure—so I went with the next best thing. Unfortunately for me, the Next Best Thing was also partly the source of the issue.

Andrew put his hand over mine, waiting until I looked up. "Don't do that."

"Do what?"

"Make a joke when you're feeling insecure."

I pulled my hand away, delving into my cinnamon roll with a vicious bite. Andrew's uncanny ability to look deep into my soul was disconcerting—even though, technically, that was the whole reason I wanted to meet up with him in the first place. Much like my feelings for Andrew, my desire to be understood by someone, anyone, played tug-of-war with my desire to be left alone.

I continued to look at my cinnamon roll, avoiding Andrew's eyes as much as possible. "I wasn't feeling insecure."

Andrew raised an eyebrow.

"Okay, so maybe I was feeling a little 'out there', but so what?" I picked up my tea and downed half of its contents. "I have a right to my feelings, don't I?"

"Yes. But you might want to acknowledge them." Andrew bit into his breakfast burrito.

"For what?"

"For yourself."

"Cut the enigmatic bullshit, Andrew." I finally looked at him dead-on. I could see the challenge in his eyes. "What do you mean?"

"It means," he said, "you need to learn how to be okay with not being okay. You need to learn how to deal with uncomfortable feelings like insecurity, guilt, grief."

"Grief? Is this about the whole Dante thing? Because I promise you, I'm fine."

"Fine, fine, fine," Andrew said in a singsong voice. "Ace, you're the most not-fine person I've ever met. What happens when it all explodes on you?"

Stupid Andrew and his stupid introspection, I thought. If there was anything I'd learned in my friendship with him, it was that I always needed to be careful what I wished for. Andrew had a knack for delivering on things I had wished for but not spoken about. Inwardly, I gave myself a rueful smile. *You wanted to talk to someone who would validate you*, I thought to myself. *Looks like you found it.*

I finished the rest of my tea and tapped the paper cup on the table twice as I got up to pay. "I guess we'll never find out," I said.

Throughout the week, I could hear the echoes of Andrew's declarations in my head. *Fine, fine, fine,* he said in my head. *Everything's* fine. *Isn't it, Ace?*

Ace, you're the most not-fine person I've ever met.

You need to learn how to be okay with not being okay.

Even in my head, Andrew's voice was irritating. And right.

Not that I had much time to think about it. Now that I was home, Mother took it upon herself to schedule meeting after meeting with all of the vendors, and even some meetings with vendors I didn't know we had.

Finally, when I thought I couldn't take any more meetings, Mother scheduled another one, at a location where I had never been. The road to the destination was unpaved, lined with tall trees that arched tall over the street. There weren't any houses or even buildings within a five-mile radius. Beyond the tree-lined road, though, fields of flowers swayed in the light summer breeze. Their tiny purple, yellow, and white heads seemed to be dancing to an unheard song.

When I pulled into the driveway of the building, I noticed a massive front yard with a garden and bubbling water fountain in the center. A cobblestone path cut through the front yard, paving the way to a sprawling mansion. The building itself was an odd sight in New England. The three-story building stood tall and proud, the second story balcony held up by pillars reminiscent of the Romans. The sign over the door said simply, *Rose Manor.*

I pulled my car around to the front of the extravagant manor and cut the engine, watching the water dribble down the fountain and spill its way into the pool surrounding it. I lay my head onto the headrest and let my body sink into the seat for a moment. *Sweet release,* I thought. *Sweet, sweet release.*

"Alicia." My mother's sharp tone penetrated the glass, and she tapped her fingernails on my driver-seat window. I jumped, my keys dropping to the floor, and I hit my head on the steering wheel as I reached for them. I said a silent curse.

"Mother." I opened the door, finally retrieving my keys. "Where are we?"

"Madam Noir's," she said. "Spa day."

I raised my eyebrows. "Spa day? Mother, this is great, thank you!"

"Why do you sound so surprised?" She walked briskly toward the front door. "You're my only living child, and this is a big event. Besides," she added, "you're starting to get frown lines."

And there it is, I thought, barely containing an eye roll. Slowly, I followed Mother to the front door.

"How did you and Father meet?"

My mother's head snapped back, surprise turning her lips down and creating those forehead wrinkles that she hated so much. The woman working on her nails stopped filing for a brief second, causing my mother's frown to swing her way. "Why the sudden interest in our love life?"

"It's not a sudden interest," I mumbled, my face heating up. I hadn't wanted to ask in the first place, but all I could hear was Andrew's voice in my head. *No holding back swears, no baby voice, no holding your tongue. Pure, unadulterated Ace.* Ace was curious about her parents' marriage, which seemed rock solid. It was entirely different from what I saw everywhere else, and I couldn't help but wonder: how did they manage all these years?

Mother sighed, tilting her head to the side as if remembering something. Her eyes took on a slightly glassy look. "It took some time," she said finally. "We were both pursuing our undergraduate degrees in sociology and pre-law. I was a couple of years older than him, quite the same difference in age as you and Michael." She smiled a bit, a rarity. "He was a freshman. I was a junior."

"Scandalous," I said and laughed before I remembered who I was with. Luckily, Mother laughed a little, too. "So you two met in class?"

"Not exactly." Mother blushed then, and I perked up with interest. "I was walking across the quad with my girl-friends, and he almost hit me in the head with a soccer ball." She looked away. "He was the finest man I had ever seen, but I didn't pursue him."

"Why not?"

She cut her eyes at me, sharp as ever. "Women shouldn't pursue men, Alicia. You know that."

"Of course." I looked down and away from Mother. "What happened then?"

"We crossed paths a few more times before he asked me out on a date," she said. The nail lady moved to dip my mother's feet in the warm bath. "He was so shy back then, despite all his bolster on the field. I was not shy."

"You weren't?"

"Never," she boasted. She laughed a deep belly laugh. "I've never been shy a day in my life."

I smiled; it was something Mother and I had in common. I couldn't think of a time where I was bashful around anyone, except maybe Andrew. I simply didn't want to be around people for too long.

"Don't get me wrong; I have my moments where I don't want to be around people," Mother said. I looked up curiously. "But, for the most part, being in a crowded room gives me energy."

"Gives me heartburn," I muttered.

"Yes, well, you were always the more introverted child." Mother sighed heavily. "Not like your brother. He was a motormouth."

We both laughed at that. Dante, for all of his perspective-taking and philosophizing, could never put a lid on it.

We both sat in silence for a while, watching the nail ladies pamper our toes, before I asked, "So when did Father propose?"

"It was my first year in law school, his junior year in undergrad." Mother yawned. "We had dated for about two years, and I was waiting for him to propose. My mother was convinced that I was going to become an old maid, and she was constantly pushing me to get married."

"Grandmother? Really?"

"Really." My mother's face took on a pinched look, her lips pursed as if tasting the bitter flavors of spinsterhood. "She couldn't stand the fact that her only child hadn't given her grandchildren yet. I think she might have even goaded your father into proposing to me." She sighed. "She was always on me about one thing or another."

Sounds familiar.

I didn't realize I had spoken aloud until Mother answered wryly, "I guess the apple doesn't fall far from the tree."

My heart started racing, my mind trying to figure out a way to salvage the situation. *Me and my big fucking mouth,* I thought.

Mother flapped a hand at me, as if dismissing my fear. "Alicia, I know I'm hard on you," she said. "You don't have to try to cover it up. I'm hard on you, but the world is so much worse."

Don't hold your tongue, Ace, I thought grimly to myself. I took a deep breath before taking the plunge. "But do you have to be *so* hard on me, though?"

Mother's head snapped toward me for the second time that day. "What does that mean?"

"Well," I said in a tiny voice. "From your admonishments about how I dress, to your criticism on my hair, I feel like I can't do anything right."

For a long moment, the only sounds in the room were that of the nail ladies working on our toes. Finally, Mother said in a quiet voice, "Do you think I think that you can't do anything right?"

I looked away. "Sometimes, it feels like if you had a choice, you would have chosen Dante to live over me."

I didn't realize that I was crying until I saw the tears hit the top of my thighs. Mother sighed long and low, and I heard something shift. When I looked up, she had moved her feet from her water basin and was facing me directly.

"Alicia Danielle Jones," she said. "How could you think such a thing?"

"Is it that hard to believe?" I wiped my eyes and huffed out a laugh. "My whole life, all I've been told is how perfect Dante was and how much work I had to do to come close to all that he'd accomplished. Nobody was as good as Dante, and nobody deserved to be with him, according to you and Father."

"You know as well as I that Dante isn't—wasn't— perfect. He had Obsessive Compulsive Disorder, which made it impossible to get him out of the house on time. He had to check every appliance three times, move every chair four times. He would have a fit anytime anything was out of place. He couldn't stop talking; it was incessant. And then, when he and Ana got together, they were practically unbearable. They were always involved in some cause or another, always trying to rope people into their missions.

And Dante gravitated toward those types of people all the time. I didn't want to have to hear them go on and on about the environment, for goodness sake." She sniffed. "And he—and you, too—always stuck his nose up at my acquaintances."

"Because they don't even know us. They didn't care to know us. And they go on and on about being the Black Elite."

"Yes, because it is a mark of honor," Mother said. "To live this long in this life, and to be successful as a black person, is a miracle. We wear our elitism with pride, because at the very least, we're alive. I'm sixty years old, Alicia. Many black people don't make it this long. Do you know how monumental that is?"

I thought about that for a moment. She had a point. "But why can't they ever remember my name? Or Dante's?"

Mother shrugged, smiled a little. "They're old, Alicia."

We laughed at that.

Mother's nail lady gestured for Mother to put her feet back in the water, and she obliged. "Never for a moment think that I love you less than I loved Dante," she said. As her eyes met mine, I could see a fierce pride burning. "You are my only daughter, and a gift from God. Never forget that." She inspected her fingernails and added, "And maybe, don't be so judgmental."

––––––––––

For the rest of the day, all I could think about were my mother's words. *You are my daughter, and a gift from God.* It was still hard to believe that those words came from my mother.

"Are you sure it was your mom that said that?" Cat said, a dubious look playing between her eyebrows.

We were in the car, on our way to The Home Store, otherwise known as my happy place. In my dreams of living in holy matrimony with Michael, our place was splendid. It had beautifully decorated rooms, complete with lush carpets to dig our bare feet in, a roaring fireplace, comfy couches, and throw blankets to wrap ourselves in on chilly New England nights. It would be somewhere between elegant and cozy, the perfect blend of Michael's bachelor décor and my warm but minimalist vibe.

Of course, to do that, we needed the décor. And, you know, furniture. That's where The Home Store came in.

My favorite place in the world was located in a not-quite-outdoors-mall just off the main road in our home-town. It spanned the square footage equivalent to four city blocks and had just as much packed in. There was Ned's Tavern, which served everything from cheap bar food to the best beer west of Route 9; Everything Toys, which was self-explanatory; the best shoe store known to man; and, of course, my little slice of homemaker heaven. The rest of the stores that made up the collective were a bunch of chains, like Barnes and Noble and the Hallmark store.

"It was Mother," I said to Cat as I backed the car into its space. I took the keys out of the ignition and stared through the windshield, wincing as I thought back to earlier that day. "Definitely Mother."

"Were you dreaming?"

"Possibly. But probably not." I watched a boy chase after his sister in the parking lot with a small smile. The mom looked less than amused. "The rest of the day was a litany of criticism."

"Sounds about right."

"Yep."

Cat was silent for a moment. "Wow. This changes everything. Mama Jones out here giving compliments. I didn't know she even knew how to smile at you genuinely."

I snorted. "Who are you telling?" I thought back to all the times I wished she would congratulate me just once on doing a good job without adding tips on how to be better. "I almost fell out my seat when she said I'm her daughter like it was something she was proud of. Do you remember that time when we went on the field trip to the New England Aquarium and someone asked if I was her daughter?"

"And she looked like she was gonna deny it?" Cat shook her head. "Who could forget?"

"I still can't believe she almost didn't claim me!"

Cat fought a smile by biting down on her bottom lip. "To be fair, you were sobbing hysterically about the museum feeding live fish to the penguins."

"I was six!"

"Girl, you were fourteen."

I sucked my teeth. "Man, whatever. It's the principle. They don't even kill the poor guys first! They just let them die when they get chomped on. Death by eating."

We chuckled at the bleeding heart I used to be. As we stepped out of the car and closed our doors, Cat mused, "I wonder what else we don't know about your mom."

"Right?" I walked to the line of shopping carts, took one, and pushed it through the opening doors. "How many other gems is she hiding?"

Cat shrugged as she followed me into the store. "Who knows?" A wry grin overtook her face as she caught my eye. "Maybe your mom actually loves you."

I rolled my eyes as I stopped to inspect a vase with intricate detail. "Sure," I said. "Okay. Which version of me? The one that follows all of her rules and marries *her* dream guy? Or the one that goes on tour with a band whose lead singer has pink hair?"

"Isn't it just a few streaks of pink?"

"Tell that to Quinta Jones."

"Right. But think about it." Cat tapped her finger to her lips, a gesture she picked up from Jeremiah. Her eyes grew unfocused as she started thinking about an alternate future. I braced myself for impact; Cat's daydreams, while mostly based in reality, sometimes took us on a journey.

"What if," she said finally, "your mom really does love you? The you that you are presently? What if she does have a heart that we didn't know about"—at this, I snorted —"but she's been motivated by wanting you to have a husband and a good life?"

"There are other ways to have a good life," I said. "I don't need a husband to do it."

"True," Cat conceded, "but what if she doesn't know that? What if her ideas about what makes a good life are based in the traditional? Back when your parents got married, that's what was considered having a good life. Get married, have kids, buy a house, blah blah blah. What if she is the way she is because she wants you to have all that?"

"Regardless of the intention, the impact is the same," I said. I placed the vase in the basket a little too roughly and a sales associate passing by gave me a sharp look. "Even if what you're saying is true—that she just wants to make sure I have a good life—she's been hard on me my whole life. She can't possibly think that I would know that's how she shows love."

"Hey, we didn't know she was even capable of giving you a compliment up until today, much less showing you love," Cat pointed out. "Who's to say what she believes?"

I paused at that. What Cat said could be true, or it

could not. But in order to believe this alternate reality—to believe that Mother really did love me, and she did what she did so I could have the best in life—I would have to believe that my mother's intentions were pure. I didn't know if I had the capacity to believe that. Not after all these years of feeling unloved, unwanted, and emotionally beat down by her and my father alike. It took too much faith to believe in that which had no physical, tangible evidence. You can't see intention. I simply couldn't believe in what I had yet to see or feel.

I couldn't even hope for it.

Fifteen

We were hanging out on the couch at my place one night when Michael turned to me and said, "Why not get the marriage license while you're home?"

The thought made my back slick with sweat and my heart race. Ever since The Leroys' tour got cut short and I had been home, I had been less and less sure about my impending nuptials. I couldn't tell if Michael had always been overbearing or if it was a new development. He always wanted to know where I was or where I was going. He used the key to my apartment more often than he did before, and it felt like he was always in my space. Even the physicality of our relationship grated my nerves. Every hug felt suffocating; every kiss felt wet and sloppy. The smell of his cologne was too sharp and not at all like the smooth, smoky chimney scent I was now used to.

It didn't help that he was unbearably self-absorbed. Everything was about football—the summer training, the new season, the NFL draft picks. On and on and on. And not once did he ask me about being on tour with my favorite band of all time.

All of this was in juxtaposition with how infrequently we saw each other. He seemed to be using work and practice as a way to avoid me; yet, when he actually made time for me, he was all over me—literally and figuratively.

But I couldn't back out now. The closer we got to the wedding ceremony in front of 200 of my parents' closest "friends," the more real it became. When Michael wasn't working, at practice, or with me, he was meeting with my father about who knows what. I hadn't realized how wholly my parents had accepted Michael as their own until my mother started wondering if she and I should go to the Family Day that his team held. The thought of Michael joining my family through marriage caused my skin to feel tight, my chest to feel like bursting. It all seemed so fast even though we had been together for over two years.

So even though my mind was ready to implode with the possibility of getting our marriage license much earlier than expected, outwardly, I smiled as if this was the best idea he'd ever had. "You're right," I said. "We should do it. Tomorrow."

"Yes!" Michael looked at me, excitement bright in his eyes. "I mean, I don't know why we were going with the month-before deadline anyway." He pulled me to his side and I grimaced. "It's so arbitrary. I can't wait to make you my wife, so why wait?"

You want to make me your trophy. The thought dug its teeth into my mind and refused to let go, no matter how much I tried to shake it.

I shivered. The pure, unadulterated Ace that I had gotten used to was buried under the weight of my public face. They each fought for purchase in my mind and in my body. *Don't make a fuss,* my public persona told Ace. *Let's not make waves.*

But who just wants a puppet? Ace snapped back.

"I'm excited to be married, too," I ground out with a smile. "This license…it's one more step toward what we both want."

Well, at least it wasn't a lie.

Too bad we want different things.

"Exactly." Michael laid a wet kiss on my cheek, and I forced myself not to wipe it off. "Then, we'll be one."

"Yes," I said, even as Ace and my public persona wrestled. "And it will be perfect."

I thanked my lucky stars that Michael wanted to wait until marriage before staying over my place. As soon as he left, I put my shoes on and drove to my hometown. Though it was dusk, and I could see just fine, the scenery passed me in a blur. I couldn't quell the rising sense of panic at being chained to Michael forever.

I found myself at the most peaceful place I could think of—mine and Andrew's park. I breathed a long sigh as I followed the path up the hill to our bench. Our now wooden bench. Part of me grimaced at the fact that even parks don't stay the same. But I needed, now more than ever, a place I could recognize. A place Michael wouldn't follow me.

A place to truly be the unadulterated Ace that Andrew had called me to be.

Once I sat down on the bench, I texted Andrew. ***Busy?*** I asked.

The response was immediate. **Not really, why?**

Care to meet me at our park? I have some exciting news.

Sure. Be there soon.

As I waited for him, I looked out over the hill. Memories of us lying up there looking at clouds, or sitting on the bench eating ice cream, flitted through my mind with no real purpose or destination. I sighed in contentment at the familiarity of the memories, like a favorite worn shirt, or a baby blanket that had been with me since birth. My mind cherished the memories, turned them around and around in my mind, leaving no detail unexamined.

And that's how Andrew found me, looking up at the sky lit up by the sunset. When he approached, he stopped just short of the bench. I could tell he was frowning, mostly because it was his facial expression of choice, but also because I was not usually the silent one of the two of us. Finally, he said, "Didn't you say you have exciting news? Like a positive thing? Because this doesn't seem positive."

"Michael and I have moved up the date to get our marriage license." I tried to dry my palms on my jeans as I stood up to pace. No luck—my hands felt like I immersed them in a pool. "To tomorrow."

Andrew waited.

"I don't know if I'm ready." My pacing grew more erratic. Andrew watched me carefully. "This is happening too fast."

"You two have been engaged for months, Ace. You knew this was coming."

"Yes, but we hadn't planned to do the marriage license thing this soon. It's too soon. It'll be all official."

"Isn't that the goal?"

"Yes, but why does this have to happen right now?" My pace quickened. "Why can't we stick to our original plan? What if we're making a mistake? What if *I'm* making a mistake? I won't be able to take it back and—"

"Alicia Jones, stop." I stopped immediately, my eyes drawn to his. Somewhere between his arrival and now, he had sat down on the bench.

He looked at me steadily. "Do you love him?"

What a loaded question, I thought. It was also one I didn't know how to answer. I didn't know if I loved him. I thought I did, but could I really call it love if the thought of being with him forever made me have a panic attack? Was it love if I looked at Michael and could only think about what this marriage would do for his career and my relationship with my parents?

Could I call it love if Holy Matrimony seemed more like The Road to Hell Paved with Good Intentions?

I sighed. "I don't know. Yes?"

"Yes with a question mark?" Andrew said sharply. Something about the tone of his voice and look in his eye told me that this was the wrong answer.

"Yes," I said finally. "Yes, I think so. I think I'm just freaking out a little bit." *Or, I hope that's what it is,* I added silently.

"Does he love you?"

"Yes—"

"And was this part of the plan all along? To get the marriage license?"

"Yes, but the timing—"

"Then nothing has changed." When I opened my mouth to protest, he repeated, louder, "Nothing has changed, Ace. You're just scared."

As my pacing continued, but at a slower speed, I noticed a change in Andrew. He watched me, same as before, but there was something darker behind the gaze. He hunched over, his back rounded, his mouth resting on his intertwined fingers. It was almost as if he was folding in on himself. I stopped pacing altogether.

"Ace." He got up from the bench and stepped toward me. My breath caught in my throat at the underlying pain in his voice. He lifted his hand as if about to stroke my arm, but then dropped it quickly. In the past, Andrew never hesitated to reach out and touch my arm, tickle my armpits, give me a hug. But now, with thoughts and talk of Michael swirling in the air, it was as if a barrier had been erected between us. I felt the loss of connection as tangibly as if I had hit the barrier physically.

"What?" I said finally.

"You're gonna be fine, you know that right?"

My breathing slowed, and I felt my heart follow. "Yes." *But will you?* I wanted to ask. Instead, I said, "But how do I know if I'm making the right choice?"

He smiled, the gesture not quite reaching his eyes. "What other choice is there?"

I met Michael at a time where I was the lowest I'd ever been. After Andrew and I stopped being friends, I would spend whole days wandering the city. I would look into store windows of places where we had been together, but I wouldn't go in. I would travel on the train or bus to places that we said we'd visit together but hadn't gotten around to seeing. And I was always, always crying or angry. I vacillated between the two with dizzying speed. It got to the point where the owners of my favorite Thai restaurant knew me as "the crying-angry girl."

I was sitting in that very restaurant when Michael saw me through the window. I was crying that time, and I was a god-awful mess. I heard the soft wind chimes at the door but paid them no mind. Even as I looked to the tablecloth, though, I could sense someone sitting beside me, watching me.

"Hey," the voice said. "Are you okay?"

When I turned my burning, painfully red eyes toward the voice, a pair of hazel eyes met mine. Blond, seemingly baby-soft hairs thickened the line of his jaw, feeding into his sideburns in one smooth slope. His hair, loosely pulled up into a bun, reflected the golden light of the afternoon as if shining a halo over his head. His eyes blinked behind a pair of black, square-shaped glasses. Full, pink lips expressed concern as two identical dimples near his mouth winked in and out.

Even in my despair, I sensed the momentous nature of sitting here with him. A man this glorious was sitting beside this sad, pathetic wisp of a person. The thought of my sadness—and everything that caused it—made the tears fall once again.

"Hey, you know that whatever it is…you're gonna get through it. You know that, right?" His golden brows came together as he tried to convince me.

"It's just…you're just…so beautiful," I sobbed. He and I both laughed—him, joyfully, me, tearfully—at how absurd this whole thing was. Or maybe he didn't, but I did. Here I was, crying over one guy and laughing with another.

"I'm Michael," he said, sticking out his hand. "And you are?"

"Other than a mess? Alicia." I shook his hand firmly.

"Do you go by Alicia, or by a nickname?"

I immediately thought of all the ridiculous nicknames that Andrew had given me through the years. As my eyes welled up with tears once again, I took a deep breath. No more crying over Andrew, *I thought firmly.* At your most vulnerable, he left you. It's time to toughen up. Never let them see you sweat, and never be vulnerable. Andrew is just like the rest of them, just like every other man. And they simply can't be trusted.

I pasted on a smile through my tears and wiped my eyes as gracefully as I could. "Nope," I said. "It's just Alicia."

Because Michael and I changed the date of our courthouse "wedding," none of the people who were supposed to be there could make it.

"It's the big one that counts," my mother said, flapping her hand dismissively.

"I have to work," Jeremiah said, shrugging.

After I begged and pleaded, Cat rolled her eyes. "I'll be there," she grumbled. "But I won't like it."

Michael didn't have any luck with his side of the family and friends, either. "They're all working or busy," he said, shrugging. "Guess we go without them."

"I mean, maybe we should hold off," I suggested. "Since barely anyone can go."

"No," Michael said. "We can do it tomorrow instead. It'll give us one more day to find someone."

I sighed.

"How many people usually attend the marriage license signing, anyway?" I asked Andrew later on that night. We were sitting in the coffeehouse that we met in when we reconnected. I was starting to think of it as "our coffeehouse"—even though it was a chain.

I knew Andrew would be there for me, no matter what. Despite the fact that he left me two years ago, he had always been a constant in my life. I called him to ask him to meet me in the coffeehouse because I needed his help, and I knew he wouldn't abandon me.

Or at least, that's what I hoped.

Andrew shrugged as he fiddled with the sleeve on his drink. "Couldn't tell you. I've never been married before."

I gave him a sidelong look before taking a gulp of my coffee. Putting down the cup, I sighed.

"Well, I guess it doesn't matter anyway," I said. "We need two witnesses, and we only have one, so we'll just have to go with the original plan. Unless," I said, looking at him briefly before looking away, "you'll be our second witness."

"Your what?" Andrew startled, turning his gaze on me with furrowed brows. "You want me to do what?"

I fiddled with my own cup. "Be our second witness?" I repeated, a question in my voice.

He sighed. "Alicia—"

"I know it's a big ask." I pleaded with my eyes as I started to shred my napkin. "I know you don't agree with this marriage, and you hate Michael—"

"Hate's a strong word. I don't like the guy, but I don't hate him."

"Then do it for me, Andrew. Please. I wouldn't ask if it wasn't really important to me."

"Alicia, ask me to do anything else. But don't ask me to witness you throwing your life away."

"Andrew, please," I said this on a whisper. "Please."

Andrew was silent for a moment, chewing on his bagel slowly. After swallowing, he finally said, "You're sure you love him?"

I grimaced even as I said the word. "Yes."

"And he loves you? You're sure?"

"Yes, he loves me. I'm sure."

"Then I'll do it."

"Do what?"

He rolled his eyes skyward for guidance. "Be your second witness, dummy."

"No need to call names," I said. "You'll do it though? Really?"

"Under one condition."

I braced myself. "What is it?"

"Tell me the truth, no bullshit." He met my eyes. "Are you marrying him because you love him, truly? Or are you doing it for some other reason?"

He held my gaze as a blush crept up my neck and spread throughout my face. My watch beeped frantically, and I took a deep breath. No number or depth of breaths could stop my heart's crazy, erratic pounding.

I'm doing it to forget, I wanted to say. *I remember everything about us, when there was a possibility that we could be something great together. Every laugh, every hug, every touch. I play it over and over in my mind to see if I could've predicted it. To see if I could lessen the blow.*

I felt like we could've had a shot at love. Did you feel it, too?

It was on the tip of my tongue. I knew that if I said yes, that I was doing it for some other reason and not love, Andrew would stop me from making a mistake.

But I had to marry Michael. He was already so ingrained in my family. And Andrew would never love me like I loved him.

Instead, I said, "Of course I'm doing it because I love him." It was my turn to fiddle with the sleeve of my coffee. "I want to spend the rest of my life with him."

Maybe I imagined it, but a little more of the fire went out of his eyes as he sighed. He pasted on his awkward kid smile, and my watch beeped again.

"Well," he said. "Good. Then I'll do it."

My heart broke a little more. He didn't realize it, and I didn't want to admit it, but I was hoping he would give me a reason not to marry Michael. I wanted him to give me the only reason that counted: because he couldn't stand to see me be with someone else. Because he, Andrew Parker, loved me too.

Michael insisted that we dress up for the courthouse wedding.

For once, Cat agreed with him. "This is supposed to be a momentous occasion," she said. Her voice fell a little flat. "Emphasis on 'supposed to.'"

I caught her eyes in the mirror as she applied gel to my curls. "Cat. I need you to be my support today."

She stopped doing my hair and turned me around. When I looked at her, she smiled a sad smile identical to Andrew's. "You know I just want you to be with someone who makes you happy," she said. "Whether it's Andrew, or Michael, or some complete rando, as long as you can look at this part of your life and be content with your choice, I will support you. Can you say that you will be content with your decision to marry Michael?"

I thought back to the last two years with Michael. Between the play pillow fights, and the dinners he made, and all the romantic gestures in between, I knew in that moment that I would live quite the content life with Michael.

But the fabric of my life had been gathering wrinkles and small rips, sullying the perfection that was my future. While some of those rips were caused by my time with the Leroys—when you tour with a band, even for a little while, what life is there afterward?—most of those wrinkles held a particular essence. An essence of cherry-wood-colored eyes and bonfire smoke.

Tell the truth, no bullshit, he had said. *Do you love him?*

If only I could tell him the truth, I thought. *But we can never go back. It'll always be different.*

And he'll never love me the way I need to be loved. He doesn't believe in love that lasts forever; he told me himself. And I can't abide by that.

I met Catalina's grave look with a cheerful look of my own. "Yes. I am content. For all of his flaws, and all of my history with men, Michael is the love of my life. And I can't wait to be his wife."

Cat's gaze fastened on my hair as she went back to fixing it. "I sure hope so."

When she finally finished with me, I felt way too luxurious to be the bride at a courthouse wedding. My hair fell gently to my shoulders in looser, elongated curls. Somehow, Cat had found a non-wedding white dress that was actually my size—a feat in and of itself. The dress hugged my curves and fell just below my knees. Pearls sat primly on my collarbone, matching the pearl drop earrings Catalina let me borrow. My mascara, eyeliner, and lipstick were perfect; my dress was regal. Yet and still, it felt like all for naught; it covered the body of a fraud. It was the costume of someone who just wasn't willing to admit that marrying to gain a parent's love and approval, or to fulfill some misguided fantasy, or to outrun feelings for someone who would not return them, was not the right reason to get married.

"Despite what your mom thinks, this is a big day," Cat sniffed. "This is the day you legally become Mrs. Alicia Smith. You have to look like a boss-ass bitch. I won't have my bestie looking busted out in these streets."

I rolled my eyes and shook my head. "All right then," I said. "Time to go."

We arrived at the courthouse exactly at 1:30 p.m., thirty minutes before Michael and I agreed to meet. As Cat and I walked up the steps, I could feel my feet getting heavier and heavier. Soon, I was wading through molasses with nothing but tunnel vision—which was getting rapidly narrower.

Suddenly, arms wrapped around me. "Breathe, Ace. Slow, deep breaths."

I closed my eyes and followed the instruction. Andrew's

scent wafted over me in a haze of comfort. Without thinking, I leaned into him. He gave me a light squeeze before steadying me on my feet. I turned around to face him.

"Thank you for being here." I looked down at my hands, watching them squeeze each other. "I know you don't agree with me marrying Michael."

He tilted my chin up and held it firmly in his grasp so that I couldn't look away. "Ace," he murmured. "Of course I'm here. I'll be here no matter what."

We smiled at each other, the joyless smile of two people who refused to say the truth aloud. Andrew may be reliable in the sense that he was always my constant, but I was always, reliably, a coward.

Michael arrived shortly after us, looking distinguished in his navy-blue suit and bow tie. He opted for his glasses instead of his contacts and had gathered his shoulder-length hair into a neat bun. His dimples, like mischievous children, tugged on the corners of his mouth as he smiled at me.

"Babe," he said. "You look beautiful."

I smiled. Now that he was here, in front of me, it was hard to keep hold of my doubts. *Michael is probably just as freaked out as you are,* I tried to assure myself. *That's probably why he's been so overbearing and distant. Everything will be fine. This is the happily-ever-after you've dreamed of.*

"Thanks, so do you." We smiled at the ongoing joke. "You ready to do this thing?"

"Of course." His hazel eyes twinkled. "I've been ready to marry you for a long time now."

"A year is a long time?" I smiled. "Then forever's gonna feel like—"

"—an eternity?" he finished. We laughed.

He held out his arm, and I linked mine through it.

"Last chance to back out," I murmured. He patted my

hand and led me toward the main room.

"Alicia, you're my forever," he said. "I can't wait to marry you."

The actual paperwork process took about fifteen minutes. However, as these things go when facing the thing one dreads the most, time seemed to crawl, stutter, and stop completely. Every minute spent waiting in line felt like an hour; getting in front of the Justice of the Peace took days.

Finally, once we completed the paperwork, we were brought to a sad little room located off the main hallway. The off-white walls were dingy and a little gray; the wooden lectern stood at an angle. The carpet looked like the carpet that time forgot, threadbare at best, nonexistent in patches.

Catalina surveyed the room with obvious disdain. "What in the name of all Fuckery is this," she muttered. "You'd think they would spruce this up a little, instead of letting it look like the place where all happiness goes to die. Wow, this a depressing room."

Naturally, Andrew didn't say anything. But his eyes blazed when he caught mine. *Are you sure?* he seemed to ask. *Is this really what you want?*

I hoped my returning look said, *Of course*. Instead, I feared it asked, *Why isn't this you and me?*

"We are gathered here today to witness these two young folks, Michael John Smith and Alicia Danielle Jones, join in matrimony as approved by the state of Massachusetts," the JP intoned. "They have decided not to exchange rings at this time, but would like to say a few words. Who would like to start?"

"I'll go." Michael cleared his throat and pulled out a sheet of paper. Beads of sweat immediately popped out on my forehead; fuck me, but I hadn't thought to write vows for this ceremony.

"Alicia." Michael paused and gazed at me with ador-
ing, twinkling hazel eyes. "From the moment I saw you
with tear-filled eyes in that Korean food restaurant, I knew
that we would be together forever." He smiled. "There was
something magical about the way you looked at me, the
smile you gave me, and the laugh we shared that day. I
knew we couldn't spend one more moment not knowing
each other."

Though I smiled, I was stuck. *How could he find one of my
most heartbreaking moments "magical?"* I thought. *And it was
Thai food, not Korean. I've never eaten Korean food in my life.*

The sense of foreboding that had been building in my
stomach grew until it almost consumed me. This marriage,
it was all wrong. And it was to the wrong person. But it was
already too late. We signed the papers.

I was in it for life.

After the ceremony, Cat didn't want to stick around.
"Now that you're a married woman, I don't want to know
what kind of business you two will get into," she said. She
tugged on Andrew's sleeve. "Come on, loverboy, let's grab
coffee before I take you home."

Andrew met my eyes over Cat's head. "Congratulations
again, truly," he said. "Call me tomorrow, okay?"

He and I embraced briefly before I pushed him away
gently. "Thanks again, Minnie," I said. "I can never thank
you enough."

"Always." A flash of sadness crossed his face before his
eyes found Cat's. "Ready?"

"Yup." She hugged me then Michael. "'Bye, you two."

"See ya," we both said.

As Cat and Andrew walked toward Cat's car, Michael
turned to me. "I have a surprise for you."

My body warmed instantly. "Oh?" I said. "What kind of surprise?"

"If I tell you, it won't be a surprise, babe." He laughed. He brought me closer to his body and gave me a less-than-gentle shoulder squeeze. I winced. "Let's head to my place."

"Sounds like a plan," I said.

Sixteen

When we parked in front of Michael's building, he turned to me. "Wait here," he said. "I have to do something first."

"Okay." My heart thrummed in my chest as I imagined everything that we had ahead of us. "I'll wait here, then."

Michael stamped a quick kiss on my lips, but I pulled him back in by his lapels. He groaned in earnest as our lips collided, sliding against each other's, speaking of things to come. He slipped his tongue between my lips, surprisingly tentative and gentle. Our tongues danced, and Michael, getting excited as he does, pressed his body against mine. He gently nibbled on my bottom lip, sighed into my mouth contentedly. I pushed thoughts of Andrew out of my mind as my husband slid his hands down my body, marking his territory, claiming me.

As he ran his fingertips across my nipples, I arched into him, pressing my softness to the harder planes of his body. I felt him grow larger underneath my hand. Though part of me ached for all of him, another part of me dimly recognized that I also ached for another.

When Michael pulled away, he smiled with semi-swollen lips. "It won't take too long," he promised. He kissed me again—punctuation at the end of a sentence, before stepping out of the car and closing the door gently.

As I watched him go, thoughts of Andrew dissipated and I sighed to myself, a content smile stealing its way across my face. *Forget Andrew,* I thought. *This is just what I imagined.* I thought back to the night that Andrew and I lay on my couch after watching Leonardo DiCaprio and Claire Danes in Romeo and Juliet.

We lay there in silence, processing for a while, before I said, "Romeo and Juliet were fools."

"Fools?" Andrew frowned. "Do tell."

"What person in their right mind pretends to kill herself so that she can run away with her lover?" I scoffed. "Who wants to set themselves up for a life of being on the run?"

"Maybe she wanted to take that chance for love."

"Love." I snorted. "Love isn't like that. That's infatuation."

Andrew waited.

"Love is about commitment," I continued. "It's waking up every day and doing what's best for the health of the two people in the relationship. You see that person and you may feel some butterflies at first, but you stay even when you don't. It's hard work sometimes, but worth it."

"Sounds like a lot of duty."

"And?"

"And where's the romance?" Andrew flicked through the channels while shoveling popcorn in his mouth. "Where's the spark?"

"The spark is infatuation, not love," I insisted. I sat up and twisted to look at him. "My ideal marriage will be comfortable, not an upheaval of my whole life. We will have built a life together, really

gotten to know one another. Our families will accept the spouse as one of their own. Life will be less chaotic, not more."

"I see." Andrew stopped at Cartoon Network. Daffy was chasing Bugs Bunny around a tree. "Sounds like you have everything laid out."

"Of course," I said. "Don't you?"

Bugs appeared in a nurses' outfit. "Not really, no."

"You don't know what you want out of a relationship?"

"If it's me and the other person, and we're in it together, the rest will fall into place."

I sighed and catapulted myself against the couch. "Sounds chaotic."

Andrew looked at me then, and my breath caught in my throat. Even then, maybe more than now, Andrew's casual magnetism always caught me off guard. I could never get used to the intensity of his eyes, how they captivated and held me prisoner. And he always held my gaze for longer than anyone else did, his eyes seemingly searching for something. They made me feel like I was on a life raft in disorderly waters, and my only way home, my anchor to this life, was through him.

Finally, he looked away, back toward the screen. "Life is chaotic, Ace," he said finally. "Sometimes, it's better that way."

When Michael came back to the car twenty minutes later, I was humming happily to myself and readjusting my hair. He tapped on the passenger window. "Alright babe, come on out."

He waited for me to carefully step out of the car, a hand out just in case I needed it. *Such a gentleman,* I thought happily. I held onto the car door instead.

He shut the door firmly and tucked my hand into the crook of his elbow. As we walked up the stairs, my heart started slamming against my chest. *This is it,* I thought for the second time that day. *This is forever.* My mind meandered through a number of daydreams in which Michael and I sat at the kitchen table of our new home, reading the paper together, laughing, joking. Later in life, our kids would fly into the kitchen and demand breakfast, which would already be on the table, perfectly cooked. I would put the coffee on, and Michael would kiss me goodbye as he headed to work.

When we reached Michael's apartment door, he turned to me. "Close your eyes." I closed them immediately, bouncing on the balls of my feet.

I heard the lock click as it unlocked and the door swing open. "Okay, open them!" Michael said. I opened my eyes, a smile already on my face.

It disappeared as soon as I looked around.

Instead of what I thought would be rose petals, candles lit all over, and soft music playing in the background, Michael had decked the place out in blue and gold. "What's all this?" I asked.

"I've been moved to the starting lineup," he said. "I just found out right before I got to the courthouse. Surprise!"

"Wow," I said, looking around. "That's great."

"Yeah!" He finally took a look at my face and his fell. "What's wrong, babe?"

"Nothing." I tried, and failed, to bring a smile to my face. "Nothing, I'm just surprised, is all. This is our first night as husband and wife. I was looking for something a little more…romantic."

"I know, babe, and that will come. But this is what we were hoping for, right?" He took my hands in his. "This was the dream. I was going to play ball and you were gonna work for your mom until you found something more

permanent." He laughed a little. "But I guess your part of
the plan has changed a little."

As much as that stung, it was true. Still, I frowned.
"Yeah." Somehow, even though we had talked about this
plan, it didn't feel right anymore. The realization of what
our next year would be like hit me all at once. My married
life fantasy faded as it was soon replaced by reality.

The truth of it was that Michael was going to be in his
senior year of college. He had been moved to the starting
lineup on his team, which meant that he had even more
responsibility. Football had to come first. On top of that, he
was involved in his family's retail chain. He was even a
manager. We were in different life stages –I was trying to
start my career while he was in the midst of following his.
*How can we truly enjoy our life together if he's constantly in practice
or in games?*

"I guess I was just hoping we could have a romantic
night tonight," I said finally.

"We will," he repeated. "But we have to talk about this
first. The season starts in a week."

"Wow," I said again. My body started to go numb. "So
soon?"

"Yeah, it's pretty much fall." Michael frowned again.
"This is all stuff we talked about, remember?"

"I remember," I said faintly. My heart picked up speed
and my palms started to sweat. I could feel my vision
getting narrow. "It's so soon. Will you still be home for the
wedding?"

"I negotiated that when they asked me to be first
string," he said proudly. "They were thrilled. They said it's
good to have a family man on the team."

"That's great." I tried gulping in some air to no avail.
"That's really great."

"Babe, maybe you should sit down." Michael looked at me, worry clouding his hazel eyes. "You don't look too good."

"I'm fine." I took a deep breath, then another. "I'm fine. It's just a lot all at once."

"Well, let's talk about it, then." He guided me to the couch and tucked me into his side. "What do you want to know?"

"How often will you be on the road?"

"About as often as I was last year, so about half the time." He stroked my head. I winced as his hands got caught in my curls. "Not much will change in that."

"And do you travel all over the country?"

"Sure do. But it'll only be during the season, and it won't be that often."

"Half the time is pretty often, Michael." I couldn't help thinking how hypocritical it was that he pitched a fit about me traveling with the band for a month when he would be out of state for a lot longer and, if he made it to the NFL, an indeterminate number of years. "How will we have kids if you're away all the time?"

"I can't afford to have kids while I'm in my last year of college, babe. But we'll do it every day I'm home after the season's over. And then, once they're born, you'll be here for them when I get that job as an agent. With your mom's and Catalina's help, everything will be fine." He frowned at me. "I thought that was your dream, to be a stay-at-home mom."

"I thought so, too," I murmured. "I guess now, I'll have to be."

"I mean, you can still work part-time and stuff," he said. "Not that you'll need it. I'll be making enough to support all of us. I have the money from the family business, and if I invest some of that money, too, then you won't ever have to work again."

"Sounds like a dream," I said faintly. *My dream life, once upon a time, or so I thought.* "Sounds like our dream."

"Right?" Michael's voice rose with excitement. "That's exactly what I was thinking!" He crushed me in a bear hug. "I knew you'd come around."

"Yeah," I said. "Everything works out in the end, anyway. It'll all be fine."

Fine, fine, fine, Andrew mocked in my head. *Everything's fine. Isn't it, Ace?*

I knew that sex wasn't going to fix anything, but I wanted to feel in control of something. At the very least, I wanted to feel in control of my own body.

I turned over in bed, slowly trailing my fingertips along Michael's arm. They glided over his chest, giving his side a gentle squeeze. I brought my hand down, traced the outline of the waistline of his briefs. I could feel him coming alive bit by bit under my hand. Though it was fairly dark, I could see the tenting effect that my hands had on his briefs. He growled deep in his chest. "Babe. Are you sure?"

"We don't have to wait anymore," I whispered. I grinned, trying to feel the happiness about this that I once did. "We're married."

As if fully awakened by those words, Michael flipped me to my back lightning-quick and hovered over me, his weight distributed onto his forearms. He trailed kisses down my neck, kissed my collarbone ever so gently, ran his tongue over the ridges. When he ran his blunted fingertips up my spine, I imagined a pair of long, gentle ones in their place. Instead of Michael's murmured tenor, I heard a just-as-familiar baritone. With every stroke, every touch, my skin came alive, but not because I was in bed with Michael. No, all I could see in my mind as my husband thrusted and grunted was a pair of cherry-wood-colored eyes and an awkward-kid smile.

"So you're saving it for marriage, then?"

I looked down at my sandwich, avoiding a pair of bright, astute brown eyes. The band had made a pit stop in a small town that was slightly off our route. Jean Lee had been complaining about feeling trapped on the bus, so it was either stop somewhere or see Danny lose his shit. Even as Andrew and I made our way to Joe's Sandwiches 'N More, I could hear Danny muttering, "If I hear one more complaint outta you, Jean Lee, I'mma strap you to the roof." The deviation from his normal reticence had me suppressing a giggle.

The sandwich shop, while big, couldn't contain the enormity of the tension that sprung up between Andrew and me. I couldn't understand how the other customers, the shop owners, even the people in the back, couldn't feel it. But talking about intimacy with Andrew felt more intimate than sex itself. For the life of me, I couldn't understand why.

"I wouldn't say I'm saving it for marriage, exactly," I said finally. "It's complicated."

"Dumb it down for me, then. Help me to understand."

I cut my eyes at him, understanding exactly what he was doing and what he wasn't saying. I looked out the window for a brief moment, watching a meter maid slip a parking ticket under someone's windshield wipers. Finally, my eyes met his again. "It's not a purity thing, Andrew. Obviously, since I've already had sex." I shrugged and blushed under Andrew's watchful gaze. "Michael wants to wait, and I respect that. Besides, with Nicholas, I did it because I thought that it was what I had to do. What I should do. I don't want to just do it to do it. I wanna do it because it feels right. Because I'm in love. Because I've finally found my soul mate."

"How ironically romantic of you."

"It's not all romance," I insisted. "It's insurance that my heart won't get broken."

"Sure, okay. Because people in love don't break each other's hearts all the time." Andrew sat back in his chair. Though his tone was casual, conversational, his eyes blazed. "Let me tell you how I think it's gonna go. You're gonna marry Michael. He's gonna do something to make you feel like he isn't the one who will keep your heart safe for all eternity, as he will inevitably do because that type of One doesn't exist."

"Talk about irony. Aren't you always chasing the all-elusive One yourself?"

"It's different."

"Right."

"Anyway, Michael's gonna fuck it up, as predicted, and you're gonna have sex with him."

"What! Why the fuck would I do that?"

"Because deep down inside, you know he's not the One. You know he's not your soul mate. I do agree, though, that he's insurance."

"What do you mean by insurance?" I crossed my arms over my chest in a futile attempt to protect myself. I hoped Andrew didn't notice.

"Insurance that you never have to admit to yourself, or anyone else, that you know you're not meant to spend the rest of your life with him. Insurance that you never have to feel the hurt of someone knowing you, truly knowing Alicia Danielle Jones and the girl deep inside who just wants to be vulnerable, who wants to be loved for the person she is." Andrew popped a fry in his mouth. "Michael will never know the real you, and you don't want him to. And sex is the best way to avoid that. A man who's getting good sex on the regular won't ask questions."

We sat in silence, staring each other down, before I cleared my throat. "What a hurtful thing to say," I said finally. "And not true."

Andrew shrugged. "For your sake, I hope I'm wrong." His mouth pulled to the side, a small frown playing on his face. "But unfortunately, I don't think I will be."

Fuck Andrew and his accurate predictions. And my stupid heart.

Seventeen

I was watching cartoons with Andrew at my place when the tailor called. I listened for a moment before hanging up. Andrew turned to me. "What is it?"

"I have to do a final fitting." I grimaced. "They want to make sure they hemmed the bottom of my wedding dress correctly."

Andrew jumped up, almost knocking over a teetering bowl of cereal. "Well, let's get going!"

I stood up, too. "You don't think you're coming with me, do you?"

Andrew frowned. "Why wouldn't I?"

I thought about it for a moment and tried to think of a reason why he *shouldn't* go. It's not like I was marrying *him*. It wouldn't be bad luck for him to see the dress.

After I couldn't think of any reason for him not to go, I shrugged. "Fuck it, why not?" I said. I grabbed my wallet and phone from the depths of the couch. "Let's go get my dress."

Andrew seemed contemplative on our way to the shop. I tried not to ask, mostly because I didn't think I wanted to know, but after a while, I couldn't stand it anymore. "Tell me what you're thinking." I sighed.

Even from the corner of my eye, I could see his resulting grin. "Couldn't stand the silence, huh."

I rolled my eyes. "Yes, I can stand the silence, but I know you're gonna tell me anyway. Might as well tell me now."

His murmur of a laugh made my face feel like it was burning from the inside out. My watch beeped. "Well, since you insist, Jones. I was just thinking about how differently everything turned out."

"What do you mean?"

"Well, for starters, we always thought I would get married." He laughed. "And that you never would."

I nodded. "True."

"And who knew that of the two of us, you would be the one who's optimistic about love."

"I'm not optimistic," I insisted. "But the fact is, my parents are still together and in love, and so are yours. The facts speak for themselves."

"Sometimes, there are things beneath the surface that we couldn't possibly imagine, Ace."

I stole a glance at him, suspicious of the tone of his voice. He seemed to be saying something, but I couldn't tell what. "Like what?"

His face remained mostly serene, but I sensed a dark cloud hovering nearby. "Like survival instincts. Or staying together for the kids. Or a host of other things that keep people together that have nothing to do with love."

"What I'm wondering is why you're fighting this so hard," I said. "Didn't you say you were still looking for love?"

"Yeah, so?"

"So why are you so hellbent on disproving its sustainability?"

"I'm not trying to disprove its sustainability. I simply don't believe it can be sustained for the long haul."

"But doesn't the Bible talk about love? And don't you believe in that?"

"I guess. But it's not the same."

"Well, either you believe in the Bible, or you think God lied. Which is it?"

Andrew remained silent. I could almost hear the gears cranking in his head.

"You know," he said finally, "for someone who doesn't believe in God anymore, you sure do go hard for him and his commandments."

"I don't," I said, making a turn. We stopped in front of the tailor, and I took the key out of the ignition. "I just believe in love. You can believe in that without believing in God."

Andrew gave me a sidelong look before he open his door and climbed out. "Sure," he said. "Okay."

Even though I had never been a ball gown type of woman, even I could tell that the dress was a work of art.

The whole bodice was an intricate dance of lace, painting a picture of flowers and belles at the ball. The sleeves stopped at my elbow, hugging my upper arms and melting into my skin. Tiny jewels rained down on the skirt of the dress, as if sprinkled there by magical elves or fairy godmothers. And, admittedly, the dress propped up my breasts in a way that no demi- or push-up bra ever did. They sat on a shelf all on their own, drawing Andrew's curiously hungry gaze.

"Ah, yes," the tailor said. "Beautiful, beautiful. It's a

good thing that you're not the groom, young man. Yes, this would be bad luck, indeed."

I blushed. "He's just a friend."

"Clearly." The old woman looked at me over her glasses, then looked at Andrew. "But you two have a history, I can feel it."

Andrew and I looked away. *If only she knew.*

Andrew cleared his throat and turned back to me. "She's right though, Ace," he murmured. His eyes traveled up the folds of the gown, around the bodice, and met the eyes living in my traitorous, burning face. "You look stunning."

"Thanks." My eyes skirted away from his to look at myself in the mirror. "It's a nice dress."

"It was made for you."

I glanced back at him. "Yeah?"

"Yeah."

We watched each other in the loaded silence. Somehow, the tailor had slipped away, but her musings sat in the forefront of my mind. I was struggling on the island that Andrew's eyes created. I couldn't tell if I was drowning, or if he was saving me.

He stepped toward me like a person sleepwalking. My heart held itself suspended, ready to jump out of my body at any moment.

My phone rang.

I snapped to attention as I looked at the caller ID. Strangely, it was Mother. *She never calls me in the middle of the day. I wonder what wedding-related hell she's concocted this time.*

I picked up the phone, never breaking eye contact with Andrew. "Mother?"

There was silence for a minute before she said in a flat tone, "You need to come quickly. It's about your father."

My father was the grumpiest old man you would ever meet. I think, once or twice, he literally grumbled about the neighborhood kids messing up his lawn. Though my mother was no ray of sunshine herself, her epic level of coldness paled in comparison to my father's utter lack of paternal warmth. And he was not shy about it.

"Children need to learn how to be useful, responsible," he always said. "Children who can't be taught, grow up to be adults who can't learn. Always remember that, Alicia." I would nod mutely, afraid to stoke his ire by pointing out that neither he nor my mother were particularly good at learning anything at their age. And they weren't even old.

But that didn't matter now.

"I don't remember the last time Father was sick," I said to Andrew as we made our way through the ICU. I very narrowly avoided being run over by a candy striper. "He never even gets a cold. But a heart attack?"

Andrew grimaced. "Heart disease is one of the leading causes of death for men," he pointed out. I reduced him with a withering glare. "Not to say that he's going to die."

"He'd better not." I stopped at room 2608 and looked at some random point on the wall. "He's all my mother's got."

Before Andrew could answer, I stepped over the threshold. There were machines beeping softly, taking vitals, I assumed. The sun beamed brightly just minutes before, but somehow seemed dimmer here. As my eyes adjusted, I tried to find my father through the brightness. What I saw made me gasp.

While Dante and I were built like my mother—all lanky muscle—my father had always been the physical powerhouse of the family. Years of football and soccer fought against his old man tendencies, culminating in my father's linebacker stature. He dug his roots deep, and even the strongest storm couldn't break him. He worked out five times a week, fifty-two weeks a year, rain or shine. And it showed.

It was heartbreaking to see him now.

It had only been a few hours since he had the heart attack, but somehow, already, he seemed to have lost muscle mass. He was dwarfed by the bed. Wires wound themselves around his arms and branched out to different machines. Half of his face was covered in an oxygen mask, helping to push air into his lungs. He sunk into the bed with every gasping breath, and somehow, he seemed to have lost inches of his height.

I didn't realize the death grip that I had on Andrew's hand until he gently squeezed back. I immediately dropped his hand. "Sorry."

"Alicia." He turned my shoulders toward him, and my body followed. "Look at me."

I found his eyes.

"I'm here." His eyes traveled along the slope of my nose, to my mouth, then back up again. "Whatever you need. No questions asked, no apologies necessary."

My eyes filled with tears, but I refused to let them fall. "Thanks, Minnie."

"Anytime." He looked over my shoulder toward the bed. "Do you need a minute?"

"Yeah."

"I'll wait in the hall."

With one final gentle squeeze, he disappeared.

I turned toward the bed, toward the shell of what used to be my ox of a father. Though his chest moved up and down, nothing else moved. There was no sign that he was even in there anymore.

"It's jarring, isn't it?"

I jumped, turning toward the voice. Mother smiled without humor. "Your father—my husband—in a hospital bed? He wouldn't hear of it."

I returned her joyless smile and turned back toward him. "Yeah. If he's still in there, he's definitely fighting this."

"Definitely," Mother agreed. She came to stand beside me near the bed. She intertwined her fingers with his. "Oh, Thomas." She sighed. "How did we get here?"

We stood in silence for several moments, watching the machines breathe for him. There was a calming rhythm to it: in for five seconds, out for five seconds. In and out—so simple.

Finally, Mother said, "He hasn't been to a hospital since you were born, you know. Says it gives him the creeps."

"Gives me the creeps, too," I muttered.

She laughed as joylessly as she had smiled. "Like father, like daughter," she said.

I turned to her. "What was my birth like, anyway?" I asked. "You two always say that it was difficult, but never tell me why."

"You always had your own mind, your own agenda," she said. A soft smile rested on her face like a promise. "You wanted to make a lasting impact on my body, and so you did.

"Dante gave me a lot of trouble when I was pregnant with him, and so did you. But Dante's birth was quick, almost painless. I went into labor with him and then eight hours later, he was born.

"You, however, were a different story. I was in labor for almost forty-eight hours before they decided that a natural birth would put both our lives in jeopardy. I had to get a C-section, and then I experienced a host of medical issues afterward. All in all, we were in the hospital with you for four or five days.

"But it didn't stop there. You didn't want to be touched as an infant. You would cry whenever anyone would pick you up. Even if someone brushed you by accident, or you had to get bathed, you would wail for hours. We took you to every doctor, every specialist. The best of the best. 'She's just fussy,' they all said. 'Might be colic.'

"I didn't know what to do. It felt like every move was the wrong move. I was on a giant chessboard whose strategy I couldn't comprehend. After a while, it felt like I was running out of ways to soothe you. So I stopped trying." She looked again at my father, with a look so intimate, I stepped back a little. "But this man, this bear of a man, pulled me through it."

"How?"

"His strength became my oasis. I held onto it for dear life." Her eyes filled with tears. "He would look at me and say, 'Quinta. You've got this. You're the strongest woman I know. You can do it.'" She took a shuddering breath. "And somehow, we survived."

"But it cost you."

"It did." She looked at me then. "It cost you, too."

We stood there for a moment, looking at each other. Part of me was filled with rage from years of isolation, of feeling ignored, criticized, cared for financially but not emotionally. My soul ached for the teenager I once was, always waiting for my family to support me at my gymnastics meets, to see how much I had achieved. I could feel the tears, angry and hot in the corners of my eyes, threatening to burst forth as I refused to show weakness, even now.

But looking at my mother, I could see that I wasn't the only one who struggled. She had fought to make a connection with me, her only daughter, and was rebuked at every turn. *You would wail for hours*, she said. Every doctor, every specialist who told her that it was nothing, that I was just fussy, was just confirming what she already believed: that she couldn't care for her own daughter. So she grew an armor so thick that even rejection couldn't break it.

And here we were now, two lost souls stitched together by the men who loved us.

I reached out for my mother's hand and squeezed it. "I get it now," I said. She nodded and squeezed back.

"Yeah," she said. "Me, too."

Mom and I stayed there for a few hours more, watching my father, relaying the past. It was stilted, at first. It's hard to know what lines can't be crossed with a person when you spent a lifetime avoiding each other. Soon, though, we invited Andrew in the room, and that made all the difference. He would ask her a question, and she would answer it, and he would bring me into it, forging a connection. The fibers of the connection strengthened the more he stuck around, and soon, we were laughing and joking in a room infused with warmth and love. When we left, I felt lighter, though it was a somber occasion.

"We'll do something together, you and me," Mom said. She smiled when I frowned. "Not wedding-related."

We laughed.

"Who knew my mother had it in her," I said happily as Andrew walked me back to my apartment.

"Had what?" he asked.

"A sense of humor."

Andrew smiled as I sighed again. My heart was so full, I was ready to burst. When we stopped in front of my apartment, I hugged him spontaneously. He laughed, the sound bursting forth in a startled bark. "What's that for?"

"For being you, for helping me to see my mom in a new light," I said. "For being here."

"Here for what?"

Andrew and I turned to see Michael's stony face.

Andrew looked at me, and then glanced at Michael. "I'll go." He reached out to shake Michael's hand. "Good to see you again, man." Michael looked at Andrew's hand but didn't shake it, so Andrew dropped it. "See you later, Ace."

"See ya."

"Ace?" Michael said as he watched Andrew walk away. "What's that?"

I sighed. I could tell I was in for a long night.

"So your dad's in the hospital, and you call him? Why didn't you tell me?"

I sighed for what felt like the millionth time. "He was with me when I got the call, Michael. I didn't want to bother you, especially in the middle of the day when you could be working or at practice."

"Why was he with you?"

"I was getting the final fitting done on my wedding dress. You know, for that big event we're having in a little over a month?"

"Well, I don't like you hanging out with him so much, babe. Something's off about him."

I laughed. "Something's off about Andrew? Really?"

"Really. You can't hang out with him anymore."

"You're telling me who I can and cannot hang out with now? What is this, a monarchy?"

"I'm your husband now. I'm the head of our household. Something doesn't feel right about him. I think he has feelings for you, and I don't want you getting caught up in that. I don't want him to even have the chance of making a move on you."

"What happens when we go back on tour?"

"You're not going back."

"*What?*"

"Alicia, he's not safe." Michael frowned. "He's trying to get between us. And he's starting to."

"Andrew's the last thing to get between us, Michael! If anything, he's encouraging me to stay with you, to work out our differences."

"Our differences? What differences? We didn't have any problems until he showed up."

I scoffed. "Michael, the fact that you just tried to forbid me to hang out with him shows just how many differences we *do* have." I started picking at my fingers. "I will not be commanded like one of your employees. We are *partners* in this relationship."

"Don't pick at your fingers, babe."

"DON'T TELL ME WHAT TO FUCKIN' DO, MICHAEL."

He stopped pacing and frowned. "Alicia—"

I held up a hand. "And no, I will not watch my language or my tone. I'm angry, Michael, and I'm anxious. My father is in the hospital, in pretty bad shape. This is what anxiety looks like."

He let out a slow breath. "We should take a break from this for the night, clear our heads. I'll cook, we'll open a bottle of wine, and we'll just hang out."

I bit my lip as I mulled it over. *That* does *sound pretty good.*

But you know what will happen if you do that. You'll cave. You'll continue to strive to be the good, little wife who doesn't make waves and doesn't stand up for herself. And you can't be that anymore.

Finally, I shook my head. "I think I need to be alone tonight, Michael," I said quietly. I looked down at my fingers. "Maybe we shouldn't see each other for the next couple of days."

"Alicia, that's an overreaction. Everything will be fine by morning."

"I don't think it will." I looked up at him. "We've been married less than a week and already, you're trying to get me to hang out with my friends less. I'm already losing my temper with you. That's a warning sign, don't you think?"

"Alicia—"

"I want to be alone tonight, Michael. I will call you when I'm ready."

He sighed and ran his fingers through his hair. "Fine." He picked up his bag. "Call me when you're ready."

He slammed the door on his way out.

I knew Michael for about two months before he started telling me how to think, dress, and act. The first time he started in on me was a rainy Wednesday morning. I had donned my long, black raincoat, black rain boots, and burgundy-colored dress. I did a once-over in the mirror, satisfied with the way the outfit came together. I gave myself a little nod and picked up my umbrella.

"Babe, are you sure you want to wear that?"

I stopped short of opening the door and turned to him. "What?"

"It's a lot of black." He frowned as he examined my outfit. "You should wear brighter colors. It's happier, and all the girls I see wear them." He puffed out his chest. "I'm the

assistant manager at a clothing store, so I'm kind of the authority on these things."

I looked down at my outfit, now unsure where I was once confident. "It's that bad?" I picked at my cuticles. "Shit."

He put his hands over mine, frowning deeper. "And the language, babe. What's up with that?" He uncovered my hands, examining my fingers. "Whoa, we need to get you a manicure."

I blinked at my hands and then up at him. "Is it that bad?"

Michael grimaced.

"Sorry," I whispered.

"That's okay, babe, I'll take care of you," he said. He brought his arm around my shoulders and squeezed a little too tightly. I grimaced. "No need to worry about it ever again."

"He did what?" Though I couldn't see her face, I could tell there was a fire igniting in Cat's eyes. "He said what?"

"Cat," I warned. "Don't make this bigger than it is."

"Don't tell me what to do—this is a big, fuckin' deal, Alicia!" She blew air out of her nose, and I held the phone away from my ear. "Your dad is in the hospital! Did he even address that? Or was it all about hurting his fragile-ass male ego?"

I frowned; I hadn't realized that we barely discussed my father's heart attack. As Catalina spoke, it made me angry all over again.

"And then, there's this whole staying away from Andrew thing," Cat continued. "It was bad enough that he policed your language, but now he's trying to police your friends? What if I tell you what an ass I think he is? Is he going to cut me off, too?" She growled. "What the fuck is this, a monarchy?"

"I told him the same thing," I consoled. "We're taking a break from each other for a few days, to cool off."

"Try taking a break from him permanently." There was some shuffling. "I'm coming over."

"Cat, that's not necessary—"

"I'm coming over, Alicia Jones." She blew more air out of her nose. "You're lucky I'm not going over to his place to let him know just what I think of him right now."

"Okay, okay, come over here. Please don't go over there."

"I thought so. I'll see you in twenty minutes."

I rolled my eyes. "Looking forward to it."

As I waited for Cat, I paced my apartment. The truth of it was that Michael's demands were wholly reasonable, if Andrew was in love with me. If Andrew had been a threat, if he had been interested in me, Michael had every right to feel the way he did. But I knew Andrew didn't feel for me what I had once felt for him. Sure, he was attracted to me. I was a challenge, and if anything, he liked a good conquest. He might have even thought I was pretty. But he wasn't in love with me.

My unrequited feelings didn't change that.

As I paced the floor and battled with my despair, I heard a knock on my door. The moment I opened the door, Cat burst through. I shook my head, trying to hold back a smile. Though Cat was terrifying when she really got on a roll, she was so small that it was hard not to think of her as a cat. *Like a kitten with very sharp claws,* Jeremiah said once. It made her nickname more than a little fitting.

When her eyes met mine, though, I quickly divested myself of that notion. She looked ready to rip someone apart.

She looked through the living room window, then at all the corners of the room. I frowned as I watched her. "What are you doing?"

"Making sure he didn't bug the place," Cat muttered. "I have things to say and I don't want him overhearing." Satisfied that we couldn't be overheard, she turned to me, smoke coming out of her ears. "What the actual fuck, Alicia."

"I know," I sighed. "It's a little crazy."

"A little crazy?" She barked a laugh. "He's fucking insane. Doesn't he care at all about your father? Weren't they super close?"

A pang of sadness hit me as I remembered my father in his hospital bed. He looked like a shell of himself, but I didn't want to think about the implications. "Cat, don't talk about my father in the past tense. He's not dead."

"But he came really close. Like, really close." I flinched but she continued, "And all Michael could think about was the fact that you were with Andrew."

"I know," I said. "It's not like Andrew even likes me like that. Michael has nothing to worry about."

Cat paused, looking uneasy. "I don't know about all that."

I staggered as I looked at Cat. "What?"

"On my way here, I started to think more about it," Cat said. "I think Andrew is a threat. Have you seen the man? Like I said before, *he is a snack.* And he absolutely does like you like that. At the very least, he's attracted to you, and that can be dangerous. To be honest, I'm shocked it took Michael this long to see it."

I groaned. "Not you, too," I said. "Listen, Andrew could have made his feelings clear—"

"—all those years ago, but he didn't," Cat finished. "Yeah, I know. But it's been two years, and Andrew has had a lot of time to think about what he lost. He probably realized what a good thing he had."

"Yeah, he had ready-and-willing tail he could've been chasing," I muttered. Cat shot me a curious look, as if she was trying to suppress her amusement. "Listen, Andrew does not want me. And even if he does, it's purely for sport. He doesn't love me."

"Do you know that for sure?" Cat asked, skeptical.

"I didn't ask him, but I don't need to," I said. "And anyway, the bigger issue is Michael's attitude about everything. He's becoming more and more possessive, more self-absorbed. I'm starting to feel more like a trophy than his wife."

"This doesn't just happen overnight, though, Alicia," Cat said. "Please tell me that Michael wasn't always this ridiculous and you haven't been hiding this all along?"

I grimaced. "I might have not told you all the ridiculous things he's said." Cat groaned. "But it was never this bad, I swear."

"You let me feed this man, and he was insane this whole time?" She turned her accusing eyes on me. "How could you?"

I laughed. "Are you really about to be mad that he had the audacity to be a misogynist while he ate $5 pizza?"

She joined my laughter. Finally, she shook her head. "But seriously, what are you gonna do about Michael? You two cannot possibly sustain this pattern. It's not healthy."

I sighed. "Well, we'll have to work it out somehow," I said. "We vowed to be together through sickness and health, better or worse. Our worse just showed up a lot quicker than I was expecting."

"A lot quicker," Cat agreed. She shot me a sympathetic look. "Look, I know Michael is out of his mind—almost literally—with jealousy and caveman tendencies right now but you should talk to him. Y'all can't start out like this; it'll cause problems down the road." She stood up and stretched. "And if you're ever gonna get over Andrew"—I shot her a look but she continued as if she didn't see it —"you're gonna need to have one, strong fuckin' marriage."

<hr />

"He's not wrong."

I turned to Andrew with my ice cream halfway to my mouth. It was the day after my big blowup with Michael and subsequent conversation with Cat, and I had needed to clear my head. So, as usual, I picked up my only vice— ice cream—and headed to the place that had always comforted me. Unfortunately for me, Andrew had the same idea.

My heart raced as I thought about the implications of what Andrew was saying. Against all reason, I hoped that Andrew's statement meant that Michael wasn't wrong about Andrew's feelings for me. I shot down this hope with one thought: *It's too late; I'm already married.*

As I gathered myself, I looked at Andrew. "What do you mean by that?" I asked.

"I haven't been his best advocate." Andrew considered his ice cream for a moment before taking a casual swipe at it with his tongue. I watched the movement, trying not to be envious of the dessert. "He wants you to live and die here. He sees no issue with telling you not to be yourself. He doesn't seem to want you to be better or to do better. If he could, he would convince your mom's old firm to rehire you so you can be the good little trophy wife he wants, with no ambition and no other options. He consistently puts his feelings first, even when you have something tragic happen, like your dad being in the hospital." He shrugged, looking out over the field at our park. "I'm starting to feel like I hate the guy."

I frowned at my Converses, kicking a patch of grass near the park bench. "How can you hate him when you barely know him?"

"I know enough." He looked at me from the corner of his eye. "And I know you."

"Used to know me." I steadily avoided his eyes. "Things change, Andrew. Maybe I like the way things are with Michael." *Maybe if I deny it to Andrew,* I thought, *I can put this notion of Andrew liking me to bed once and for all.*

"Maybe? Or you do?"

"I do." I avoided his eyes.

"Alicia."

My eyes immediately found his again.

"No bullshit. Do you like the way things are with Michael?"

I sighed, giving up the ruse. I couldn't lie to Andrew any more than I could lie to myself. "No." My voice was quiet. "I don't."

"What do you *really* think about all of this?"

I sighed. "It's like I'm moving from one leash to another." Andrew looked at me with raised eyebrows. I frowned. "Wow. I didn't mean to say that aloud."

"Well, you did, so..." He leaned forward without breaking eye contact with me. "What's going on with you, Ace? Why are you with this guy?"

I thought back to that day two years ago, when Michael found me crying. "Michael's been there, you know?" I sighed and toyed with the end of my sleeve. "He and I met when I was in the worst of it. The aftermath of our friendship," I said, gesturing between me and Andrew. "He helped me feel whole again. He's safe. And despite what you may think, he does actually love me for the person that I am."

"Okay, and I can see that you truly believe that," Andrew said. I frowned again. "But you do realize that he didn't actually make you whole, right?"

"I didn't feel like a whole person before then, so who's to say?"

"Ace, you are your own person, a whole person, and you've been that way all your life." He turned to me, his eyes adamant, his shoulders stiff. "You didn't need him to make you that way. You don't need him to do it now, either. And other than him being there in hard times, being "safe," as you say, what else has he done for you? And was he actually helpful, or was he just there?"

I sighed again. "I know what you're getting at, Andrew, I do," I said. "But you don't get it."

He shrugged and faced forward again. "Maybe I do get it," he said. He was quiet for a moment before he said, "What happened between us, Ace? How did we get here?"

I laughed, the sound falling flat on the pavement. I stood up to stretch my hands to the sky and turned to him, the scorn making its way into my voice.

"Honestly, Andrew," I said. "The fact that you even have to ask speaks volumes about how clueless about me you really are."

When I finally made it to the park, my heart began to slam against my chest with the force of a WWE wrestler. My palms slipped against each other, slick with sweat as I paced by our bench. I couldn't wait for him to get here even though I knew that, true to form, he would be late.

Nicholas and I weren't together anymore. Andrew wasn't with anyone, either, now that Thalia broke it off with him. Everything was laid out perfectly. We had already graduated from college. We could travel the country together this year. I could maybe start my photography career.

The moment he showed up, though, I knew my suspicions were spot on; something was definitely wrong. A storm cloud brewed above his head, and I knew that this would be one of his bad days. My watch beeped, and I took a breath. It's okay, *I thought.* We can still make it work.

"Andrew, hey," I said, feeling a little breathless. He plopped down on our bench without looking at me, elbows pressed into his legs and hands steepled. My breath quickened, and my watch beeped again. I ignored it and sat down next to him. "What's wrong?"

"Everything." He glowered at his hands. "Let's talk about something else. What did you want to meet for?"

"Well." I cleared my throat, more nervous than I've ever been around him. I fiddled with my sleeve. "I broke up with Nicholas."

"I thought it was mutual."

"Same thing." I cleared my throat again. "We're not together anymore."

"So?"

"So I wanted to tell you something." I took a deep breath and an even deeper plunge. "I'm in love with you."

Andrew's head snapped up. "What?"

"I'm in love with you." Our eyes met and I blushed. "I think I've been in love with you for years, actually. I can't stop thinking about you. I always want to be around you. I've been waiting for you to kiss me for years, and when we finally did the other night, something clicked within me. When we

hug, everything's right with my world. We fit perfectly together. You make me feel like I can do anything. I love you."

We sat there in silence, my heart racing as Andrew's glowering grew. Finally, he said, "Fucking unbelievable."

"What's wrong?" The sinking feeling in my stomach got *worse.* Something bad is about to happen.

"You get out of one relationship and you try to hop into another. You don't want to be with me. You want to be with anyone. You're just lonely." He got up from the bench to glare down at me.

I stood up, too, facing him with a frown of my own. "That's not true, and not fair—"

"It's true and fair, Alicia. You love the idea of being with me. You love who you are with me. But you don't love me. You never have."

"Andrew, wait, let's talk about this—"

"No, I will not fucking wait. And we are talking about it. Finally. Finally! Because you never want to fucking talk about it, but you choose this day, the day after your relationship with Nicholas ends? How convenient."

"Andrew, it's not like that—"

"I bet it's not."

"Will you stop for a minute and let me finish my goddamn sentence, Andrew Parker!"

We faced each other, chests heaving, both of us out of breath. I had been trying to stop the snowball from stampeding down the hill of despair, but even I couldn't save Andrew from himself, or save myself from getting sucked into it. Again.

This was not the way this was supposed to go, *I thought.*

"I do love you," I said. *"And yes, the timing might seem convenient—"*

"Real convenient."

"—but that doesn't mean that my love is any less
genuine." I took a steadying breath. "And yes, it was a quick
breakup with Nicholas, but everything is fine now. He and I
are fine. There's no loose ends, nothing to worry about."

"Fine, fine, fine," Andrew mocked. "Everything is fine.
Isn't it, Ace?" He sighed and ran his hands over his head.
My heart melted and wept at the same time. "But the thing
is, it's not fine. You don't love me. And even if you did, so
what?" He turned his back to me as he walked toward the
entrance of the park. "So-the-fuck what?"

"That did happen, didn't it." Catalina let out a deep
breath. "Shit."

"Indeed," I said. I picked at my cuticles, my eyes on the
stadium seats in front of me. Cat and I were sitting in the
bleachers at the field at our old high school. I could
remember, so clearly, the day we graduated on this field.
We were so hopeful then. *I* was so hopeful then. I
wondered what that version of me would think of this one.

"It was tough," I continued. I looked down at my
hands as I remembered. "He was the one best friend I had
in this city. You were on the other side of the country when
it first went down, so you didn't see me going to places,
hoping to find him there. When you came by for the
weekend or when we talked on the phone, I was able to
fake it, but then I would break down afterward. I cried my
way through the rest of that year, which Michael helped
me through.

"See, that's the thing that you, and Andrew, and
whoever-the-fuck else don't understand. Michael wasn't
just there, physically. He was supporting me emotionally,

no questions asked. He didn't know who or what I was crying about, and he didn't care. 'You'll pull through this,' he used to tell me. 'No matter what.'

"More than that, Michael proved to me that I could be loved without being fetishized or hated for my skin color. All of my life, I've been told I'm too black to live in this world. Even my own parents ground that message into me. 'You have to be better than even your black peers,' they said. 'Your skin is too dark for you to be anything less than excellent.' As if my skin color was a barrier to success. As if it was something to overcome.

"So I overcame it. Even while being fetishized and hated simultaneously. I crawled my way to the top of everything that I did. I became the best in school, in gymnastics. I earned every major academic award that one can earn at the high school level. But even that wasn't enough. I still got rejected by every boy I came across, regardless of his race. I even got rejected by Andrew. I was my best, most authentic self with him. He spit on my declaration of love for my troubles.

"And then Michael found me. He loved me at my most broken. I was able to be Alicia, the person, not Alicia, the gymnastics franchise. Or Alicia, who must have good hate sex with all that attitude. And yeah, I had to make some sacrifices, but who doesn't? It was the least I could do."

Cat was silent for a moment, looking out over the field. I looked over it, too, lost in the depth and breadth of my nostalgia. It was easy to imagine the girl I once was: while not completely carefree in love, I had wished, so badly, that I had even a taste of romance. Too bad I didn't know that it also came with a multitude of dissatisfaction and heartbreak.

"You're right, Alicia," she said. She shrugged. "You're right. Michael was there for you in a way that Andrew

wasn't. Michael helped you put your life back together."
She met my eyes, sadness mingling with determination.
"But think about this: is Michael the man you think he is?
Or are you just settling because you don't think you can
have security and a soul mate with Andrew?"

I didn't have an answer for that.

Through all of this, my father remained in the hospital.
The doctors were somber when they met with us, despite
delivering seemingly good news. *Your father will be okay,* they
told me. *But it's a long recovery process.*

I agreed to meet up with my mom at the hospital the
day after Michael and I decided to take a break. I dreaded
having to talk about Michael and all that had happened.
Despite all of the progress she and I had made, her feelings
about Andrew—and Michael—hadn't changed. It was
odd, considering how we had laughed and joked with
Andrew in the hospital.

Still, I knew I had to tell her how I felt. I dragged my
feet as I approached my father's room, knowing how she
would take the news.

As I approached, I could hear her laughing softly.
When I peeked my head in, I could see her head dip
toward my father's in a chaste kiss. Her face lit up as he
reached out to touch the back of her hand. They both
sighed in unison.

"So he was here? Andrew?" My father said.

"Yes. And I still hate him."

"Why?"

She sighed again. "I guess I'm being hard on the boy.
It's not him that I hate, really. It's his lifestyle. He seemingly likes to pick up and go. From what I gather, he

doesn't like to be tied down to one job. He only has health-care because he'll get taxed otherwise. He's with a new girl every time I see him in the city. Even though Alicia's a married woman now, that won't stop her from trying to pursue that kind of life, that unfettered life. He's no good for her, Thomas."

"But you see her with Michael."

"Michael is protection," she said. "He is safe. Their relationship is not a perfect fit, sure, but he well connected, privileged. Look at our daughter, Thomas. Really look at her. She doesn't have the benefits that I have. I'm a light-skinned black woman. I still face persecution, but not nearly as much as she will. She is beautiful, but she is considered ugly in this world. She is considered 'too dark.' People will forever wonder how to put makeup on her and will ask *does it even show up?*

"And her hair. Her hair adds another layer. I love her curls. I love that she's not afraid to wear it in an afro. But she won't get a real job that way. They will take one look at her and throw her résumé in the trash. Think about the partners at both of our firms. What would they say to a person like Alicia? 'Not a culture fit.' You've heard it. And when we show up to those networking events? They are surprised. When they hear us on the phone, they're expecting someone else in person. 'But you're so well-spoken,' they say. Haven't you heard that?

"She will even be shunned by black society. Black men will turn her away because she has 'too much attitude.' She's a strong woman but she has already been hardened by life, by circumstances. As black women, even when we're not yelling or cussing or fighting, we're told we have an attitude. At least Michael tries to love her, as best as he can."

"My love," Father said. He smiled, tears pooling in his

eyes. "Don't you get it? If she's murdered, if she's hurt by this world, she will be forgotten no matter who she's married to. She walks through this world as a black woman, which means that nine times out of ten, she will step into a room with a target on her back. No one stands up for black women the way they stand up for white men, white women, or even black men.

"But she shouldn't live her life in fear. She can't be a lesser version of herself just to protect herself. You get that, right?"

My mother's expression matched my father's. "But how will we protect her?"

I stepped back from the room, not wanting to be seen. Though I understood what my father was saying, to a certain extent, my mom and I agreed: it was simply too risky to *not* be with Michael. And he loved me. That had to count for something, right?

I sighed. I knew what I had to do.

Eighteen

Yasmine sighed, grimacing at the diner window. "Are you sure about this?"

I had called Yasmine to let her know what was going on, in as little detail as possible. She suggested that we meet at a diner in our hometown, just off of Route 9. When I had stepped into the diner, I closed my eyes and breathed in the familiar smells of buttery pancakes and sizzling bacon. I looked around at all of the happy diners, sitting in booths, laughing with friends and loved ones.

I brought myself back to the present moment, to Yasmine's question. I wasn't sure, but I had to do what I had to do to save my marriage. I bit my lip as I nodded, trying not to speak, trying to delay the inevitable. Finally, I said, "Yeah. At least for the next month while we're getting ready for the wedding. Michael is on edge, and what with everything happening with my dad, I can't afford to be away from home right now." I didn't want to add the real reason I wasn't going back on tour with her and the band: Michael was forbidding it, holding it over my head as an ultimatum. *Either you stay here, or we get a divorce right now*, he said last night. I sighed, dropping my head into my hands. How I had managed to gain my dream job and lose it in the span of months, I couldn't explain. Maybe after the wedding, Michael would calm down.

Hopefully.

"Okay." Yasmine turned back to me, a small smile playing on her lips. "The job will be waiting for you when you get back. We'll make do for the time being. I know a photog that can stand in for the month. *Claro*, it's not as good as having you." She smiled again. "But we'll make do."

"Speaking of shitty situations, how are you?" I itched to touch her, to assure her that I understood the complexities of her grief. I refrained. "How's your family doing?"

"They're doing. I'm doing." She sighed. "*Abuela* was the toughest of all of us, so to not have her here really shows us how much we need her. But we're managing, somehow." The tears welled up in her eyes, fell to her cheeks. She swiped them away as if resigned to the grief.

"I've been there. My brother was the glue that held my family together. It's been a hard five years without him."

Yasmine's eyes found mine, a question evident in them. "Your brother? I didn't know you have a brother."

"Had." I winced as I was assaulted with all of the images of him in hospice, wasting away into the sheets. "He died years ago."

"He's still your brother, even when in Heaven." Yasmine smiled a weary smile, the edges folding like an old newspaper. She held up a hand as I started to protest. "I know, you don't believe in Heaven and Hell, nor in God. *Ya se*. Regardless, him being dead doesn't make him any less your brother. It doesn't stop him from being a part of you."

The weight of that conclusion—that he would always be a part of me—fell on my chest. She was right, of course. Every step I took in this world, I carried Dante with me. It was in the joy I experienced with friends, the lightheartedness I now shared with my parents. It was in my love for Andrew.

Your love for Michael, I corrected. *Andrew never loved you. And you hardly had time to love him before he rejected you.*

I cleared my throat, mentally grasping at ways to change the subject. "I guess. So when do you all officially get back on the road?"

Yasmine tapped her fingers as she thought. "Soon. A couple of days." She caught my eyes again. "You have a couple of days to change your mind."

I smiled, knowing the feeling didn't reach my eyes. "Sorry, Yas. I'll come back as soon as the wedding's over."

She shrugged, resigned. "Just figured I'd try again to get you to come." She put her hand over mine. "Come back to us soon, *sí?*"

I smiled at her, hoping my sadness didn't dim it. "*Sí,*" I agreed.

With one thing off my checklist, I was so hurried to get to the other that I was not watching where I was going. I bumped into a human barrier with the force of my hurried walking. "Sorry," I muttered without looking up.

"Where you off to, squirt?" The familiar voice had my head snapping up and my eyes searching for his. *So much for putting off the inevitable.* I wanted to save this conversation for last, maybe not even have it at all. I wondered if Andrew would leave it be if I just slowly, gradually stopped talking to him for a month.

Sure, I thought sarcastically. *Okay.*

"Andrew. Just the person I wanted to see." I straightened up, trying to infuse steel into my spine and my voice. I thought I was doing a pretty good job of it, especially when I caught the everpresent frown on Andrew's face. I took a steadying breath. "How's things?"

"'How's things?' Ace, you saw me like yesterday."

"I know. Just trying to see how you're doing."

"Why don't you tell me how you're doing? Since I was just the person you wanted to see."

I grimaced. "I did say that, didn't I?"

"Stop stalling. What is it?"

The velvety command had me pulling up short. I searched his cherry-wood eyes, looking for a way out of this very painful next step. Instead, what I found there was understanding, compassion. As if he knew what I was about to say. He had braced his body, his legs spread in a square stance, arms crossed. The longer I stared at him, trying to memorize this face that I was so used to seeing and loathe to forget for even a moment, the more he narrowed his eyes.

"Ace." His murmur wrapped around me like a blanket. I started to unravel. "What is going on?"

"I can't hang out with you anymore," I blurted. The words hung in the air, clanging their death nell. "I'm not going back on tour, either."

"What did he say to you." Not a question. I closed my eyes against the hard edges of his voice.

"It's what we need—what I need—at least just for this month." I heard the plea in my voice as much as he did and did nothing to cover it. "Please, Andrew."

"Alicia." He sighed the long sigh of the eternally disappointed. "Are you giving up your dream for this man?"

"Just for a month. Then I'll get back into it."

"If he allows."

"When he calms down a bit."

"I see." He paused. Though I wasn't looking at his face, I already knew what expression lay there. "And us?"

"That's a little more complicated."

"Complicated?"

"Yes." For once, I didn't tease him about echoing me. I didn't know if I had enough joy to pull it off. "Michael doesn't understand our history."

"Or maybe he understands it better than you think." I pulled my eyes up to his and he sighed. As he pushed his hair back, the tug of pain in my chest only grew. "Ace, don't do this."

"I have to, just for a little while." The pleading worked its way into my voice again. "Maybe we can be reconnect again after the wedding is over."

"Maybe?"

I didn't answer.

He looked at me for a beat, two beats, three. My heart protested by slamming itself into my body. He didn't have to say it for me to know. I felt his answer as sure as I knew myself. Because Andrew didn't engage in fights. Except that one time.

"Sure," he said. "Okay."

That night, I packed up everything that reminded me of Andrew. Every momento gained on tour, all band-related paraphernalia. I closed and sealed the box, and I pushed it to the back corner of my closet and of my mind. *I have to make this marriage work. I have to be a good wife.*

Even if it burns off every last piece of the old me.

Nineteen

"Well, that's the last thing to be done." My mom closed the wedding binder with a flourish. "Congratulations, Alicia, you are now officially done with wedding planning. Now all you have to do is show up on the big day."

"Great." I played with my napkin, shredding it to pieces. While I knew this was a momentous event—the finalization of the biggest event I'd ever host—I couldn't bring myself to find joy in it. What did it matter if I lost my best friend?

"Alicia? What's going on?" My mom's eyebrows pulled together, concern trickling into the wrinkles around her mouth. Her expression was so similar to Andrew's, I had to close my eyes against it.

This is what you wanted, though. Closeness to your parents. Marriage to a man who wouldn't leave you. Try to smile.

I plastered a wooden smile on my face. "Nothing," I said. "I know I had to stop touring to get the rest of the wedding stuff done, and to be here for Father. I just miss the band, is all."

"Are you sure?" Mom wrinkled her brow. "You have that look that you get when you think about Andrew."

"What?" I yelped. I blushed. "I don't have a look when I think about Andrew."

"Yes, you do. Like you've lost a piece of you." She sighed and pushed the binder to the side. "Tell me what's going on, Alicia. Let it out."

"I'm no longer friends with Andrew," I blurted. I flushed even harder. "Michael has an issue with him, so we stopped hanging out."

Mom's eyebrows shot up in surprise. "Really. I thought I'd never see you stop being friends with him for a second time."

It was my turn for my eyebrows to raise. "I didn't know you knew about the first time."

"Of course I knew about the first time," she sniffed. "Catalina told me. Although I don't suppose I was much help back then."

"Only back then?" I looked at the remains of my napkin. "It's no secret that you hate Andrew."

"I don't hate him." She sighed, looked toward the window. "I just don't think he's good for you."

Though I knew why, I wanted to hear her say it. "Not good for me?" I asked. "What's not good about Andrew? He's funny, he's caring, and he's industrious. He always lands on his feet."

"But how many times does he put himself in situations where he needs to land on his feet?" Mom sighed again. "Alicia, I know that you're somewhat in love with the boy. Don't deny it," she said when I opened my mouth to protest. "There'll never be another like the first boy you fall in love with. But he's part of your past. Michael is your future. Michael has access to resources that Andrew can only dream of. Michael has a real job, with real benefits.

He's forward thinking, and he can take care of you. Most importantly, he will love you forever. Can you truly say that about Andrew, who is with a new girl every week?"

"But what about the passion? What about romance?"

"Does Michael not shower you with romantic gestures? I heard about your anniversary date. Was that not romantic?"

"It was, but…" I put my head in my hands, effectively covering my expression. "Look, I know that Michael is the one I want to be married to. I agree, Andrew may have been my first love, but not the one for me now. But I don't understand why it meant I have to give up a friendship with him, as well."

"Because men are territorial," she said. "They can't exist in the same space without having to mark their territory."

My head shot up. "I'm not Michael's territory!"

"It's a figure of speech, Alicia. Don't be so sensitive."

I grit my teeth. *Don't be so sensitive,* I grumbled in my head. *You don't know what sensitive is.*

Aloud, I said, "It's not a matter of sensitivity. I'm irritated, rightly so, about someone trying to take control of my life. Regardless, I'm giving up my friendship with Andrew, for Michael. It just sucks, is all."

My mom made a noise of understanding. "Of course, dear. It always sucks, as you say, when you must clear out the old to make room for the new. Andrew is your past. Michael is your future."

Yes, I couldn't help thinking, *but who is my present?*

After that rousing conversation with my mom, all I wanted to do was go home and burrow under the covers. But when I turned the key in the lock and opened my apartment door, Catalina was waiting for me. Until that moment, when I wanted to be alone more than anything else, I had never given thought to giving my best friend a key to my place. It was supposed to be for emergencies. *Emergencies.* But I didn't doubt that Cat thought that whatever she had to say was, indeed an emergency that required use of the key.

I sighed; I knew what was coming.

"Andrew told you, I'm guessing." I dropped my keys on the counter and dropped my bag in the chair. "Go ahead and say it."

"So you did it. You gave into the demands of that Neanderthal of a fiancé—"

"Husband," I corrected.

"Whatever he is now, I don't care. How could you? This pissing contest has gone on long enough. When will it end? What, am I next?"

"Probably," I joked. She narrowed her eyes and I stepped away, hands in a conciliatory gesture. "Sorry, too soon."

"Way too soon."

"Cat," I sighed, "you yourself admitted that Andrew is a threat to my marriage. What other choice did I have? I'm with Michael."

"Exactly," she said. Her fists looked like they were digging into her hips. "You already chose him. You're already *married to him.* Why does it matter if you're friends with Andrew?" She frowned. "You just got Andrew back, only to lose him again."

"'Got him back'? Cat, he wasn't mine to lose."

"That's bullshit and you know it," she shot back. "Don't forget, I remember the utter desolation you experienced after you and Andrew stopped being friends. I may not have been here physically, but I still had to endure weeks of weepy behavior. I don't know if I can do that again."

"It wasn't that bad."

"You're right, it was worse." She stood in my living room with her hands still on her hips. I sighed.

"Look, you're right, it was bad the first time around." I shrugged. "But this time, it's different. I know what I'm getting myself into. And it's my choice."

"But what about Andrew? Shouldn't it also be his choice?"

"He made his decisions a long time ago without my consent," I said. I crossed my arms. "I think he'll understand."

For the first couple of weeks, I tried not to torture myself with it. I avoided all social media platforms at all costs; I didn't even listen to my favorite album because I knew it would elicit memories of being on tour. But finally, I couldn't resist the pull anymore. I had to see how they were doing.

I started with their social media pages. Clicking through the photos, I watched Yasmine's eyes first. Even though I could tell that she was putting everything she had into the songs, grief had stolen the light from her eyes. Pain coursed through her every movement on stage, from the way she gripped the mic, to the way she stared into the crowd as if searching for her *abuela*. Her fans might not see what it cost her to be on the road, to be in front of them, but I knew. The death of a loved one never really fades.

The rest of the band also fell short of playing at their best. Opening up another tab, I watched their videos. From the first video clip, I could hear it. Jean Lee missed the beat several times by a hair. Kevin slumped over his guitar as he did his best to play it off as part of his persona. Even Danny, usually smooth and steady as lake water on a summer day, showed signs of strain as he plucked his bass strings. All of them gave such a good performance that no one else would be the wiser. But I wasn't just anyone; this was my family. It wasn't until I was staring into the computer screen with tears threatening to fall that I realized just how close one could get to people in a couple of weeks.

It was clear they all felt the loss of Yasmine's grand-mother. It brought my mind back to what I'd overheard just before we arrived home. *It's definitely better than the way Leroy went, wouldn't you say?* Philip's question grit into the ridges of my mind, like sand that you couldn't quite get out of your car. Maybe what I was seeing was the echoes of leftover grief from losing Leroy; maybe it was a new shared grief that washed over them. But now I would never know.

As I closed their video page and resumed clicking through their photos, I felt my breath lodge right below the lump in my throat. Someone had taken a group photo of the band and Andrew. It was a typical hasty photo—Jean Lee's hand was a little blurry, as well as the corner of Kevin's face—but the one person whose eyes I could never look away from was perfectly clear. He stared into the camera with his typical intensity, as if he knew that I would look at this photo someday. Eyes alight with mirth, with mischief, or both, found mine, almost caressing the depths of my denial. The corners of his mouth lifted slightly, a smirk that was so familiar and so foreign that it made my heart twist. He held up a hand with just the pinky and thumb extended from the fist, a typical laid-back gesture that both fit him so succinctly but was also out of place. Before I could stop myself, I traced the outline of his lips, the face I knew better than my own, hurting at the nonchalant slope of his shoulders, the lure he wore so easily. I longed for this one, the boy I knew, instead of the man I married.

Fine, fine fine. I couldn't tell if the refrain mocked me in Andrew's voice or in my own. *Everything is* fine. *Isn't it, Ace?*

Twenty

Even though I thought I would never make it to the wedding, finally, it was the week of. Catalina and my mom teamed up to make sure that I didn't have to worry about any other details before the big day, which meant they arranged a bachelorette party, a couple of days before the rehearsal dinner, against my wishes. Cat came over to my place a few hours before to do my hair and makeup.

"Who's even gonna be there for it?" I asked as Cat arranged my hair around my face. She gave a sharper tug than I felt was necessary and I winced. "Sorry, besides you."

"I guess you'll just have to wait and see. God, were you always this insistent on not being surprised?"

"Were you always this unwilling to give me the goods?"

She smirked at my reflection in the mirror. "Shouldn't someone else be giving you the goods?" I rolled my eyes and her smirk grew wider. "Speaking of the king, how's he doing these days?"

I sighed as I fiddled with my sleeves. Cat refused to see

him more than was necessary these days, which meant that she never saw him. *I can't hold your secret for long,* she said. *I can't straight-up lie to the man and not tell him you're also in love with someone else.* "He's good. Nervous, it seems."

At the word *nervous,* her hands stilled and she frowned. "What does he have to be nervous about? Y'all are already married. The hard work is done; now all that's left is the fun stuff."

I shrugged, my shoulders lifting in as much apprehension as I felt coming from her. "Fuck if I know, Cat. The man's an enigma these days."

"Hmm." She came around to squat in front of me with a makeup brush. She swiped it in the powder and dusted it across my face. "That's strange. Michael's the last person I'd expect to be mysterious."

"I know." I closed my eyes as she got closer to them with the brush. "Usually, he's an open book. Lately, not so much."

Cat hummed her concern as she closed the makeup container and picked up another. Though I tried to make eye contact with her, she kept her eyes down as she asked, "What do you think it could be?"

I lifted my shoulders again. "Work? Practice?"

"The fact that he knows he has competition?"

I grunted my irritation as I closed my eyes again.

"What?" I could hear the defense in her voice. "Your attraction for Andrew is apparent. And his for you is undeniable. It was only a matter of time before Michael put the pieces together and felt some type of way about it."

"That's the thing, he's not around enough to *see* anything. Besides"—I scoffed, trying not to fidget—"Andrew and I don't hang out anymore. He's on the road with the band. And most importantly, Michael wouldn't only be able to see something if it was more than attraction. I would need to have feelings for Andrew. And he would need to have feelings for me."

Cat's long-suffering sigh was her only reply. I focused on the jangle of her bracelets to distract my mind from indulging in the memory of Andrew's body so close to mine. "But whatever. I'm sure whatever Michael's struggling with will be over by the time he sees me walking down the aisle."

Cat's eyes met mine in the mirror. "Girl, for your sake, I hope so."

Not surprisingly, Cat was only able to round up a few of our mutual acquaintances from high school. My mom, thank God, bowed out at the last minute, citing "you shouldn't have your old mother hanging around" as her reason. I knew better than to say it aloud, but I'd much rather have my mom hanging out with us than a bunch of people I barely spoke to even in high school.

Cat, keeping up the secret, ordered me to blindfold myself when we got in the limo. "Either you can do it, or I'll do it," she said, watching my hesitation with sharp eyes.

I rolled my own eyes before taking the slip of fabric from her. "Fine, fine, I'll do it." I pulled the proverbial wool over my eyes and sighed. "Better?"

"Much. Now sit back, relax, and have some champagne." She gently placed a glass in my hand. "And yes, it's actual champagne. Drink up."

Without hesitating, I tipped the glass back and did just that. The cool, bubbly liquid poured down my throat at a rate I didn't think was possible without choking. As the alcohol effervesced in my system, I tried not to fidget with the glass. "Now what?"

"Damn, girl, I didn't think you'd drink it *that* fast!" Catalina's disembodied voice came from my right side. "Want another?"

Ignoring the mischief in her voice, I held my glass out. "Yes, please."

By the time we arrived at wherever we were, I already had two more glasses of champagne and not nearly enough hors d'oeuvres. I stumbled out of the limo, teetering precariously on pinheads-for-heels. Catalina took it upon herself to untie my mask with a flourish. I blinked as I looked around.

"Welcome," she said, "to bachelorette paradise."

All around us, groups of women—also teetering on tiny heels—flooded the streets. *Get the perfect mani-pedi combo here!* one sign shouted. *Best bar in town!* another yelled. The thumping baseline seemed to come from everywhere and nowhere and provided a weird backdrop to this bache-lorette hellhole.

Cat sidled up to me, eyes on mine to gauge my reac-tion. I remained motionless to take it all in without falling headfirst. "Where would you like to go first?" she asked.

I didn't know which was worse: letting her choose for me or choosing something and not knowing what I was getting into. After a while, I realized that I probably didn't even have enough working brain cells to make any type of decision. I waved a drunken hand in her direction. "You choose."

She grinned and took my hand, pulling me in the direction of the mani-pedi craze. "I thought you'd never ask."

The funny thing about being more than slightly drunk is that everything starts to feel somewhat okay. I was no longer touring with my favorite band? No problem. I had to give up my soul mate of a best friend to please the love of my life? Not a care in the world—give me another drink. The higher my blood-alcohol content level, the less I cared. *Maybe if I drink enough, it'll numb all the pain.*

After our mani-pedis, we stopped at a store that was exclusively for brides and bridesmaids. The windows were lined with tiaras that spelled out messages like *Bride to Be* and *Head Bride in Charge.* The T-shirt and tank-top messages ranged from simple—*Bride,* —to obvious—*Here Comes the Bride,* to outrageous—*Spend One Night with Me—I Get Married Tomorrow ;).* At the last one, I turned to Cat with a side-eye. "Really?"

She shrugged. "I don't make these things, so don't blame me."

I sighed and picked the least offensive of the T-shirts, one that simply stated *Bride.* I turned it over in my fingers clumsily and was struck by how different my fingers looked than Andrew's. I was assaulted by the memory of those fingers attached to the hands that bracketed my body on the wall, that wrapped around my curls and held me in place with little else than gentle pressure. *But I have a feeling that you already know what that's like,* he had said. *An unexplainable longing. Missed opportunities realized.*

"You ready?" Cat's face swam in the corner of my vision, her voice somewhat muted in my head. I turned to her, waited for my vision to catch up with the motion.

"Sure," I said. "Okay."

We spent a couple more hours in bride hell before Catalina looked at me and told the girls to call it a night. Turns out that it wasn't a moment too soon; once everyone agreed, I promptly looked for a bush to throw up in.

The trip home in the limo was unmemorable for me though everyone else seemed to have a good time. Champagne and drinks abounded, and Catalina, at the very least, looked like she was having the time of her life. I crawled into the quietest corner of the car that I could find and curled up, trying not to vomit everywhere.

We dropped off the other three first, and then Catalina had the driver drop me off. We pulled up to the curb in front of my apartment building, tired and only a little worse for wear. Catalina eyed me with some trepidation. "You done throwing up?"

I rolled my eyes, remembering how much she hated vomit. "For now. Thanks for your concern."

She grimaced. "Come on, let's get you out of the car." She opened her door then walked briskly to my side and opened that door, as well. She reached in and pulled me to a standing position.

"For someone so small, you're awfully strong." I smirked down at her.

She rolled her eyes. "Yes, I work out specifically for moments like this."

"Last I heard, you didn't work out at all." The familiar voice rose up from the shadows and, despite my drunkenness, my head turned toward the sound. Andrew, like a figment of my imagination, pushed off the building's edge and walked toward us.

"You actually came," Catalina said. When I turned toward her, she shrugged. "Listen, girl, you're like twice my height and outweigh me by a good fifty pounds. I had to bring in reinforcements."

"You could've called Michael. Or even Jeremiah."

"Couldn't get a hold of them."

I pursed my lips, disbelieving. Jeremiah always picked up Catalina's calls. *She probably didn't even try to call him.*

It didn't escape my notice, even in my drunken state, that I wasn't surprised that Michael didn't come.

"No matter now," she said. "I'll leave Andrew to it. Thanks, babe."

"Anytime. Come on, you." Andrew wrapped an arm around my waist. "Let's get you inside."

Everything feels a little different when you've had too much to drink. It wasn't so much that the room spun; rather, I felt a quaking in my stomach, a tumultuous roll that threatened to take me with it. I closed my eyes, made my body heavy to indicate that I wanted to stop moving for a bit. Andrew made a noise as if to protest, but I held up a hand. "Trust me, you'll want me to stop."

We paused on the stairs for a moment, my heavy breathing the only sound between us. Finally, I opened my eyes. "Ready."

As we journeyed up the stairs, a thought occurred to me. I turned to look at him, and he watched me with a hint of exasperation. "What?" he said.

"Why aren't you on tour with the band?" I asked.

"You mean, you don't enjoy being in my presence?" He smirked.

I rolled my eyes. "Even though we're not supposed to be hanging out together, it's not that. It's just—I just saw you in the band photos." He frowned and I waved my hand dismissively, somewhat off-kilter. "Online. Social media."

"Ah." He nodded. "We were always planning to come home at this time. It was a short tour, remember?"

Memories came back to me as he said that. *But you'll be back in time for your wedding, no prob,* Yasmine had said, that first day. "Right," I said. "Now I remember."

"Yup."

When we got to my door, Andrew patted my jacket pockets. When I frowned at him, he rolled his eyes. "Your keys, Ace. Where are your keys?"

I grinned at the notion that he would ever find my house key. I reached between my breasts, watching

Andrew track the movement. I tried not to think about how even in my current state of drunkenness, I could feel the heat of Andrew's gaze on my…hand. It also didn't help that I had buried the key deep within the depths of my bra.

When I finally produced the key, I dropped it in the palm of his hands. "Here you go."

"Took you long enough," he grumbled as he fumbled to get it in the lock. He opened the door and maneuvered us through the doorway. "Welcome home, Ace."

"Are you welcoming me to my own apartment?" I gave him a lazy sidelong look as I kicked off my shoes. I burrowed my toes into the carpet, loving the way it felt on my bare skin. I loved it so much that I laid down spreadeagled and moved my limbs around as if I was making a snow angel. "How kind of you."

"Ace, get off the floor. We gotta get you changed and ready for bed."

"Nope, I think I'll stay here for a bit." I almost rolled side to side but thought better of it. The room suddenly had a pulse, and I knew that if I were to move just then, I'd probably regret it.

"I'll join you, then." I heard a quiet thump as Andrew took off his shoes and lay next to me. "Better?"

"I guess." I laughed, my voice teetering on the cliff, slightly off balance. When my laughter died down, we sat in the expectant quiet of my apartment. The clock ticked off every second, the floors creaked, and I could hear Andrew's soft sigh from next to me.

The feeling of panic, that soft suffocation on my chest and burning sensation in my throat, overtook me. I wanted to say that I didn't know why, but I knew. Even my drunk brain knew. It might be the last time I ever saw Andrew. I was struck with the sudden urge to get it all out there. I turned my face to him, waited for him to catch my eye. "Hey."

"What?" Momentarily, I got lost in the browns of his eyes, those eyes that had tracked my every movement from the moment he saw me tonight. The same eyes that clouded over when I told him the fate of our friendship. The same eyes that lit up when he found a new adventure or discovered another "favorite" food.

"Ace?" he prompted. "What is it?"

"This may be the last time we see each other, so I wanna ask something."

"Sure. Okay."

"Did you really not love me all those years ago? When you rejected me?"

He regarded me with cautious eyes. I held my breath as he brushed a curl back from my face. "Maybe we should wait till morning to have this conversation."

I closed my eyes as the urgency of it all overtook me. "We don't have time for that. You won't be here in the morning."

"I will."

I opened my eyes, now regarding him with the same cautious look he had just moments before. "I can't leave you like this, Ace. You could choke on your own vomit. Plus, I promised Cat."

"And those are the only reasons you'll stay?"

"Yes."

"Liar."

He looked away.

"So, answer the question. Did you? Not love me?"

"I've always loved you, Ace." He smoothed a hand down my arm. "You were my best friend."

"You know that's not what I mean, Andrew. Come on." The drink in my system emboldened me. I met his eyes without fear of repercussion, the usual urge to fidget not hitting me. "Answer the question. Did you really not love me?"

He sighed, pushing his hair back in the way that I adored. Andrew's resolve was hard to break most of the time, so it did something to me that I could unravel him with a question. "I don't know, Ace. I didn't give myself time to explore that."

"You have time now. Explore it."

"You're married, so what does it matter now?"

"It matters to me." He held my eyes as I bit my lip. "I need to know that I wasn't imagining things. That you felt it, too."

We watched each other in silence as Andrew thought about it. I could see him weighing his options in his mind, considering things, turning them over in his mind, rejecting something. I scooted closer to him, resting my hand on his chest. Maybe it was the drink, or maybe I wasn't imagining it, but his heart was racing. Like mine would have been if I wasn't so far under.

I knew what his answer was when he covered my hand with his. My heart dropped in the alcohol-infested depths of my stomach. *He hadn't loved me then. He just doesn't know how to tell me. Catalina was wrong.*

His fingers curled around mine. "Come on," he said. "Let's get you to bed."

I barely made it to the bathroom before I vomited everything left in my stomach. Admittedly, it did feel better, almost as if I also threw up all of the worry, despair, and sadness. I gargled mouthwash then brushed my teeth, the relief almost immediate. When I finally wiped all the makeup off and opened the door, Andrew was waiting by the bed with a glass of water and two aspirin. Seeing him set off a fresh wave of emotions within me: anger and embarrassment for being rejected yet again, sadness at a dream lost, and finally, the slow sludge of shame at hoping that this man wanted me when I was already married to another.

"You look a little better," he said. I nodded and he smirked. "This is good, because your face was killing me."

"Ha." I opened my pajama drawer and took out a shirt. "Jokes on jokes on jokes." I pulled my dress over my head, not caring that Andrew was in the room or even caring if he looked away. I unhooked my bra, letting it fall to the floor, and dropped the shirt over my head. When I pulled my arms through, I found Andrew watching me. I felt my breath get trapped in my throat. Despite knowing that he was not, had never, been in love with me, I could still see the desire warring in his eyes, in his body. He gripped the water glass so hard, I was surprised that it didn't shatter. Barely contained fire in his gaze seared me, and it was all I could do not to run to him, wrap my legs around him. I wanted, so badly, to be desired. But the need to be loved, to be seen, was much stronger.

The thing was, if Andrew had told me he loved me all those years ago, it would have been different. I could almost imagine the life we would have had: a life of creative energy, of love, of passion. I would never have met Michael, never fallen in love with the idea of a stable life. I would have given up everything for Andrew.

But it hadn't happened that way.

I didn't want a hook up. I wanted his heart. Anything less was a travesty.

Twenty-One

As promised, Andrew stayed the night. Luckily for me, I didn't throw up again. I drank water and went to sleep, hoping that whatever alcohol was left would wipe the night straight from my memory.

But it didn't. I woke up to light streaming through my window and onto the bed where Andrew lay facing me, fully clothed. His peaceful face made all the night's events come crashing back into my memory. The heated look he gave me after I undressed in front of him. The look of sympathy and pity as he avoided my desperate, pathetic question. *I might as well have asked him what made me not good enough for him to love.* Inwardly, I groaned.

I must have made some movement because Andrew stirred. He grumbled something in his sleep, his deep frown causing quiet laughter to bubble up in me. He seemed to gravitate toward the sound, even in his half-sleep state. He groped around until he found my hip and pulled me in, tucking me into his chest. Knowing that he would never know, I inhaled deep, taking his scent deep into my body, trying to commit this moment to my memory. After all these years, he still smelled like my favorite combination: bonfire smoke and mint and home. I indulged in my secret desire to get physically closer to him, wrapping an arm and a leg around his body, burrowing into his chest like he was mine. Like I was his.

His arm tightened just a little around my waist, accepting the contact, encouraging it. His hand kneaded my side, a low groan escaping from him. I held my breath as another part of him stood fully awake between us, despite its master's slumber. I couldn't help noticing that, despite being with Michael in every romantic and physical sense, I had never felt as intimate with or close to him as I did Andrew. Michael's body reacted just as quickly as Andrew's did to our proximity, but with him, it was less passion, more safety, more deliberation, more about duty —and on my part, more wrestling for control over my rights to my own body. Andrew felt what he felt—sadness, anger, lust—freely and with his whole body. And he encouraged me to do the same.

With Andrew, I was free. And there's an intimacy in that.

I tried to take my attention from that and just focus on being close to Andrew, having what I dreamed about within my reach and yet, so far outside my grasp. If worse came to worst, if Andrew woke up and realized what was happening, I would pretend to be asleep.

But I froze once I felt Andrew's eyes open.

At first, he stiffened. His eyes, when they found mine, were a muddle of confusion and apprehension. But then, something changed. Maybe it was the pleading look he saw in my eyes, the utter desperation I felt to just be seen and loved for the person that I was in the moment. Or maybe he was feeling his own longing. Whatever it was, we both felt the shift, an inevitable draw toward the end of the cliff.

"Ace." He only said my nickname, and it was steeped in the remains of sleep, but it was also layered with everything I had hoped for from Michael. Joy. Need. Boundless desire. I closed my eyes as I fought the urge to taste the lips that made this oath, fought the part of me that raged against the promises that I had made to another.

He said it again—my nickname, sounding more strained, teetering on the precipice. His fingers started a brushfire across the expanse of skin on my hip, my neck, my face. He made a small sound in the back of his throat, so unlike him, then a hiss as I accidentally brushed against his crotch. My breathing sped up as I made a decision, right then and there, knowing it would be impossible to go back, to drag us out of the abyss.

I kissed him.

Twenty-Two

In romance novels, they talk about the hesitation before taking the full plunge that first time around. The one surprised by the kiss always hesitates, always tries to stop the protagonist from going too far and hitting the Point of No Return.

Andrew did not hesitate.

The moment I pressed my lips against his, he pressed back, the contact making my body come alive. His tongue demanded entry almost immediately, finding mine, insistent, naughty and sweet, wanting.

His hands glided over my body, reverent. "I dreamed about this," he said. His nose nudged my collarbone. "About you."

"Yeah?" I closed my eyes as I held my breath, waiting for his lips to find mine again. "Why's that?"

He murmured a chuckle, sending his breath across my earlobe and tickling the side of my neck. "You still don't see it, do you?"

I frowned, opening my eyes to meet his dancing ones. "See what?"

His hands made their way up my sides until finally coming to cup my face. "How irresistible you are."

I closed my eyes again, tilting my head up to receive his kiss. He delivered it gently, lingering at the corners of my mouth like a lover sailing out to sea.

He pulled away, studying my face as if looking for an answer. I squirmed under his gaze, not wanting to see the weight of what we were doing—what we might end up doing—on his face, as well. As if sensing this, he drew my face to his again, taking over my body and my thoughts entirely. Every brush of his hands down my body erased the litany of awkward touches and almost-painful squeezes endured from Michael. Andrew made a choir come alive in my head—the sweetest of melodies. And no matter how urgent his hands, or how firmly he pressed me into the bed, or how tightly he fisted my hair, or how he grabbed my ass, he held me like I was a queen.

His hands traveled from my face, down my neck, over my shoulders and arms, linking his hands with mine, never breaking the contact between our lips. Our kiss shifted from gentle to urgent as he brought our arms above my head, pinning me to the bed, his body running the length of my own, his legs tangling with mine. He groaned when our bodies made contact, the sound sending pleasant shivers down my spine. I breathed heavily through my nose, embarrassed at how worked up I sounded but not caring enough to stop. Realizing and getting the ingredient that was missing in my relationship with Michael was intoxicating and I couldn't get enough.

I moved slightly away from Andrew, just enough to fit my hands between our bodies. Trailing my hands down his chest, I moved to unbuckle his belt. I fumbled with it, finally unclasping it and unbuttoning his pants. My breath hitched in my throat as I started to run through the repercussions of having sex with my former best friend, while being married to another. My stomach lurched.

After fumbling with the belt and button, I made quick work of Andrew's zipper. He lifted his hips to help me remove his jeans, and I dropped them unceremoniously on the floor. Almost as if by magic, both of us were down to our underwear in what felt like seconds. I blushed deeply, looking down at my plain, cotton panties and unremarkable flesh-colored bra. I wasn't expecting anyone to see my underwear tonight, so I hadn't worn one of the three pairs of sexy lingerie I owned. My bra and panties didn't even match.

But it didn't seem to matter to Andrew. His hungry gaze swept over my body from toes to eyes, taking it all in. Though the heat of his gaze warmed me, it was the adoration and appreciation that permeated my skin. His feelings, and the transparency of them, filled me with liquid sunshine.

"Well, what are you waiting for?" I demanded uneasily. I was so unused to being appreciated for my looks that Andrew's attention became downright unbearable. Where moments before, I felt warmed by it, I now became supremely uncomfortable. Even water, a life-giving substance, can drown you when in excess.

But Andrew refused to be rushed. In his deliberate, kind, unhurried way, he brushed his fingertips across my skin. "We've been at this precipice for years now," he said. His eyes caught mine and I once again felt the heat of his longing. "Let me enjoy going beyond it."

His words filled me with my own keen longing, but also, a deep understanding. From the moment he and I met on that wintery Monday evening in our senior year of high school, I knew there was something different about him. Something in me joined with something in him, fusing us together in a way that was unbreakable. This physical joining was as inevitable as the sunrise.

When his eyes finally got his fill of me, he brought his lips to my forehead. I closed my eyes against the tenderness of the gesture, and I breathed in his scent. His lips glided over my temple; his nose created a path along my jawline. He brought his lips to the space behind my ear and pressed a gentle kiss there. The gesture brought tears to my eyes and warmth between my legs.

I could feel our hearts speed up, mine racing after his. When Andrew finally noticed that my breasts were pressed up against him, he groaned softly. It was his turn to move back a little, this time, to cup my breasts in his hands. He considered them for a moment, rubbing gentle circles around my nipple over the thin fabric of my bra. I gave a surprised little yelp at how wonderful, how sensual it felt. My sex clenched at the gesture, wanting more, needing more. I pressed my breasts into his hands, the gesture making Andrew catch my eye. The fire that lay there burned a little brighter as he saw the desire in my eyes that matched his.

Things suddenly sped up, the urgency becoming an itch across my skin. I took his mouth into my own, running my tongue along the seam of his lips, demanding entry as he had done moments before. He readily permitted it, his tongue finding mine once again. As our tongues danced, he rolled me over so I was beneath him. He pressed himself against my center, letting me feel just what I did to him. His hardness against my softness sent me into a frenzy, had me gasping for air. He rolled his hips against mine again and again, the friction becoming almost unbearable. Finally, I rasped out, "Condom?"

"Condom," he confirmed in a murmur. His breathing slowed as he reached into his jeans pocket and pulled out a small foil square. He looked at me with apprehension, a small frown creasing his brow. "Are you sure this is a good idea? I don't think—"

"That's good," I said, pressing a kiss to his lips, palming his erection, rubbing the tip. "That's exactly right. Don't think."

He groaned low in his throat, the sound reverberating between us. His pressed himself into my hand. "Do it again."

I grinned, enjoying the effect I had on him. Watching him come undone was about to be my favorite activity in life. Slowly, tantalizingly, I made a circle around the head once more. I watched Andrew's expression, delighting in the fact that he bit his bottom lip, closed his eyes, cursed under his breath. His hips moved in time to my circles, almost as if they moved of their own accord.

Finally he stopped me with a curt, "No more." When I looked up in surprise, he grumbled, "You will make me come before I even get the condom on. And I wanna be inside you when I do." A shiver ran up the length of my spine at the timbre of his proclamation. I immediately stopped circling and he chuckled. "We have the same goal," he said. "Good."

"Enough talking," I said. I linked my hands behind his head, bringing his lips to mind once more. "We've talked enough for the last seven years."

"Noted," he murmured.

I wrapped my fingers around the waistband of his boxer briefs, pulling the fabric down his legs as best as I could. He helped me once they got to his knees. He looked at me then, his eyes dancing with mischief, joy, and dominance. "Put the condom on me."

I shivered at the velvety demand, reveling in it. He had always been a little bossy, but this was different. This was the full force of it with a sprinkling of possessiveness. I may have been married to another, but in this moment, Andrew made no qualms about making me his.

I rolled the condom down slowly, ending the motion with a kiss right above his belly button. His abs contracted, and he shivered. I guided him to my entrance, lining us up perfectly. With an inhale, he entered me in one smooth motion. We exhaled together.

Andrew started out slow, watching me as if he thought I would disappear. Behind the fear, though, was a look of total reverence. Whether he loved me before, loved me now, or could love me forever, he at least adored me. And for now, that was enough.

Our bodies were horribly out of sync, though. It wasn't because we didn't have the chemistry—God, I wish that were the case—but we had different ideas in mind. I was eager to feel his release, to chase mine; Andrew wanted to savor every stroke. "It's as if—"

"As if what?" His grip under my ass loosened so he could finger my curls. "As if this is the last time, Ace?"

I cringed because we both knew: this *would* be the last time.

He continued his slow ascent to bliss, and I slowed down to match him. With each stroke, I felt more and more bonded to this man. This man who I loved. Who I was in love with. Who was not my husband.

As we got closer to our release, finally, Andrew picked up the pace. He reached between us and rubbed slow circles around my clit. I bit my lip to keep from crying out but a small moan escaped regardless. Andrew's gaze fell on my lips, watching my breath move from between them. "Tell me I'm yours," he demanded.

"You're mine," I gasped.

"And you're mine."

"Yes. *Yes.*"

"Yes what?"

"Yes, I'm yours."

He squeezed my ass as his hips rolled into mine, and I almost went blind with pleasure.

"Andrew," I begged. "Please."

"Please what?"

"Don't make me say it. Don't make me beg."

"Alicia." I shivered at the authority in his voice, his tone demanding obedience like a hand cupping my throat. "You may be married to Michael, but right now, you're mine. Say it."

I said the words he so desperately wanted to hear on an exhale. "Andrew, make me come. Please."

As he fulfilled my pleas and also set off his own release, all I could think of were the words I didn't say. *Fall in love with me the way I am with you. And make it forever.*

I could tell I was in for it when I heard, "What on God's green earth am I seeing right now?!"

I bolted upright in bed, my vision not quite in focus but swerving to where I heard the shriek. It was coming from the doorway, and fuck me, it was coming from my mother.

At first, I thought it was just because I was naked. My mother was a woman of great modesty, so anything less than a full nightgown to bed was seen as a ticket to Sluttown.

But then I realized: Andrew was still in my bed.

Also naked.

"Alicia Danielle Jones, you get up this instant! And you too, young man! Put some clothes on, both of you!" Mother, more distraught than either Andrew or I, searched the floor for our clothes. "Michael will be here any minute and he can't see you like this—"

"Michael can't see me like this? Are you serious??" My outrage raised my voice an octave or two, to the point where my shriek almost matched hers. "You just caught your daughter in bed with a man that's not her husband, and you're worried about appearances?"

"Yes, Alicia, I'm worried about appearances. Get up right now!"

"What's happening?" Andrew's low, sleepy murmur came from a spot right behind me. He pressed a soft kiss to my shoulder and I smiled.

"I second that question." A stony voice came from behind my mother, and Michael pushed through the doorway.

"Shit," Andrew muttered.

"Am I seeing what I think I'm seeing?" Michael's voice rose more with every word. "Is there another man in bed WITH MY WIFE?"

"Michael, I'm sure it's not as bad as it looks," Mother tried to say. "Maybe a misunderstanding—"

"What kind of misunderstanding could there possibly be?" Michael thundered. "They're both naked in the same bed! Seems pretty straightforward to me!"

"Michael, I'm so sorry—" I started to say.

"Not a word from you, Alicia," Michael cut in. "There's nothing you could say to make this better. And you"—he turned to my mother—"you were gonna try to cover it up. Unbelievable!"

"Now wait just a minute," my mother begged. My skin itched to hear the pleading in her voice. She'd rather plead to a man not even related to her than to try to understand her own daughter. "I'm sure we can fix this."

"Oh, we're gonna fix it," Michael said. "Effective

immediately, Alicia and I are no longer together. We will get an annulment. And the business deal is off." Michael turned to me, a sneer on his face.

"When you're done getting dressed, make your way to my apartment. You have three days to get your stuff."

Mother followed Michael out, probably to try to talk him off the ledge. Andrew stayed and slowly got dressed.

I could tell when his moral compass kicked in because he sat on the edge of the bed, closing his eyes. Judging by the tightness in his jaw, I could tell that I wasn't the only one having trouble stopping the train of irrational thought from running us over. It looked like he was counting.

After a while, he caught my eye. "I'm sorry. That should have never happened. You're married, and I got caught up."

"Yeah, you did. Leading me off the beaten path." He frowned at the slyness in my voice. I frowned, too. "Too soon?"

"We can't do this, Ace. You're married. Like actually married. As in, legally, and two days away from being spiritually tied, too."

"You heard Michael. He wants an annulment. I hardly think I'm gonna be walking down the aisle in two days." I snorted. "But you're right." I repositioned my scarf on my head. "We should stop."

"What are you gonna tell Michael?"

I startled, my head rearing back. "What?"

"You're planning to get back together with him." He turned to face me fully. "You were planning on telling him something, right?"

"What should I tell him?" I snorted. "That I cheated on him in a brief act of insanity? That this meant nothing and was a quarter-life crisis? I think he already knows that."

"Really, Alicia, you're gonna joke right now? Do better."

"What do you want me to say, Andrew?" I threw my hands up in frustration. "I realized that my life as I know it is deeply unfulfilled?" I rolled my eyes to mask the storm of emotions roiling within me. "Give me a break. Like you so kindly pointed out, *I'm married.* You said it yourself: what we did was a mistake. Chalk it up to bad decisions made after a long night of drinking and forgetting."

"Forgetting that you're married?"

"Yep."

"So that's what you're going with?" he asked again. "That this was nothing?"

Like always, I knew there was a double meaning in his question. With Andrew, one question is always two, or three, or several, like a seven-layer dip with nothing but bad surprises and regret.

But I just didn't have the time nor inclination to figure out what he meant. I knew that telling him that I was in love with him would yield nothing but my own broken heart, and I had no desire to relive the pain that caused. So, instead of reaching for him like I longed…instead of telling him I've been in love with him for years and I feared that I would never love anyone else, including my husband, the way I loved him, I let the dust settle over our shared moment and prepared to lie.

"Yes," I said. "This meant nothing to me."

The hurt in his eyes doubled, and I could see him take a sharp inhale. His mouth became small, pinched, as he looked around without seeing, held his body taut without knowing.

Finally, he shook his head and started putting his socks

on. I could see a muscle tick in his jaw as he slowly, methodically finished getting dressed and stood to look at me.

"Call it whatever makes you feel better, Ace," he said. "Mistake, misplaced passion, a shit show. But when you're ready to have a conversation about what this all really means, you know where to find me."

I knew that what happened between me and Andrew would be a one-time thing, and I knew he would stay away, because he didn't fight. Even still, I couldn't shake the feeling of uncleanliness. The fact that I cheated on my husband in a brief moment of senselessness was no one's fault but my own. Though I knew that having sex with Andrew was a mistake, and despite knowing that Andrew would never love me the way Michael was capable of, I also knew that I couldn't live in a passionless marriage.

But I still had to try to win Michael back.

I felt the sweat slide down my back, leaving an icy trail in its wake as I raced to what would have become our apartment complex. I had already mostly moved in with Michael because my lease was up soon, but I hadn't gotten a key from him yet, so I was forced to wait in the lobby.

He entered the complex whistling, smile ready on his face. When he saw me pacing, he stopped near the front desk.

I sighed. "We should talk," I said.

"Yeah," he said, slowly walking toward me but coming to a stop six feet away. He crossed his arms. "We should."

He looked toward the guard desk, where the man sitting behind it seemed to be trying not to overhear. He turned back to me and nodded in the direction of the front of the building. "Let's talk outside."

"Can't we just go upstairs?" I tried not to plead but failed. "Maybe make some lunch and talk while we eat?"

"Alicia, I don't want to make any more memories with you in my apartment." He gestured to the outside more emphatically. "Outside will have to do."

With that, we both made our way to the entrance of the building—him, steadily, and me, following shamefully behind.

When we got outside and sat on a window's ledge, Michael sighed.

"Alright," he said. "Talk."

"First, let me say I'm so sorry," I started. "I had no intention of sleeping with Andrew, and he was just there to make sure I didn't die in my sleep. I was super drunk, and things just happened—"

"Save the excuses, Alicia," Michael said. "Regardless of intention, you slept with the guy. I only want to know what happened. Start from the beginning."

I sighed, running my hands over my hair. "Okay," I conceded. "Okay, I can do that." I paused for a moment to gather my thoughts, to put things in chronological order. My head hurt from the effort, and I realized then that I hadn't eaten anything to counteract the alcohol still in my system.

"Cat saw that I was too drunk to function, so she called Andrew. According to her, she also called you and Jeremiah, but neither of you picked up. Andrew was the last resort."

"She never called me."

I frowned at him, indignant and anger building in equal measure. "Are you calling Cat a liar?"

"I'm not saying it's intentional, but she definitely didn't call me. I would have picked up."

"You can check your phone later," I said finally. I took a deep breath to quell my irritation. "That's not the point."

"It's definitely the point," Michael cut in. "I want to know how many people were complicit in all of this. It's clear that your mother was. How many other people didn't want us to get married?"

I reared back, my anger taking over. "It's not about you, Michael," I shot back. "Everyone but you seemed to see that we weren't happy, that we shouldn't get married."

"So, what, I'm just supposed to *accept* the cheating then?" Michael asked. "We weren't happy, so that makes it right?" He got up from the window ledge and stood in front of me, arms crossed. He looked down on me with a sneer. "It's *not* my fault you were so unhappy that you slept around on me. You could have left at any time. Did you have sex with anyone else?"

"How dare you," I said slowly. I rose from the ledge, not willing to have him look down on me any longer. "How dare you treat me as if I'm willfully unfaithful, that I am indiscriminate in my infidelity."

"How do I know any differently?" he shot back. "If you were so unhappy with me, who's to say you didn't sleep with anyone else? Who's to say you didn't cheat while you were on the road?"

"I'm gonna pretend that you didn't just accuse me of sleeping around with multiple people and move on," I said through gritted teeth. "Anyway, Andrew showed up to make sure I didn't die. Because *that's what friends do*. He made sure I made it through the night. And then I kissed him."

"So let me get this straight." He pulled at his beard.

"Andrew slept over to make sure you didn't choke on your own vomit."

"Yes."

"And then you two kissed."

"This morning, yes."

"After all the alcohol had left your system."

"Well, there might have still been a little—"

"Alicia, please don't lie to me. Please. Were you drunk when you kissed him or did you know what you were doing?"

I sighed, any residual anger leaving my system and leaving me exhausted in its wake. "I knew."

"And he kissed you back?"

I hesitated, weighing my options. It was one thing for me to confess; it was quite another to drag Andrew into this any more than he already was. I didn't want him to get implicated. It wasn't his fault I couldn't control myself around him. When I met Michael's stony look, though, I knew I had to come clean. "Yes."

"And then you had sex."

I stayed silent, knowing that wasn't a question.

Michael broke our gaze and shook his head. "I still can't freakin' believe this."

"I'm so sorry I hurt you, Michael." I wrung my hands. "I didn't realize I had lasting feelings for him until this morning—"

"Wait, *lasting?* What do you mean lasting?"

With a lurch, I realized that I hadn't mentioned my feelings for Andrew, only explaining the sex. I closed my eyes as I felt more than saw Michael's fury double in size.

"You mean to tell me you've been in love with the guy this whole time?"

"Yes, but I didn't know," I pleaded, opening my eyes. I

was disgusted myself with how much I sounded like Mother. "It wasn't until I kissed him that I knew for sure."

"Oh, how lucky!"

"Please, Michael—"

"Please what? Not be upset that my wife is in love with another guy? What am I supposed to do with this information, Alicia?"

"Now that I know, I can fix it. I'll overcome it!"

"How long?"

I blanched, knowing what he was asking but trying to avoid it anyway. "How long what?"

"How long have you been in love with him?"

I sighed, trying to stall for as long as possible. Finally, I said, "Since before you and I met. We had just stopped being friends when you met me."

"You were crying over him that day, weren't you?"

I didn't say anything, but the silence spoke for me.

"Unbelievable." He got up and stalked toward the building entrance.

I followed. "Where are you going?"

"I'm gonna stay with one of my buddies for a few days." Michael stopped at the door but didn't turn to look at me. I didn't have to see his face to hear the hardness in his voice. "When I get back, I want you and all your stuff gone."

"What do you mean?" Panic rose in my throat and I almost choked on it. "Where will I go? How will I get into the apartment?"

He handed me a key out of his pocket. "Here's the spare I was planning on giving you this morning," he said. "As for where you'll go, I don't know and honestly, I don't care." Michael turned to me, his face a mask of hardness. "But you can't stay here. This marriage is officially over."

I stood in front of the entrance of his building, looking

at the spot he once occupied. Something in me broke, though not for the reasons I imagined. No, something in me knew that Michael and I were just not meant to be. But it wasn't as if not being with Michael meant I was with Andrew. He didn't want me either.

Finally, I turned toward the road, intent on calling an Uber. Tears blurred my vision as I methodically unlocked my phone, searched for the app, and called for a car. I felt the tears finally fall, but I did nothing to stop their descent. What was the point in stopping it when more would just take their place?

As if that weren't enough, Mother called me as I was walking into to my apartment. I closed my eyes and sighed before I picked it up.

"Hi, Mother. I take it that you want to discuss what happened today."

"You haven't been married for more than a month and already things are imploding."

I paused, staring at the phone in disbelief. "Mother, it just wasn't working out. I couldn't keep up the ruse. I'm a different woman than I was when he proposed. Granted, I shouldn't have cheated on him—"

"Did you know you two were being filmed?" Mother interrupted.

My heart stopped. "What do you mean?"

"Search for Michael Smith and Alicia Jones online," she said.

With shaking fingers, I opened my laptop computer, opening up a web browser and typing in our names. The first video clip had over 200,000 views in the last two hours, and was titled *Michael Smith and Alicia Jones Go Nuclear.* With lead fingers, I clicked on it.

As I watched with mounting horror, I heard my conversation with Michael repeated back to me as if from a distance. The person filming had some damn good audio equipment, because even though they seemed to be several yards away, the audio quality was pristine.

When I heard Michael's final words to me, I exited out of the browser and sighed. Putting the phone to my ear, I said to Mother, "What do you suggest I do?"

"Alicia, this is a disaster that I knew was coming. I told you to keep him happy so that this wouldn't happen and instead, you go and screw up everything."

Resignation set into my bones, as weary and endless as time. "Well, at least he didn't have a chance to go to the press."

"And that's a good thing? At least if he went to the press, we could have some control of the narrative. Now your infidelity is out there and on tape for the whole world to see—with you readily admitting to it!" Mother sighed, exasperated. "Alicia, how could you be so careless? You knew what this venture meant to your father. And he can't afford any additional stress. For goodness sakes, he just had a heart attack!"

I paused as the implications of what my mother was suggesting caught up to me. "Are you really saying this is solely my fault?" I asked. "Are you actually telling me that you'd rather I spend my life in a miserable marriage to help out Father's business? You'd rather see me in pain than see me be free? Mother, your loyalty, your *support*, should be for your own flesh and blood, not someone you wanted to go into business with. And yes, admittedly, I made some mistakes along the way, but so did Michael! With this alone, he made a mistake. He was the one that wanted to talk outside in the first place!" I growled in frustration. "Have you ever thought that maybe this was the way it's supposed to turn out? I couldn't do it anymore. Michael is not The One. I couldn't be with someone who wasn't meant for me or whom I wasn't meant for. And if it weren't for you two walking in on me and Andrew, maybe we would have never known before it was too late."

"Meant for him? The One?" Mother scoffed. "Alicia, come back to reality. Sometimes, you must make small sacrifices to get the thing that you ultimately want. Security. A loving husband. You were going to gain all of that, but instead, you decided that you'd rather follow a pipe dream. That romantic notion, while cute, fades quickly after you say, 'I do.' It's the willingness to be another's partner that gets you through the hard times, not romance."

"I'd much rather forsake security and follow, as you so lovingly called it, a 'pipe dream' than stay in a marriage where ultimately, I'd have to give up my dreams for my husband's. Michael wanted a trophy, Mother, not a wife. He wanted to restrict me, to control me, the way he does his employees. I'm supposed to be his actual partner, not some bauble on a shelf."

It was my mother's turn to sigh. "Alicia, I'll call you later. When you're not so irrational."

I felt the tears fall down my cheeks, felt the scream building in my throat. "Then don't bother calling. Because I'll never be reasonable enough to understand how a mother could choose business over her own daughter."

I hung up, feeling of sting of my mother's betrayal in my tears. I knew my mother was ruthless, but deep down, I thought that our recent shared moments meant something more to her. I thought it meant that her love was unconditional, but instead, I found that the saying was true: when someone tells you who they are, believe them.

All my life, my mother had told me that I had to be worthy of her love, to prove myself to garner her favor. Time and time again, I leaned on everyone else—Catalina,

Dante, Andrew—to fill the void that my parents never filled. Before, when Dante was alive, I had come to expect it. But in these last couple of weeks, I started to believe that maybe I was wrong about my parents. Maybe they could love me.

My hope made the fall to reality that much more painful.

I don't know how long I sat in my living room before I heard a pounding on the door. "Alicia, I know you're in there. Open up."

Without knowing how I got there, I opened the door to Catalina's startled face. I grimaced. "How did you hear?"

"I saw the video," she said. She watched me with sad doe eyes. "Oh, Alicia." She shut the door and opened her arms.

Usually, I hesitate to give anyone a hug, even Catalina, whom I've known pretty much my whole life. This time, I didn't hesitate. As her arms wrapped around me firmly, everything I had been holding in—fear of my feelings for Andrew, panic at how it made me look, anger for not being able to overcome it, sorrow for what I lost, betrayal by way of my parents—came rushing to the surface in a maelstrom of tears and snot. I wailed against Catalina's shoulder while she made comforting humming noises. "I know," was all she said. "I know."

"It hurts," I sobbed. "Why does it hurt?"

She rubbed circles on my back as I hiccuped and finally trailed off in a pitiful-sounding sniffle. She led me to the couch, had me put my head in her lap as she stroked my hair.

"This is gonna sound absolutely ridiculous," she said. "But you're gonna get through this."

"How?" I wiped my nose with my sleeve. "I have no money and no steady income; my husband wants a divorce; my infidelity is all over the internet; and I'm practically homeless. Where do I go from here?"

Catalina was silent for a moment, a peaceful look on her face. She smiled down at me.

"That's the good news," she said. "The only thing you can do is move forward."

Once I was settled enough and not breaking down into tears every few minutes, Catalina convinced me to pack a bag and sleep at her place. I didn't fight her.

I thought I was fine until we reached her place and Jeremiah opened the door. Seeing the look on his face, I couldn't helping breaking into tears again. This time, Catalina let Jeremiah take over as I cried.

When I was finally able to speak coherently, Jeremiah looked over my head at Catalina. "Thai food for delivery?" he asked.

She nodded. "Thai food," she said.

We ordered Thai food whenever any of the three of us was going through a tragedy of some kind. We got it the day I told Catalina and Jeremiah about Dante's diagnosis, then when Catalina was fired from her full-time job —"With the benefits!" she had wailed over her Tom Yum —and again when Jeremiah's grandmother, who was a second mother to him, died.

So it was no surprise that we were going to usher in the beginning of the end of my marriage with Thai food. As Catalina went to scrounge up the takeout menu, Jeremiah regarded me with a thoughtful, curious look. "So, you left Michael."

I gave a small chuff of a laugh. "*He* left *me*. Spectacularly and thoroughly. You see the video?"

Jeremiah shrugged a little, nodding at a thought playing through his mind. "But did he really leave you? Or did you leave him a long time ago?"

I frowned at him. "What do you mean?"

He shifted forward, bringing his elbows to the tops of his thighs. "Well, there are some people who are there for a season, or who have a specific purpose," he said. He stroked his face, his dimples appearing like a captive audience as he carefully chose his words. "Michael was here for a very specific purpose, to help you through your breakup with Andrew."

"But Andrew and I weren't together romantically."

"Doesn't matter. You still loved him romantically, and your feelings weren't returned, and you two stopped hanging out. For all intents and purposes, y'all broke up." I sighed because I knew he was right. "Anyway, you and Andrew broke up, and Michael was there to help you pick up the pieces. He was also, I think, there to show you that you can in fact fall in love again and live a full life even without Andrew. But he wasn't meant to stay so long, and you definitely weren't meant to marry the guy. I mean, look at what he tried to get you to do, all you had to give up to make it work.

"But I think subconsciously, you knew that his time and purpose had run out. It's why you went on tour, why you got so physically close with Andrew." When I frowned at him, he raised an eyebrow. "Anyone with eyes could see that if you two hadn't hooked up already, you would soon enough." Jeremiah leaned back, linked his hands behind his head in a relaxed pose but watched me with knowing eyes. "Listen, I'm not here to tell you what to do with your life. I think you have too many people doing that already, honestly, including my own wife." He shot a wry glance over his shoulder when Catalina called out, "I heard that!" I laughed. "But just remember to listen to what God's telling you above all else. And then, after that, listen to yourself."

Though I was pretty sure I buried my belief in God along with my brother, I nodded. Jeremiah was right: I spent too much time listening to the voices outside my head, and not enough time knowing what it was that I wanted to do. I knew that with this understanding came more work, work that I didn't want to do. But it wasn't going to go away just because I wanted to suppress it.

Catalina popped her head out of the kitchen. "Everyone ready for Thai?"

I smiled. "No," I said. I looked at Jeremiah, and he bestowed a rare smile on me. "It's not necessary."

Twenty-Three

After a long night of Jeremiah's fantastic cooking, and Uno, and bad teen TV shows, I fell asleep in a haze of good feelings. When I woke up the next morning with Catalina and Jeremiah's couch imprint on my face, though, I knew I had to get up and get out.

My first stop was the gym. Even though Yasmine wasn't there to guide me through the workout, I could still remember the general idea behind it. I started my warm-up on the bike, feeling the slow burn that comes with missing a few weeks' workouts, loving the power I felt in my legs anyway. Of course, by the time I dismounted, I was slick with sweat.

I shrugged off my impending self-consciousness and moved toward the weight racks. Yasmine always started us there, with either squats or deadlifts. *You wanna be fresh for these,* she had warned. *Doing deadlifts at the end of a workout is a recipe for disaster.*

Well, I guess my body is calling me to the weight rack first. I grabbed my warm-up set of weights. Just as I was readjusting a stack of 5 lb weights, I heard behind me, "Well, I'm glad I made it to the gym this morning."

I turned to see a broad-shouldered, mountain of a man just barely holding back a leer in his dimpled cheeks. His light brown eyes flashed in a way that was all too familiar but none too welcome. In the past, I might have been flattered, maybe even scared to say what was on my mind. But after all I had experienced in the last twenty-four hours, I was in no mood to entertain the likes of another Cro-Magnon.

I squared my shoulders, looking him dead in his eyes. "Can I help you?"

"I sure hope so." He grinned as I barely contained my eye roll. "Care to share the bar? I can do my sets between yours."

"I bet." I looked around at the three empty Olympic bar stations. "But lucky for you, you don't have to. There are plenty of bars available."

Caveman scratched the back of his neck in a clear and transparently fake show of getting caught. "I'll admit, it was a lame, not thought-out excuse to talk to you. A girl as pretty as you is hard to approach in a place like this. I'm sure you get that a lot."

"I don't." I crossed my arms over my chest, waiting.

A moment passed, then another, before I spoke again. "Look, I don't even know your name—"

"Alan."

"Alan, then. I'm sure you're a great guy, but I'm just getting out of a relationship and not looking to get into another one, of any kind, anytime soon. So as much as I'm flattered, I'm gonna get back to my workout, and I hope you have a great day."

Alan nodded his appreciation and stepped back. "No worries, I hope you have a great day too," he said. He turned to walk away and turned back. "And the guy who left you had no idea what he was leaving behind."

I smiled. "Probably not," I said.

Despite the feel-good feelings from my workout, I knew I had to visit my parents and come to terms with their reaction to my impending divorce. As I stepped up to knock on the door, a flurry of nerves unleashed their wrath. I knew that I couldn't count on their love to be unconditional. While that stung more than a little bit, this reality was one that I was used to, instead of the alternate universe I had been inhabiting where my parents actually loved me.

By the time my father made his way to the door, I had composed myself. As if he sensed this, he ushered me in stiffly and quickly. "Your mother's not home," he said, by way of explanation. "But if she sees that I'm walking around, she'll have a heart attack herself."

My laugh sounded shriller than I liked, so I coughed to make up for it. "Sounds about right," I said. He rewarded me with a half-smile, wariness and curiosity blazing in his gaze. As we sat in the sitting room, I braced myself for the obvious question.

But my father surprised me. He watched me for a few moments before he cleared his throat. "So you and Michael broke up. Can't say I'm surprised."

I turned to him, startled out of the dialogue happening in my head. "What?"

"You heard me."

"Yes, but I don't understand."

Amusement warmed his eyes as he regarded me. "Anyone could see that you didn't love the boy. That it would be a marriage of convenience more than passion or warmth. And frankly, watching and listening to you interact was painful. What'd you talk about with him anyway, the weather?"

I snorted before I could stop it. "Catalina asked the same thing."

"Well."

We sat in silence as I processed this. Hearing my father's acceptance wasn't just startling; it was downright counterintuitive. This was the man that went on and on about practical matters, which was completely at odds with current society's thoughts on marrying for love. If anyone should understand what it means to marry for pragmatic reasons, it should be him. Yet, here he was, approving of the end of my very practical marriage.

Finally, I said, "Well, this is a surprise. Of all people, I thought you'd understand why I married Michael."

"Oh sure, I understand it." He watched me, not afraid to meet my eyes. "Doesn't mean I agree with it. Like I said, watching the two of you together was painful, borderline masochistic. You two didn't even have mutual respect for each other."

"But what about your business deal with him?"

"What about it?" He shrugged, and I almost fell off the couch. My father was not a man prone to shrugging; I couldn't believe he even knew how. "There will be other business deals. Granted, this one was a big one. We could've made a lot of money off the guy. But I didn't like interacting with him either, so for that, it's not a big loss."

"But what about the bad press he's threatening? And did you see the video?"

My father grinned then; the expression was more threatening than jovial. "I've had bad press before. I'll manage."

"But Mother made it seem that I would tank the entire

business if I didn't keep him happy and encourage the relationship."

He sighed a long sigh, as if continuing a long-standing argument. "Your mother still operates in the mindset that we are want for money. She's not used to having it." He leaned forward as if telling me a secret. "She used to be poor, you know."

I raised my eyebrows. "Really?"

"Really. It's why her mom encouraged her to marry me." A small smile played on his lips as he stared off into the distance. "She practically begged me to marry her only daughter. Funny, because I was going to do it anyway, approval or not."

I laughed. "Mother did tell me that her mother begged you to marry her." I sobered as I thought about the rest of what he said. About her being poor. "But she didn't tell me it was because she was poor."

"Of course she didn't," he said. His smile was gentle as he thought of his wife. "She probably also didn't tell you that my parents didn't want me to marry her. They saw her as precisely the type of woman that didn't belong in our world."

I raised my eyebrows so high that I thought it would hit my hairline. "What? Why?"

"Not only was she poor, but her family was involved in gang activity and drugs." Father grimaced. "When her father died, her mother had to do some questionable things to make ends meet. I found out one day after overhearing a business deal between her mother and one of her associates. When I looked to my parents for advice, they told me to leave her. But I knew in that moment that no matter what her mother was involved in, I couldn't risk leaving your mother. I had fallen head over heels in love with her and I knew that I had to marry her.

"When I proposed, I told her as much. I told her I'd give it all up—access to my parents' money and resources —if it meant that she would marry me." My father's laugh was a small chuff of a sound, the evidence of years of fighting against my mother's practical ideas of marriage. "But I know she won't tell you that. That would require her to admit a few things that she doesn't care to admit."

"Like what?"

"Like the fact that it's okay to marry for love, and that sometimes, it works out. Our marriage started with it and it still has it now.

"She would also have to admit that she's afraid for you. She doesn't want to admit that because it would require her to also tell you that she has been affected all these years about your lack of closeness. And God forbid she admit to being hurt in any way."

I felt the tears in the corners of my eyes and tried to ignore them. My mother, afraid for me? What a novel concept. "I could've really used that information. From either of you."

Father nodded, a weariness seeping into his shoulders. "I know. It wasn't until I was laid up in a hospital bed that I realized how far off the mark I was with both you and your brother." He threaded his fingers together and propped his arms on his thighs. "You needed more from me and, misguidedly, I thought financial provision would be enough."

When he looked up, a newfound fierceness, so like Dante's, filled his face. It took my breath away to see that like my brother, my father would do anything to protect the ones he loves. "But that stops here. You are my only daughter, my only living child. And she's my wife. I have to make it right."

Though my dad didn't seem worried about Michael's threat, I had to confront him anyway. The fact was that no one should suffer for my mistakes. Not even my parents.

As I walked into the store, I steeled myself for the second time that day. One of the things that had attracted me to Michael was how formidable he was—on and off the field. When he was interacting with his employees, you could tell that there was a healthy distance between them, both physical and psychological, that was borne from deference and a tiny bit of fear. It was an attitude I was used to seeing in reference to white men, but the sheer size of Michael also kept many at bay.

I finally found him in the shoe department, giving instructions to a guy with tousled black hair and insolent green eyes. He couldn't have been older than twenty-one. His posture indicated that he wasn't bothered by anything in life, particularly this job, and judging by the firmness in Michael's voice, this was not the first time this particular employee needed to be spoken to.

"Now, Rafael, if I have to ask you to do this again, we will have to discuss if this is the right department—or even the right job—for you. Do you understand?"

"Aye, aye, captain." Rafael gave Michael a mock salute. His eyes rested on mine. "Looks like we have company, so can I get back to it?"

Michael sighed. "Sure." It was only then that he turned, his turbulent hazel eyes meeting mine. "Hey, Alicia, what a surprise." He pulled on his beard. "I didn't think you knew where the store was."

I laughed, the merriment not quite reaching my voice. "I did have to put it into the GPS," I said, a tinge of chagrin in my voice. Michael had been working at the store since before we met, but I couldn't recall a time I had actually even visited him there. "Can we talk somewhere private?"

"Sure," he agreed, steering me toward a door off to the side. He pulled out a ring of keys and unlocked it, ushering me in. "What's up?"

I straightened my spine, looked him in the eye. "I wanted to talk about the threat you made." I crossed my arms. "It's one thing to punish me, but another to bring my family into this."

Michael sighed, cupping the back of his neck with his hand. "Yeah, ignore that. When I saw the leaked footage of our fight, I knew I couldn't do it. I knew I shouldn't have spoken out of anger, but I was furious with you and didn't know how to handle it. I mean, how could you be in love with another guy for a whole fucking—" Michael's eyes widened to almost comical levels and I giggled. "Oops."

"Michael, we're grown," I said. I smirked. "Besides, what's a little fucking between husband and wife?"

We both laughed at that.

Finally, Michael sighed. "Look, I'm sorry about the threat. Consider it retracted. But only under one condition."

"What's that?" I tilted my head in curiosity. Michael was not one to put conditions on agreements, so I figured it must be good.

"You have to tell Andrew how you feel."

I reared back, the sting of the surprise hitting my skin. "What?"

"This"—he gestured between us—"all this fighting and marriage and then breaking up. It has to be for something. It can't just be so that you can spend the rest of your life alone."

"So I have to be with a man for it to be worth the trouble?" I raised my eyebrows.

Michael sighed, pulling at his beard again. "No, that's not what I meant." He started pacing in the small space, and I watched him the way one watches a tense lion. Finally, he stopped, looking in my eyes.

"I always knew that I wasn't getting all of you." He laughed without humor, the sound sharp in the small space. "I could feel that there was a barrier between us, like you didn't ever fully trust me. I figured it would go away with time, but here we are."

The waves of hurt coming off him were so strong that I wanted to reach out and touch him. I drew my hand up toward his shoulder, then stopped and dropped it back down. "Why didn't you say anything?"

He barked out another laugh. "And what? Admit that I was failing as a boyfriend, then as a fiancé?" He shook his head. "No way."

"But maybe that could have saved our relationship." I shrugged. "Maybe it would have kept us honest and genuine."

"Or maybe it would have broken us apart." He regarded me, his eyes a concoction of sorrow and bittersweet feelings. "There was no way of knowing."

"But at least it would have been honest," I said. I leaned against the wall, my arms still crossed. "We spent these last two years trying to be the image of the perfect couple, Michael. But the truth is, we can't be the perfect anything. If given the opportunity, I cuss more than you'll ever be comfortable with. I prefer to wear a lot of black, and multiple bracelets, and converses. The very opposite of what you want from me. And you…" I hesitated, feeling the curiosity and wariness from Michael. "You are a sports guy. You want a trophy wife, someone you can show off to your friends and teammates. You like the parties, and the surface-level stuff. And your work ethic reaches insane heights, to the point where you can't see anything else. None of these are terrible traits, but they are imperfect, and real. And we needed imperfection in our relationship."

Michael nodded, considering this. "I hear you." He grimaced as he caught my eye. "So, you love him, then?"

I picked at the skin around my fingers as Michael looked on with a slight frown. "I think so, yeah. I guess I owe it to myself to at least explore what's going on between me and him."

"I think you owe it to him, too."

I tilted my head, a frown now playing on my face, as well. "What do you mean?"

He brushed a curl back from my face, the gentlest gesture he's ever bestowed on me. "Every man deserves to feel loved," he said. "And if the love you feel for Andrew is even a tenth of what you showed me, he deserves to feel loved by you." He stepped away and shrugged, hurt evident in his gaze. "You know, I think you're right—I think it's better for us not to be together. We don't bring out the best in each other, and I don't think I could ever get used to the swearing."

I rolled my eyes and laughed. "Great, thanks for your blessing."

"Of course." I shook my head and laughed some more. He had no idea I was being sarcastic—typical Michael. He puffed his chest out proudly. "Consider it my wedding present to you."

We smiled at each other. I knew that things would still be a little messy, especially given that now we had to navigate a divorce, but somehow, things seemed okay between us.

"Hey."

He looked up, all of the messy things reflected back at me in his gaze.

"Thanks for everything, Michael. Really."

He shrugged, a rare moment of shyness from him. "Anytime." He grinned. "Now, get out of my store and find your boyfriend."

Twenty-Four

The funny thing about Andrew is that he finds you when you don't want to be found, but when he doesn't want to be found, he simply falls off the grid. Spectacularly.

I texted Andrew three times to no avail. After two hours had passed, I made my way to Catalina and Jeremiah's place. Something told me that they would know where Andrew was. Jeremiah had opened the door as if he was expecting me.

"Why won't he answer his texts?" I wailed to Catalina. "What the fuck could he be doing that he can't stop for a minute to say, 'Hey, never speak to me again'?"

Catalina put her hands on her hips as Jeremiah regarded me carefully. "Alicia, please don't tell me that you still believe he doesn't love you."

I typed out another text, growing frustrated with every word. ***ANDREW, WHERE THE FUCK ARE YOU????
ANSWER YOUR DAMN TEXTS.***

"The proof is in his ignoring my texts. And the fact

that he basically implied that he wasn't in love with me when I asked him the other night."

"Consider the possibility that he *is* in love with you and he's just afraid."

I snorted as I went through Andrew's social media pages to see if he had posted anything in the last two days. "Right. Andrew, afraid of love? That's like saying Cupid's afraid of a bow and arrow."

"No, really, think about it." Cat rounded the dining room table and stood in the path of my pacing. I came up short, glaring down at her. She put her hands back on her hips and met my eyes. "Would you want to profess your undying love to a man who's tied to another woman? And who asked you about your feelings while he was drunk off his ass?"

"I wouldn't want to, but I would do it anyway." I picked at the skin around my nails, tapped my hands against my thighs. "Besides, even if he does love me right now, who's to say that he can love me forever, or enough to marry me? I don't wanna be in a dead-end relationship, Cat. And he basically told me that he didn't believe in a love that lasts forever."

"So it's either all or nothing, then?" Cat tilted her head. "It's either 'love me for eternity' or 'don't love me at all'?" I nodded and she sighed. "Alicia, he probably said that because he was afraid. Besides, I have it on good authority that he *does* love you—romantically and permanently."

I rolled my eyes. "Right. And what authority is that?"

Cat grinned. "Andrew's."

By the time Cat finished telling me about her conversations with Andrew—which, unbeknownst to me, happened over a period of *years*—I was so impatient to find him that I was ready to crawl out of my skin to do it. The fact that Andrew could build a wall so high to keep out the one person who could love him the way he needed—and apparently wanted—infuriated me.

At the same time, I understood. Sometimes, the thing that seems to be the most helpful can also feel like the most hurtful.

"What day is it, anyway?"

Catalina and I looked over at Jeremiah, Cat's body language mirroring mine. Jeremiah had been silent this whole time, choosing instead to flip between the different channels for something to watch.

"It's the tenth," I said finally. "Why?"

Jeremiah sat in a contemplative silence as he scrolled down the list of shows on Hulu. I could feel Catalina's rising impatience.

"Why do you ask, babe?" Catalina prompted.

"Because Andrew might be getting ready to get on the bus. The Leroys leave tonight. And you probably already know this, but they won't be back in town for a while."

I turned fully to Jeremiah. "You knew where he was gonna be this whole time and didn't say anything? What the fuck, Jeremiah."

He shrugged, biting back a smile. "Didn't seem like the right time to tell you."

I groaned. "Jesus. Fine. Do you know where they're leaving from? And what time?"

Though Jeremiah's shrug was nonchalant, I saw a small smile play on his face, the expression of a person watching a happy ending unfold. "From your favorite park. In twenty minutes."

They were exactly where Jeremiah said they would be.

I sighed as I recognized the outlines of several people milling about. Philip seemed intent on his mission to get everything into the bus, with Danny loping behind him. Jean Lee and Kevin, always the procrastinators of the group, were kicking a soccer ball in the parking lot, pretending to dodge each other, faking each other out. Yasmine was talking to two people in a huddle, her clipboard in one hand, and gesturing wildly with another. One of the people in their threesome, a woman, was the only one I didn't recognize. I guessed this was the stand-in photographer who took my place with the group—and apparently, with Andrew. As I came closer, I could hear the delicate tinkle of female laughter, and I bristled as she laid a hand on his chest with more familiarity than I would've liked. Andrew leaned into her and was murmuring something in her ear as I came up to the group and blurted out the first thing I could think of like I had no fucking sense.

"You love me."

All three of them stopped, looking at me with three different degrees of startled. Andrew and Yasmine exchanged glances before Yasmine muttered, "*Coño.*" She looked at me then at Andrew again. "We'll be on the bus. You have ten minutes or we're leaving without you. Come on, Sandy, let's give them some privacy."

I glared at Sandy as she squeezed Andrew's arm gently then nodded in my direction. Finally, it was just me and Andrew. He turned to me, his face unreadable. "So what's this about me loving you?"

I gulped, palms sweating now that the moment was actually here. Echoes of panic and despair pulsed around me as I remembered the last time I confessed my love for him. I fought with it as I tore the words from my very soul, straightened my spine, and forced myself to look him in the eye.

"You heard me. You. Love me."

"Of course I do," he said easily. "We're best friends."

"No, Andrew, you're *in love* with me. And you're terrified of it." I sighed, forcing my hands to my side instead of picking the skin around my nails or reaching for him. "I talked to Catalina. She told me."

"That was a long time ago." Andrew shifted and for once, his mask slipped. Terror, plain as day, was stamped on his face. "I've moved on."

I squinted a little, eyebrows raised. "Have you, now?" I stepped closer. "So if I were to tell you that I'm in love with you, that wouldn't mean anything to you?"

"Of course it means something to me," he said. He shifted again as he looked away. "But it doesn't mean I share those feelings."

"You're right," I said as I stepped closer to him still. "It doesn't mean that you share them just because you care. But I know you love me, so that's irrelevant." I stepped closer still, our bodies an inch away from each other. "What is it that you're afraid of, Andrew? Why are you afraid to go all in with me?"

Despite his apparent calmness, his hands shook by his sides. I could see his pulse, strong and fast, throbbing at his neck. Heat was coming off him in waves though I couldn't be sure what emotion fueled it. It was just as likely that he was embarrassed as it was that he loved me. Doubt slashed at me but I reminded myself: he had already confessed his feelings to Catalina. His mistake was twofold because not only is Catalina a horrible secret-keeper, but she never forgets.

And Catalina was sure he was in love with me, wholeheartedly and presently. So I was sure.

"I'm not afraid," he said as my eyes roved over his face, staking my claim. My eyes fastened to his lips, seeing them move but only barely hearing what he said. "You're married. You've found your One. Even if I did have feelings for you, nothing could ever happen now. Besides, you said it yourself: what we did, our kiss, was a mistake."

"Really? That's what you're going with?" I murmured. I traced an outline on his forearm. "C'mon, Minnie, do better."

He tried to step away but I moved with him. Irritation flashed across his features but nothing could tamp down the desire, the endless summer of hope, that lay underneath it. "You're married, Ace."

"Yes, to Michael, for now." I fought to keep my voice casual as I got closer to our happily-ever-after. I could see it, wrap my fingers around the picture of us that was so strong, it was almost a premonition. "He gave me his blessing. And his reassurance that it was okay." I pursed my lips as I thought of Michael's heavy-handed way of telling me that I should pursue Andrew. "He sends his regards, by the way."

"But what about your parents? They hate me."

"So what if they did? I would give it all up to be with you. Their approval, their access to resources. Losing that is not, in the grand scheme of things, worth losing you." My throat burned as I thought about my dad's expression when he talked about his love for my mom. "Besides, they don't hate you. Or at least, my dad doesn't." I shrugged. "Fifty percent ain't bad. We'll work on my mom."

"Alicia, this is crazy. We can't just be together."

"And why not?"

"We're too different. We believe different things. You don't even believe in God."

"You're only half right. I don't *think* I believe in God. Attaching ideas of God to your dead brother would shake up anyone's beliefs. And yes, you and I are different in our sources of faith. But what I feel for you is bigger than my doubts about God. My love for you has overcome grief, loss, fears about our future together, trepidation about my relationship with my parents, a whole marriage, everything. No matter how much I tried to fight it, it persisted. It even overcame the fear that you can't love me forever." I met his eyes. "I know you love me. But you have to admit it to yourself. Do you really wanna step onto that bus not being honest with the one person who needs it?" I straightened to my full height, gaining confidence with each inch I rose. "Do you really want to go against your own morals?"

Our eyes took up the battle that our wills had started. The truth of the matter was that I was just as terrified as Andrew to embark on a relationship that might, ultimately, fail. The thought that our romantic relationship would be completely different than our friendship hovered on the surface of my conscious mind, sinking and floating, buoying and descending in equal measure. There was no guarantee that our relationship would thrive the way our friendship had. Even still, I knew that I couldn't give up a second time. I had to take it on faith.

Finally, Andrew looked away. For a moment, my heart sank. That is, until he said, "So what if I'm in love with you? What then?"

Epilogue - One Year Later
ANDREW

Ace will forever be my One.

She didn't have a fucking clue what my body did whenever she was around. Every time she stepped into a room, I knew precisely where she was. Whenever she was within even five feet of me, I felt like I was on fire. If she had ever spontaneously grabbed my hand in high school—which, to this day, I'm glad she hadn't—hers would slide right out from all the sweat. I'm glad I didn't have a snitching-ass watch like hers, because it would always tell me—and her—what her closeness did to me.

I'm surprised my dick didn't tell on me. I still don't understand how she couldn't feel it every time we hugged, and especially in the beginning, because it refused to stop pointing at her. Just thinking about her made my pants stretch uncomfortably forward, made it press against the zipper.

And yet, despite almost getting caught thousands of times, I did whatever I could to be near her, to be sucked endlessly into the gravitational pull of her wit and scorn—which she doled out in equal and generous measure. From the moment I saw her walk into our ninth grade English class—hurried, as if she was already late—I knew that I had to be near her. And once I fought against her tide of defensiveness, I knew that she was the One for me. Forever.

Because, you see, it wasn't that I believed that there's no such thing as the One That Could Last Forever. It's that I knew it was elusive and, most times, pure fucking luck. My parents got lucky and found each other by accident. My dad got on the wrong train and saw my mother sitting there "looking like God's perfect image," as he says. Cat and Jeremiah got lucky, too—they've known each other all their lives, were in the same kindergarten class.

But who was I to be so lucky? I was pretty sure Alicia was it for me, but she spent most of her effort trying to push me away.

So I dated. A lot. And I made it so nothing was permanent, not even my job, so that nothing could have the potential to hurt me. I knew it made me seem flighty. I knew that Alicia, with her desire for stability, might see me as less desirable for it. Still, I couldn't take the risk of being rejected by her. I figured, if everything else could be made transient, love could be, too. Because that's that futile shit you think and do to get over the One You'll Never Get Over.

Each time I dated someone new, I thought she would be the One That Could Help Me Get Over Alicia Jones. Some came close; Sadie almost convinced me that I could do it. But then I saw Ace fighting with someone on the phone (as usual), and the old familiar feeling of "I'll always be hers" overtook me. So I broke up with Sadie.

Even still, I didn't want to bank my hopes and dreams on that. And the moment I watched her get legally tied to that fool Michael, I thought that was the end of it.

But thank God for Cat's meddling, and for her big mouth, and for her unwillingness to give up on me and Alicia. Because of Cat, Alicia gave me a gift: she fought against my tide of defensiveness and challenged my notion of love, and my notions about her. When she showed up to the bus that day, I didn't dare hope that she was there for me. But she was. (She was also there to get her job back, which she did. But still.)

And now, here she is, walking down the aisle in a dress that was made for her. Walking toward the man that lives for her.

God, I hope my dick doesn't ruin this.

The End.

Can't get enough of Alicia and the crew? Subscribe to my newsletter for bonus content, sneak peeks, and ensuring hilarity. Subscribe here!

Language Key

One of the characters in this novel, Yasmine Torres, is Dominican-American. Her first language was Spanish, so she often uses Dominican phrases in the book. Please see below for the English translation.

- Manita - girl / lil sis
- Sí, Claro - yes, of course
- Más personas - more people
- No me preguntaste - you didn't ask me
- Bueno - okay
- Pendejo - asshole
- Díos Mio - my God
- Verdad que si - true/right
- Me oiste - you heard me
- Con los muchachos - with the kids
- Vaga - lazy girl
- Párate de ahi - get up
- Apurate - hurry up
- Estamos de acuerdo - do we agree
- Mi gente - my people / you all

- Estoy muy emocionada - I am very excited
- Padre, que siempre está con nosotros - Father-God, who is always with us
- Entienden - you all understand
- Por favor - please
- Está bien - it's alright
- Mi abuela se murio - my grandmother has died
- Mi responsibilidad - my duty
- Mi amor - my love (from a boyfriend)
- Mi Cielo - my love (from a boyfriend)
- Ya se - I already know
- Coño - fuck / holy crap

Acknowledgments

None of this would be possible if it weren't for God, first and foremost. May I continue to do good work and follow the path laid out for me.

To my husband, my favorite person: you, sir, have pushed me to the bounds of my imagination and have encouraged me to follow my dreams. If I wanted to be a band photographer, I have no doubt you would have told me to do that, and so what if I was scared, do it anyway.

To my family, who has always been supportive of my dream to become an author: we did it! And to my brother specifically: thanks for letting me bounce my ideas about Michael off of you!

To Maria, who gave me the best advice and never turned me away: thank you so much for letting me bug you with questions and author woes! I couldn't tell you how invaluable your advice has been. You were the first person I told when I decided to go public with my book baby, and I thoroughly appreciate all the encouragement.

To Kathy, my editor: you gave my words the push they needed, and I couldn't thank you more for it. Thank you for your patience with this new author, and for your kindness and thoroughness. You're the best!

To Najla, my cover designer: every time you sent me mock-ups of this cover, you helped me to bring my vision of Alicia and Andrew to the page, literally. Thank you for all the work you did - on both the novella cover and this one!

Thank you to Ana, who helped me bring authenticity to Yasmine - a woman in charge but also a leader in the true sense of the word!

To all the people who volunteered to read the manuscript before I unleashed it on the world: thank you, thank you, thank you. Your insight into and love of the characters helped to make them who they are.

And to the readers: you are the reason I do what I do. Thank you for your support, your kind words, your laughs, and your encouragement. Till next time!

About the Author

Student crisis handler by day and writer by night, Jessie often finds herself wrapped up in the tales of humanity. She cultivated an appetite for a good love story from the moment she read her first Sarah Dessen book, and it led to her desire to create some stories of her own.

When she's not writing or providing resources for students at a small SoCal film school, she can be found driving into the sunset while listening to the Foo Fighters, taking photos, sinking her toes in the sand, or reveling in the beauty of a good meal. She also enjoys hanging out with her better half and favorite tiny human.

You can find her on Facebook, Instagram, and her website.

Made in the USA
Middletown, DE
19 April 2021